IN THE SHADOW OF THE HANGING TREE

Michael A. McLellan

In the Shadow of the Hanging Tree
Michael A. McLellan

Second printing
ISBN-9781096423515

Copyright © 2017 by Michael A. McLellan

All rights reserved. No part of this publication may be reproduced, distributed, or transmitted in any form or by any means, including photocopying, recording, or other electronic or mechanical methods, without the prior written permission of the publisher, except in the case of brief quotations embodied in critical reviews and certain other noncommercial uses permitted by copyright law. For permission requests, write to the author at the address below.

This is a work of fiction. Names, characters, places, and incidents either are the product of the author's imagination or are used fictitiously, and any resemblances to actual persons, living or dead, business establishments, events, or locales is entirely coincidental.

Cover / interior layout & design by Bradley Knox (SUBATOMIC)

To Landrin Kelly.
See you in awhile, pal.

This novel is dedicated to the human race.
I fear for us.

One

1
Near Osceola, Missouri. September 25 1861.
"Get up, boy," Samuel Cromwell said as he laid a kick to the sleeping young man's bare feet. "You and your woman get up and get on your way, before I change my mind."

Henry rubbed at his eyes and looked up at his master's shadowed features. Samuel kicked him a second time and dropped something onto the splintered wooden floor beside the reed mat he and Eliza shared. He pushed himself up to a sitting position and felt Eliza stir next to him. Samuel held the lantern he was carrying over the small bundle on the floor.

"There's some bread and molasses, a little bit of salted pork, a parin' knife…and your free papers. Hers too. I was going to give them to you come Christmas, anyhow. Ownin' another man—or woman, for that matter, never felt Christian to me, you know that. I've been living contrary to the word of God, regardless of what Reverend Adams says about it, and I know I'm going to have to answer for it eventually. Now listen here. William Prescott tells me those Jayhawkers are camped not but three or four miles up the road. You can take your chances with them, if you're of a mind, but I'd head out past Chaney's crossing and stay to the woods. Follow the river northeast and get yourselves to Illinois as quick as you can. Mayhap get up to Minnesota or even Canada."

Samuel Cromwell's expression was grave.

"You understand those papers aren't going to mean a damn thing if you get caught by some of our boys?"

"Yessir," Henry replied.

"And I won't be here to corroborate your story. I'm heading out, first light. I'll be on my way out to California to join my brother. It was nice to have known you…*Henry.*"

"Thank you, sir. You too, sir."

"Go on then."

Samuel Cromwell turned away without another word and left the tiny, one-room house, leaving Henry and Eliza in the dark.

Henry stood and retrieved a small, lard candle from a shelf above the pallet by feel. "Get dressed, Eliza. We have to go," he said, then walked naked through the door. He stepped onto the small porch and watched his master's silhouette move up the path toward the big house. Samuel Cromwell's lantern caused shadows to flicker and dance in the trees bordering the path.

Henry walked out to the stone fire ring and stirred up the remnants of the evening's cook fire. He soon had the candle alight and walked back to the house.

"Where will we go, Henry?" Eliza asked while gathering up her few belongings and putting them in the embroidered drawstring bag that her previous mistress had given her.

"North, I suppose, like Mister Cromwell says. I heard tell those Kansas whites preach the abolition but don't treat our free folks no different than if 'n they were still slaves. I heard they do better up north." Henry set the candle down and began dressing.

"You hear all that from Nathaniel Clement up at John Anderson's place? You know you can't believe a word coming from his mouth."

"I heard from others, too. Now come on. Make sure you bring along that sack of flour and whatever else we got."

"There's nothing but a couple biscuits worth left."

"Bring it anyhow."

"Of course I'm gonna bring it. I was just wondering how we're going to eat."

2

The two reached the river just before sunrise and, after some debating, they chose to move a little way inland to find a suitable place to hole up for the day. They were well aware of how things would go for them if they were discovered.

After negotiating a couple of particularly dense hazelnut thickets, they came across an abandoned trapper's lean-to about a quarter of a mile west of the river.

The sun was fully up and they decided that it was as safe of a place as any.

The aged canvas lean-to was just tall enough for a person to crawl inside and barely wide enough for two. Henry was over six feet tall, but lean. Eliza was petite; just tall enough to stare Henry in the chest when they stood toe to toe. If either of the two were any larger, they wouldn't have fit inside together.

The morning was warm; the early sun rapidly burning off the night's thin layer of ground-fog. It was promising to be another hot day. Henry and Eliza both removed their coats—his wool and threadbare, hers flannel and still in fine condition—and laid them out upon the thin duff of leaves covering the ground. Eliza was able to sit upright, and she unwrapped the small cotton package that Master Cromwell had given them while Henry lay on his side looking up at her.

"I hear there's plenty of payin' work, farmin' up in Wisconsin. They say a man can make enough to buy his own piece of land, if 'n he's willin' to work hard," Henry said.

"You hear that from Nathaniel Clement, too?"

"He says his brother is up there in a place called Wooshara or Washara or somethin' and—"

"It's *something,* Henry. How many times do I have to tell you?"

"Yes, ma'am, it's Wooshara County or something. We weren't all lucky enough to grow up a house-nigger."

"Don't call me that. You know I don't like it. Besides, I'm trying to teach you, is all. You get up there around all those educated northern folk, you want to be speaking proper don't you?"

"I'm sorry," Henry said, reaching down and putting his hand up Eliza's dress so he could rub her upper calf. "I know you're jes tryin'—*just trying* to teach me."

Eliza cut two slices from the small loaf of bread then cut two thin hunks of the salted pork to lay on top of them. "Do you want some molasses?" she asked, holding up a small clay jug.

"I reckon we should save it," Henry replied, taking one of the quasi-sandwiches and biting into it. "That pork's not going to last long. Once we get further up the woods I can set a couple of snares."

"Henry, I'm afraid."

"So am I. Don't you worry, though. Once we get to Illinois, we'll be jes fine. Can't be more than a hundred an' fifty mile if 'n we just stay northeast."

"*If* we *just* stay northeast."

"That's what I said. *If* we just stay northeast we should be in Illinois in a fortnight."

Henry smiled wryly in the dark and popped the last bit of food in his mouth and lay back with his hands laced behind his head.

"*A fortnight?*" Eliza exclaimed, forgetting the ongoing grammar lesson for the time being. "It shouldn't take us two weeks to walk a hundred and fifty miles. Master Cromwell sent me up to Colonel Jenkin's place to help with the washing when his house-girls fell ill with the yellow fever, and I walked it in an afternoon. And you know that's five miles to and five miles back."

"You weren't walking at night, through the woods, and the moon ain't gonna be on our side anymore two or three days from now. We'll be lucky to get in ten mile a night. C'mon, finish your food and try to get some sleep."

"I'm not very hungry. My stomach's paining me some this morning."

Henry looked at her with concern. Eliza smiled, "It's nothing. It'll pass."

Eliza stowed the food back in the small muslin bundle, set it aside and laid her head on Henry's chest. She was soon lulled by the steady rise and fall of her man's breathing.

They slept.

3

Henry's mother died bringing him into the world, and his father had been stabbed to death by another slave just days before Henry's third birthday. Henry was told later that the stabbing was over a pair of shoes his father had allegedly stolen from the other man. It was the consensus on the plantation that Henry's father was a snake of the lowest sort, and his violent end had been a long time coming.

As a boy, Henry was raised for a time by a woman named Harriet. She had wet-nursed him when he was an infant, then saw to the better part of his upbringing—even while his father was still above ground—until he was sold downriver when he was eleven. Henry lived with her and her two daughters in a small, two-room shanty on a tobacco plantation near the Missouri River in Howard County. In addition to the two daughters, Harriet had also birthed five sons: three died in infancy, and the other two were sold off to new owners before their tenth year. The plantation owner, Alexander Fordham, kept mostly female slaves. He claimed them to be easier to handle and harder workers than the men. Fordham was a widower and was known to call on the young women of his plantation in the early hours of the morning. Refusals were met with beatings. Henry could remember Harriet's eldest daughter, Sally, being sent for by Master Fordham on more than one occasion. He would sometimes lay awake, listening to Harriet sobbing softly in the darkness after Sally left. He'd wished he could comfort her, but didn't know how. Sally was always back before sunup, and the incidents were never discussed in Henry's presence.

Harriet had treated Henry kindly, but was never affectionate in any physical way. She was a tough taskmaster and had little patience for anyone shirking his or her duties. She'd put him to work as soon as he could heft a wash bucket and worked him hard until he began service in Master Fordham's tobacco drying shed when he was seven. Harriet cared for him in her fashion but never acted the mother. On the morning he was to be taken to the travelling slave auction in Fayette, she'd given him a stiff, short hug before saying goodbye. It was the first and only embrace Henry had received from another human being in his life.

Up until the day when Master Stryker, the plantation's overseer, took Henry to the auction in Fayette, Henry's life had been routine and mostly unremarkable. He'd been treated fairly, albeit indifferently by Amos Caulfield, the drying shed foreman, and he rarely went to bed hungry. That all changed moments after the overseer—who'd said nothing to Henry during the entire ten-mile trip to Fayette— stopped the mule-cart in front of a large stable near the end of town and said, "You stay put, now."

Henry never saw Master Stryker again.

Fayette was small, but Henry had never been off of the plantation and was awestruck at how many people were about, walking from place to place, peering in glass fronted stores and loading wagons with flour sacks and parcels. Some stopped and greeted each other before moving on to whatever business they had to conduct. Two boys of about Henry's age came out from an alley between two buildings across the street. One saw Henry on the mule-cart, and after tugging on his friend's sleeve and pointing a finger at Henry, picked up a fair sized dirt-clod and threw it toward the mule-cart. The projectile missed Henry— just—and bounced off of the cart's backrest before clunking to the floorboard by Henry's feet. The two boys ran off up the dirt street, shoving each other and laughing.

"Come on down off'n that wagon, nigger, and get on inside."

Henry turned around, startled, and saw a fat man wearing a wide-brimmed straw hat with a cigar stuck in the corner of his mouth looking up at him speculatively.

"Master Stryker tol' me to stay put, sir."

"Master Stryker ain't here, and I ain't gonna tell you again. You get down offa there and get your ass inside."

Harriet taught Henry early on not to argue or be insolent with the whites—any whites. He glanced in the direction Master Stryker had gone then reached into the back of the cart and retrieved the small bundle that was all of his possessions: a second shirt, and a small wooden cross that had belonged to his mother. He jumped down from the mule-cart and looked expectantly at the fat man, who waved a hand toward the stable. Henry turned and began walking. The fat man kicked him in the backside—hard—and Henry fell to the ground.

"You move your ass when I tell you, nigger. Now get up and *move.*"

One of the two large stable doors was propped open slightly and held in place by a couple of roof shakes. Henry entered through the narrow gap at the fat man's urging. He wondered if the fat man would fit.

The stable's spacious interior smelled of fresh hay, leather, and horse manure. Tack hung here and there from the rafter beams. The rear doors were both wide open and there was a small congregation of whites gathered just inside of them, speaking in subdued voices.

"Go stand over there with them other niggers," the fat man said, pointing. Henry obeyed and walked over to where a group of about ten slaves were standing single file behind a large crate which was placed midway in the stable. They were all naked. He lined up behind a girl of about fifteen—the only female in the group—and looked around, unsure of what was coming next. After a few minutes, a man in a fine suit and tall hat strode through a door in the side of stable and approached him.

"You are ahhh…Henry?" the man asked, after briefly consulting a sheet of foolscap.

"Yessir," Henry replied.

"Remove your clothes and put them over there." The man cocked his head toward several small piles of garments lying on the dirt floor near where he'd entered. "And what is that?"

"Jes a shirt and my mama's cross, sir."

"Leave it with your clothes. Go on now, boy, then get back over here."

Henry did as he was bidden. A wave of homesickness hit him as he undressed, and he choked back the tears that wanted to come. He already missed the little shanty on the edge of the tobacco field. He wasn't going to hear Harriet's sweet singing voice as she chopped vegetables for the soup pot that night, or any night, ever again.

"Hurry on, boy. Time is money, you know. Let's have a look at you."

Henry dropped his too-small, roughly sewn, osnaburg trousers onto his little pile and hurried back to the line where the man was waiting for him with clear impatience.

"I trust you move faster at your work," the man said, taking Henry roughly by the chin. "Open your mouth…yes, good. Very fine teeth. Lift your arms…higher…good." He squatted, then reached out and squeezed one of Henry's thighs, then the other. "Now let me see the bottom of your feet…no, turn around, boy. That's right. Now the other…"

When he was finished inspecting Henry, the man stepped back and spoke to the entire group of slaves. "When I say your name, you will step forward and stand on this box. You stand up straight and you will not speak to any of my patrons unless they address you directly." He eyed the line of naked slaves for a moment, then turned and strode toward the group of prospective buyers.

4

After nearly two hours the line of slaves was down to three: Henry, the girl, and a large, muscular man whose back was a latticework of thick scars. Henry had to piss but kept silent. None of the other slaves had spoken a single word—to each other, or the whites, so he thought it prudent to follow suit.

Not long after the auction started, the fat man with the cigar returned with a milking stool and sat himself down next to Henry and the others. He spent most of the time whittling a big stick into a smaller stick, pausing every now and then to retrieve a small flask from the inside of his sweat-stained shirt and take a pull from it. He also escorted the newly sold slaves from the stable to whatever transport—and future—awaited them.

The man with the scarred back was called next.

"John Brown, step up please," the man in the fine suit called out. John Brown stepped up onto the crate and dispassionately faced the group before him.

"John Brown, ladies and gentlemen," the man with the fancy suit and tall hat began. "Thirty-two-years old, and just look at him; he's a pillar of strength and good health. This well-built nigger's a skilled carpenter and can work tobacco from sunrise to sundown seven days a week without appreciable signs of slowing…"

Henry watched with growing trepidation as his turn to stand on the crate grew closer and closer. He watched as John Brown, like the others before him, was poked, fondled, and squeezed repeatedly by the whites while they haggled over the price of owning him.

Finally, after repeated inquiries into John Brown's scars and questions as to whether or not he obtained them due to being troublesome (there were assurances that he was a passive and respectful nigger) a deal was struck and John Brown was sold to a man named Frederick Abbott, who was in the market for a slave skilled in woodcraft.

The girl, whose name was Hanna, was sold in minutes.

Henry was called and he stepped onto the crate to face his potential masters. He was shamefully aware of his nakedness as he endured the strange hands on his body.

"This monkey's gonna be right tall, I reckon, Mister Fallwell, but he looks underfed," Frederick Abbott said to the man in the fancy suit. "I'll pay five hundred."

"Oh, I'll have to respectfully decline, sir. I couldn't part with Henry here for a penny less than six-fifty. He's only eleven and already knows tobacco like the back of his own hand."

"It's not the *back* of his hands I'm worried about, Mister Fallwell. Look here…" Frederick Abbott took Henry's hands and turned them over. "This boy's hands haven't seen a single day of field work; not that I intend to use him for such, but how can I know I'm not going to have teach this boy what a day's work is? I'll pay six hundred or take my leave."

The man in the fancy suit—Mister Fallwell—quickly scanned the thinning group of possible buyers before saying: "You are a shrewd negotiator, sir. He is yours." He stuck out his hand and Frederick Abbott shook it absently.

"I'd be grateful if you'd have the niggers delivered to me by tomorrow."

"Of course, Mister Abbott. I'll make the arrangements."

5

Henry was allowed to gather his things before being led naked through the rear of the stable by the fat man with the ever-present cigar. It was a short walk past an already harvested corn field. Forgotten stalks, bent and brown, whispered to themselves in the light breeze.

They entered a smaller barn which canted appreciably to one side. The interior was dim and dusty. The fat man pointed to an open stall.

"You'll sleep over there," he said. "Sunrise tomorrow I'll be takin' you and the big one down south of Boonville. C'mon now, get dressed." The fat man waited for Henry to put on his clothes, then ushered him over to the stall.

"Over here, boy," he said, stepping over the legs of two other slaves sitting against the plank wall of the barn. "Sit on down here."

Henry did as he was told, sitting against the wall in the thick bed of sour smelling hay on the barn's dirt floor. The fat man gathered up a length of chain that was attached to the other two men's ankles and deftly fastened the cuff to Henry.

"Got to protect Mister Abbott's investments. Once I get you delivered, you'll be his worry."

Henry began to cry. The fat man looked at him with something like wonder.

"Wooo, whooo, whooo. Little nigglet missing his mama?" He slapped Henry across the mouth. "You shut that shit up, now. Mister Abbott ain't gonna take too kindly to a sniveling nigger." He leaned in close and exhaled a breath that reeked of whiskey, stale tobacco, and rotten teeth. "And hear me, nigger, you don't want to get on Mister Abbott's bad side." He gave

the chain a rough shake, then turned and walked out of the barn.

"You and me going to the same place. You a field hand?" John Brown asked, eyeing Henry doubtfully from his place a few feet from Henry.

Henry wiped his eyes. "I ain't never worked a field, yet. I tied tobacco and hung it."

"What's your name?"

"Henry."

"You ain't never wore chains before, neither." It wasn't a question.

"No, sir."

"I ain't no white boss, boy. You call me John, and I'll call you Henry. This here," John cocked his head to the man sitting next to him, "is Thomas. He'll be travellin' with us as far as New Franklin."

Thomas, who was younger than John Brown, nodded his head to Henry. "You ought'n not be crying lest you wanna git whooped."

"You never mind that," John said, looking sternly at the younger man.

The barn door opened and the fat man and a young slave woman entered. The fat man stood beside the open door with his arms crossed, and the woman, who was carrying a woven basket, walked over to the stall where Henry and the two men were chained. She removed large pieces of cornbread from the basket and handed them around without a word.

"You're right pretty," Thomas said, smiling.

"I'm not supposed to talk to you," the woman whispered. "I'm sorry there's no beans."

"Thank you for the cornbread, missy," John said.

"Thank you," Henry said, already enthusiastically stuffing the cornbread in his mouth.

The woman gave them a nod then hurried back to where the fat man was waiting. He gave her an impatient shove through the door.

After the meager meal, Thomas began singing softly, under his breath. Henry couldn't place the song but thought he'd heard it sung by Harriet. Listening to the familiar but unnamable melody, he looked forward with apprehension and a child's hope. He wondered what his life with his new master would be like.

6

"Where'd you get those scars on your back?" Henry asked, breaking the silence. He and John Brown were sitting in the back of the buckboard eating stale biscuits and waiting for the fat man to return from delivering Thomas to his new master. They were both chained to a thick, metal ring fastened to the side of the wagon. The fat man hadn't allowed any talking on the trip from Fayette to New Franklin, stating that there was nothing surer to get a man's head to aching than listening to a bunch of niggers *conversating* for three hours.

"Tied to a tree is where I got them. If you're askin' *why* I got them, it's because I'm a slave. Masters don't need no reason to give a whippin'."

John could see by Henry's expression that his answer wasn't satisfactory. He sighed. "I reckon I got the worst of 'em on account of I couldn't keep my mouth closed when I was young—not young like you, young like Thomas. I had to learn the hard way, you don't back-sass the free folks. You ain't been whipped yet?"

"No. I ain't never. Amos Caulfield sometimes swatted me with a willow switch if 'n he thought I was moving too slow."

John Brown looked at Henry with something like pity. "Well, you gonna get hit with somthin' worse than a willow branch from time to time, but not so much if 'n you do what you're told an' be quiet when you're supposed to and make noise when you're supposed to."

"When am I *supposed* to make noise?"

"Some places, they want you singin' while you're workin'. That ways they can know you ain't run off, even if they can't see you."

"Have you lived in a lot of places?"

"Yes, I have. More'n I care to count." John caught movement out of the corner of his eye and glanced without turning his head toward the big house where the fat man had taken Thomas. "Quiet down now. He's comin'."

The fat man strode up. "You two comfy back there?" he asked sarcastically as he climbed into the wagon's driver's seat. "The missus served up some fine tea and cakes."

7

They arrived at their destination less than an hour later. The house was a huge, two-story timber-frame—much larger than Master Fordham's, which Henry had thought grand—and was situated majestically among manicured hedges and a sprawling lawn. The gabled roof extending over the porch was supported by six towering, white pillars.

The fat man turned off the main road and coaxed the horses slowly up the neat drive to the house. When the wagon was close, a man strode down the porch steps and waved the fat man off to the left. "Take them around back!" he called, walking in that direction himself.

They rounded the house. The rear's appearance wasn't given quite as much care as the front, and tools of plantation living were scattered here and there.

The fat man stopped the wagon in front of a long hitching rail with two large water troughs at either end. "You niggers are home," he said, stepping down from the wagon and walking to the rear. He reached over the side and began unlocking the chains that held Henry and John Brown.

"Any trouble?" the man who had come from the front porch asked as he walked up and regarded Henry and John with a flat expression.

"No. No trouble at all," the fat man replied, continuing to work the shackle on Henry's ankle.

"Well, you can leave them with me as soon as you get them loose. You water your team and I'll have the kitchen girl bring you out a glass of beer and a couple boiled eggs."

"I'm grateful, Mister…?

"Lawrence Townley. I'm Mister Abbott's responsible order." He extended his hand.

The fat man turned from his work and shook the other man's hand. "David Cornish," he said.

"I'll see to that beer, Mister Cornish.

The fat man—Cornish— finished unshackling Henry and John Brown. He then led the horses to one of the water troughs and stood there while they drank. Soon a girl of about Henry's age came out of the back door carrying a tray with a blown glass mug full of beer and a small bowl of boiled eggs on it. The girl set the tray on a knee-high cedar round next to the water trough and hurried back to the house. Henry looked after her curiously.

"I'd like to have me some of those eggs," John whispered to Henry, who smiled and nodded his assent.

Lawrence Townley reappeared a short time later and addressed Henry and John: "You can climb down now. Follow me. Good day, Mister Cornish." Townley tipped his rather misshapen, felt hat at the fat man and started off toward a series of outbuildings several hundred feet behind the main house. He didn't look back.

"C'mon, Henry. Follow along, quickly now," John said, getting up and hopping down from the wagon. Henry glanced at the fat man, who was leaning on the front of the wagon looking at him with a smirk and also jumped down.

They followed Townley past what appeared to be two large supply sheds and a massive barn before stopping at a cleared-out area where four wood stakes had been driven into the ground to make a large rectangle. There were several stacks of planks and timbers, some as tall as a man, laid out some feet away.

"The master should be along shortly," Townley said, then pulled a pipe from his pocket and knocked it several times against the palm of his hand before retrieving a small leather pouch from the same pocket and refilling it.

"I see they made it," Frederick Abbott said walking up from the barn. He addressed Townley without even looking Henry and John's way. "Are those stakes at forty feet and sixty feet as I asked?"

"To the inch," Townley replied, striking a match and lighting his pipe.

Frederick Abbott turned to John. "You're a carpenter?"

"Yessir, Master Abbott."

"You remembered my name." He looked John up and down. "You *are* a smart one, aren't you? Are you really thirty-two years old, boy?"

John lowered his eyes. "I don't rightly know, Master Abbott, sir."

"I knew that hornswoggler Fallwell was just spinning a tale. You *can* build me a drying barn, though?"

"Yessir, Master Abbott, sir."

"Then you can begin tomorrow. This boy," he cocked his head toward Henry, "will be your helper and will remain your charge until I instruct you otherwise. I will provide you with additional labor when it is required. Do you understand?"

John's eyes darted to Henry then back to his owner. "Yessir, Master Abbott, sir."

Frederick Abbott turned back to Townley. "Lawrence, lash this nigger ten…and five for the boy, then quarter them in the tack-barn until they can build a suitable place for themselves—" Townley began to interrupt in protest, but Abbott put up a hand and cut him off.

"I don't want these two fraternizing with the field hands and I'm certainly not going to quarter them with the house help. They can work on the barn six days and do their own work on Sunday after I read from the good book. Do as I ask, now."

"I'll see to it, Mister Abbott."

Frederick Abbott started down the path toward the house. "Oh, and Lawrence, when you're finished, have Eliza tend to their wounds and get their supper."

Two

1

Henry awoke with a start. It was full dark. He gave Eliza a gentle shake and crawled out of the lean-to. He walked several feet away and urinated into the thicket. He didn't think it was very late—possibly nine o'clock—but he wanted to get moving right away nonetheless. He was a good deal more afraid of being discovered than he'd let on to Eliza.

"Do you want to eat something before we go?" Eliza asked, poking her head out of the lean-to.

"I'd like to eat everything we have," he replied, finishing his business. He walked back and crawled into the lean-to. "A little of that molasses would taste good."

"I can't see a thing and I'd just get it all over the place. Have some bread." She cut two more slices off the dwindling loaf—a thick one for Henry and a much thinner one for herself—and stowed everything away. A short time later they were on their way.

They kept as close to the river as they could, circling well around any lamplight given off by homesteads and farms. Not long after midnight, after veering inland, away from what appeared to be a ferry crossing—Chaney's they assumed, though neither of them had ever actually been there—they came across a small apple orchard. The apples had already been harvested, but they were able to find a few pithy, worm-eaten stragglers as they nervously searched the trees by the light of the moon.

"You brought me the first apple I ever ate," Henry said quietly, putting a pair of the apples in his coat pocket for later. "Not long after I first came to Master Abbott's."

"And you ate the whole thing, worm and all," Eliza said with a laugh. "And you don't have to call that wicked man *master* anymore, Henry. We don't have to call anyone master ever again."

"I know. It's gonna take some gettin' used to, that's all. C'mon, we should keep moving. We don't want to get caught stealing apples.

Even ones that have been left to rot."

As if cued, a dog started barking not far off. Henry grabbed Eliza's hand and hurried around the orchard and back down by the river, upstream of the ferry crossing. Eventually the dog ceased barking.

"I want goats," Eliza said out of the blue as they walked the high bank of the Osage river. They hadn't seen a house in awhile, and they were on a stretch of riverbank that was more high grass than trees and brush. They were making good time.

"What do you want an ornery old goat for? All they do is eat."

"For the milk. Adeline Holm brought some milk from her goat when she came to call on Missus Abbott one time. She allowed I could try some of it. It was wonderful."

"I expect we'll be raising a goat or two then…once we get settled. Anything else you want?"

Eliza stopped. "Yes. One thing."

"What's that?" Henry walked a few more steps before realizing Eliza wasn't next to him anymore. He turned and walked back to her; a dark silhouette against a moonlit sky.

"This." She took his hand in hers, pulled him close, and kissed him in the hollow of his neck, tasting his sweat and savoring it. Tightening her grip she lowered herself down into the grass, pulling him down with her. The grass was dewy but neither of them noticed. The love was heated, urgent—much more so than what had become routine for the young pair. All of the growing tension and uncertainty caused by their new found freedom was relieved, temporarily at least, in a few frantic moments. And for those moments, they felt truly free.

Afterward they held each for a time, staring at the moon and listening to the musical chirping of a thousand crickets. But as their bodies and their passions cooled, both Henry and Eliza soon felt the need to get moving again.

"I love you, Henry," Eliza said, kissing him softly on his temple before standing up.

Henry stood and pulled up his trousers, cinching them tight with the hank of hemp rope that served as his belt.

"You're all I've ever loved. Now c'mon, we should look for a place to stay the day so's I can set some snares before the sun comes up. It sure would be nice to catch us a couple rabbits for breakfast."

2

They weren't as lucky as the previous night and had to travel quite a distance away from the river to find a location where they felt confident no one would come across them while they slept. They settled on a large, downed hickory. The deadfall was in a fairly dense, mixed stand of trees and was surrounded by a lot of underbrush. Henry thought it looked like a fair spot to try some snares.

It was still too dark for Henry to confidently set any snares that actually had a chance of working so he risked lighting a small torch he fashioned out of a stick, some dried moss and a bit of the salted pork. He rubbed the piece of pork all over the moss, then tied the moss to the stick with a bit of thread Eliza had included in her drawstring bag. After tearing off a small hunk of the bread to use for bait, he headed out.

He walked several hundred yards from the downed tree— Eliza stayed behind to prepare their meager meal—and lit the torch with the chunk of flint and scrap of steel John Brown had given him before running off into the night three years before. John Brown; his only friend, outside of Eliza. He couldn't believe it had already been three years since he'd last saw him. He wondered what became of him. He wondered if John had fared as well as Henry and Eliza had after that night.

He rubbed at the jagged scar running from just behind his left temple to midway down his cheek.

He wondered…

3

"Jes don't wail too much, if you can help it," John Brown whispered as he and Henry walked ahead of Lawrence Townley toward the split-rail pasture fence.

"That's good, now. Take off your shirts and just spread your arms out on that top rail. That's it, reach up there, boy, you can reach it," Townley called from behind them.

Henry, although tall for his age, couldn't spread his arms across the fence rail so he just reached his hands up and grabbed on. Townley came up and tied John Brown's hands to the rail then began with Henry's.

"My, look at that back," he said as he tied Henry's hands. "You ain't been whipped yet—at least not by someone who cares about what they're doing. Well I'm gonna whip you now, so I don't have to whip you later. That's so if down the road you get to thinking about being a lazy nigger, or stealing from Mister Abbott, or running off somewhere, you think about this whippin' and imagine it being tenfold. That's fifty lashes for you, boy. You think about that."

Townley walked off and the next thing Henry heard was a loud crack, and simultaneously his back exploded into blue fire. He glanced over at John, who was staring at him intently, as if willing him not to cry out. Henry gritted his teeth together and closed his eyes: *Craack!* the lash hit him again, tears welled up in his eyes and his vision blurred. He could feel blood running down his back and down the cleft of his buttocks. *Craack!* Henry screamed, his knees came unhinged. *Craack!* Townley missed his mark and the whip spun around Henry's face, tearing a deep gash into his left cheek. Now, hanging limply from his bindings, he stared at a brilliant late summer sky, impossibly blue and scattered with big puffy clouds resembling ripe cotton. He heard the crack again but it was far away. The sky went gray, then black.

Henry came around with his face in hay. He was on his stomach. He tried to roll over but two hands pressed down on his shoulders.

"You just lie still now," the female voice spoke softly. "We have to take care of these so as you don't get the rot in them."

Something cool touched his back and it stung fiercely. Henry gasped.

"There now. You can sit up, I have to look at your face."

Henry slid his hand up to his face and touched it gingerly. His fingers came away bloody. He pushed himself up, wincing at the pain in his back, and was looking at the girl who'd brought the beer and eggs to the fat man. John Brown was sitting behind her, shirtless, on a milking stool. He was looking at Henry, his expression was grave. Henry averted his eyes.

"There's no shame. You did fine. You let that girl get you fixed up. The master's gonna 'spect a whole day's work out of you tomorrow an' this here's a whippin' master."

"Am I gonna get whipped every day?" Henry asked, his hand reflexively darting to his face with the fresh flare of pain from speaking.

"Not so long as you work hard an' do what you're told. Now be quiet an' let her finish."

"I'm Eliza," the girl said, kneeling in front of him and gently daubing a damp cloth on the cut on his cheek. She rinsed the cloth several times in a small clay bowl full of water. She was wearing a plain white housedress and had a white scarf on her head that was patterned in tiny blue flowers. Henry thought she was beautiful.

"This is going to hurt some," she said as she scooped some foul smelling mixture out of a second bowl and began applying it to the cut. It looked like mud to Henry.

When she was finished she smiled at him and said: "I don't have enough cloth for a proper poultice, but it should be fine if you keep your fingers out of it."

She picked up the two clay bowls and stood. "The missus says I can bring you all some supper once I'm finished here. I'll tend to the other one now."

Eliza walked over to John Brown and set the clay bowl with the poultice mixture in it next to him. "I'll just fetch some clean water, then I'll see to your back."

"Thank you, missy." John said.

Eliza hurried out of the barn.

"That girl was born a house-nigger. She talk almost jes like one of the white folks."

"I like her," Henry said.

"I like her too. But you be careful how much you be trustin' house-niggers. Sometimes they ain't the same as we are."

"All right," Henry said, sounding dubious.

A few moments later Eliza returned with the fresh water and knelt behind John.

"Don't you worry over it too much. My back's so scarred up it's about as tough as a bull's hide anyhow."

"It don't look as bad as his does," she agreed.

"His name's Henry."

Eliza looked over John's shoulder at Henry and smiled. "Henry's a good name."

About an hour later Eliza returned to the barn with several ears of hot corn and some biscuits on a wood plank.

"This is about the last of the corn," she said. "It's tough but sweet."

4

Six years later Frederick Abbott's plantation house burned down. Master Abbott, along with his wife, his daughter, and two of his house slaves died in the blaze. Eliza and two other women who worked in the big house managed to escape.

Eliza ran to the tiny but neat looking house that Henry and John Brown had built from scrap wood at about an hour after midnight. Frederick Abbott had allowed Henry and John to build themselves the place with cut-offs and discards from the drying shed and a secondary tack-barn they'd built. Since they were carpenters, they were treated slightly better than field slaves, though not nearly as good as house slaves.

The plantation was in chaos, and Henry and John were already running out of the house when Eliza arrived.

"Master Townley wants everyone to help with the bucket line," Eliza said, out of breath.

John looked up at the big house, which was fully engulfed in flames. It was at least three hundred yards away but it lit Henry and John's little porch like sunset. "Ain't no bucket line going to save that place. Did the family get out?"

Eliza shook her head. "Mathilda and Old George neither." She began to weep and Henry took her hand.

"Good," John said bitterly, then added: "Course not Mathilda and Old George—that's a sad shame—but I don't feel a lick of sorrow for Master Abbott nor none of his folk. That man's already in hell, if there is such a place. And for his sake I'm hopin' there is. Now I'm quittin' this place. You two comin' with me?"

"Where are you going to go, John?" Eliza asked.

Henry started to retort, "If 'n they catch you—"

"Then they can goddamn kill me," John shouted. "There ain't nothing left for them to take but my life, an' that's all they're gettin' if they catch me. An' I tell you I ain't givin' *that* up without a fight. Now you're a long sight from that wet-nosed boy they shackled me with six years back but you're still a young man an' you ain't broke yet. But you will be. You'll be a broken down ol' nigger jes like me, an' Eliza'll jes be a sad recollection you weep over on cold nights when you think no one can hear.

"Now you look at that house. They's all gone. What do you think the chances are that you two stay together through this? By tomorrow one of you could be on your way to Arkansas and the other a mile up the road from this very spot. I heard we can live as free men—and women—down in Mexico. That's where I'm going and you both should come with me."

Just then Norman Smith, one of the field foremen, came running by shouting, "C'mon, get a move on, now! We got a fire!"

John grabbed Henry by the wrist and nodded his head in the opposite direction of the burning house. Henry looked at Eliza. She shook her head slowly back and forth. "Henry, I can't...I'm afraid."

John tightened his grip and looked at Henry intently. "It has to be now," he said urgently.

"I have to stay with Eliza," Henry said.

"It's been good knowing you, then. Both of you...wait a minute." John ran back into the little house and was back out in seconds. He had a grain sack (much like the one Henry carried three years later) and he fished around at the bottom of it and pulled out a small, folded scrap of leather. "It's a flint and steel. Been meaning to give it to you for some time, jes kept slippin' my mind. You take care now."

John Brown ran into the Missouri night.

Three

1

There was about two hours of daylight left, and Eliza was already sitting up with her back against the downed tree. She was thinking about how good some rabbit would taste and hoped Henry's snares worked as well as they usually did. She rubbed the top of his head, massaging his skull through his closely cropped hair. He opened one eye and looked up at her.

"I'd say good morning but it's evening," she said, then leaned down and kissed him. "Now are you going to go see whether we're eating salted pork again or rabbit or squirrel?"

"On my way, missus," Henry joked. He reached up and patted her belly then sat up. "I know you must be real hungry." You just leave that pork wrapped up. My snares never miss…leastways back 'round Lawson's Bend they didn't."

Henry was gone less than ten minutes when Eliza heard breaking branches and voices coming from behind her. Dropping to her hands and knees she raised her head and peered over the fallen tree. She could see men moving through the woods—four or five—and they were coming straight for her.

Seized by panic, Eliza scrambled to her feet and began running through the brush. She struck off in the general direction she'd watched Henry go but was soon only following the path of least resistance and running blindly away from danger like a frightened animal. The inevitable happened, and she tripped over a hidden branch and went down, tearing her dress from hip to hem on more woods detritus. She lay there for a moment, breathing heavily and gingerly running her fingers over the nearly foot long scrape down her right thigh. She heard movement from her left and froze, staring into the deepening twilight. Snatches of a familiar tune being whistled low came to her and she leaped up and ran toward the sound.

Henry looked up, startled by the sound of something moving fast. He caught movement in the shadows nearly dead in front of him and raised his hands reflexively—dropping the two rabbits he'd been carrying in the process—just as Eliza collided with him.

"Henry...oh, Henry," Eliza panted, with a frightened whisper-shout. She threw her arms around him and clung to him while twisting her head around to look back the way she'd come. "There's men, we have to run—"

Henry didn't wait for further explanation, he just reached around his back, grabbed Eliza's hand and headed off in the opposite direction of their makeshift camp. Fighting the urge to run, Henry steered them back a few yards to the animal path he'd followed to set his snares.

Once there he dropped her hand; the path was too narrow for them to move side by side. "C'mon, stay close and be as quiet as you can," Henry said before setting off at a jog.

They'd only moved a dozen or so steps when two men appeared from behind a thick stand of trees and stepped onto the path.

"What are you doing out here, niggers?" One of the men asked while the other leveled a musket at Henry.

"I'm not going to ask you a second time...James, shoot the woman."

"Pa?" The man holding the musket, who was obviously younger than Henry's twenty years, sounded unsure.

"I said—"

"We're free!" Henry blurted. "We was given our freedom two days ago by Master Samuel Cromwell down by Lawson's Bend. We have our free papers."

"That so?" The man walked a few steps closer, rubbing his salt and pepper beard thoughtfully. Henry backed up until he felt Eliza then stood in front of her protectively. "You keep still, nigger," the man said, leveling a finger at Henry. "Now, show me these papers."

"Yessir. They're right back there a ways."

"Well, let's go and see 'em, before it gets too dark." The man put his fingers in his mouth and whistled twice. It was a melodic *heehoo heehoo* like a birdsong.

He cocked his head as if listening, then whistled again. Seeming satisfied he looked back at Henry."Go on, get moving." Then: "My boy here's going to shoot you if you try to run."

Henry turned and gave Eliza a nod, pointing in the direction of their makeshift camp. He walked behind her, keeping himself between her and the men.

About a third of the way back to the deadfall, four more armed men came tramping through the brush and joined the other two. None of them appeared to be older than seventeen.

"More runaways, Emmet?" one of them asked, falling in step with the older man.

"Looks that way."

"What're you going to do with 'em?"

"Just get the horses, Bob," the man replied flatly, without taking his eyes off of Henry's back.

A minute later they were at the deadfall. Henry retrieved the papers from his grain sack and handed them to the man named Emmet.

"I can't read these," he said, indifferently stuffing the papers in his coat. "We'll go up the road to our camp where I can have some light. If you're telling the truth, you can be on your way."

Henry looked around apprehensively at the men, then at Eliza. "Let's get our things."

"You can leave your things here. They'll be waiting for you when you get back. Let's go."

Emmet led them through the brush. There was a road less than two hundred feet from the deadfall, and Henry felt the fool for missing it the previous night. *Might as well camped right in the open,* he thought grimly. The one named Bob was waiting for them with a string of horses a short distance up from where Henry, Eliza and the others exited from the trees.

"Tie their hands," Emmet said when they reached the horses.

Eliza began to sob. "Henry—"

"And shut that bitch up, unless you want me to," he added, mounting a horse.

"Gimme your hands, boy," Bob said, grabbing Henry and spinning him around so his back was turned. Another yanked

Eliza toward one of the horses where he removed a length of rope from a saddlebag. Eliza let out a cry as he pulled her arms behind her back and began roughly tying her wrists. Henry shook free and started toward Eliza but was stopped short when James, the one holding the musket, stepped forward and clubbed him in the side of the head with it. Henry went to his knees. Bob came up behind him, cursing under his breath, and planted a boot in the middle of his back, pushing Henry down face first in the road. James spun the musket back around and put the business end to Henry's head.

"You move again, I'll put a ball in your skull," he said, tapping the barrel of the musket on Henry's head.

Bob sat on Henry's legs and tied his hands tightly, then he yanked Henry to his feet by the rope. Henry tottered and almost fell but Bob grabbed him under the arm and steadied him. "That knock some sense into your dumb runaway skull? Well, I reckon not."

They'd marched Henry and Eliza—who were tied together by a short rope and then tethered to Bob's horse by another, longer leader—about two miles when Emmet stopped the group just short of a sharp bend in the road. He whistled twice; the same melodic sound as before. This time Henry heard the response coming from some distance away. It was a similar whistle to Emmet's only the notes were reversed. After a moment they continued on.

Some hundred yards or so past the bend they came upon a small group of armed men sitting in the back of a horseless wagon. The wagon was blocking all but a narrow strip of the road—just enough to allow horses to pass single file. Emmet cued his horse over to the wagon and exchanged words with the men there as they passed. Henry could see campfires and lamplight up ahead.

The camp was set up in the middle of the road. There were several wagons and dozens of horses and mules. Campfires burned here and there. Henry's stomach rumbled from the smell of cooking meat and beans, despite his fear. He guessed there were around forty men, most as young or younger than he was. He looked back at Eliza; the only thing in the world he'd ever cared about. Her face was a mask of despair. Seeing the hopelessness there made him feel as if his heart was being ripped out. He tried to give her a reassuring smile but knew it missed the mark. She could always tell exactly what he was thinking.

Emmet stopped just inside the camp and a boy of about ten came running up. "I'll take your horse, Mister Dawson," he said eagerly.

Emmet Dawson dismounted and handed over the reins. "Mind you rub her down, and get someone to help you with the saddle." He gave the boy's hair a quick ruffle then turned and walked past the spot where Bob was standing, holding the reins of his own horse in one hand and the rope leader tied to Henry and Eliza in the other. He was looking at Emmet expectantly. Emmet ignored him and walked up to Henry and Eliza.

"What is your name?"

"Henry, sir, and this is Eliz—"

"I didn't ask you *her* name," Emmet interrupted.

"Yessir."

"Henry, did you see that boy?" He nodded his head in the direction the boy had taken his horse.

"Yessir."

"That boy's house was burned to the ground by bloodthirsty unionist jayhawkers two days ago along with every other house and farm between here and Osceola, including your…" He pulled the crumpled sheets of Henry and Eliza's free papers from his coat and held them close to his face, squinting. "…Samuel Cromwell." He held the papers out. "Can you read these?"

Henry averted his eyes. "No, sir," he lied.

"No, of course you can't. It's not only near to impossible to teach a nigger to read but it's also against the law—God's *and* man's." He lowered the papers to his side. "These jayhawkers are burning and pillaging their way across our great state. They're murdering innocent Missouri families in their sleep then setting niggers loose on the land like a pestilence. That boy's an orphan. His father, his mother, and his little baby sister were inside the house when it was set ablaze. They were unable to escape. We found their niggers a few miles away, riding their horses and leading their pigs just like they had the right to. We are at war, Henry. We are at war to save our families and our way of life."

Emmet turned and looked at Bob. "Hang him with the others."

Eliza let out an anguished wail and dropped to her knees where she began screaming hysterically. Henry tried to kneel down with her but Bob yanked the rope tight and wrapped it on his saddle horn. This left Henry standing at an awkward lean as he tried not to drag Eliza.

"What about the woman?" Bob asked.

Emmet Dawson looked down at Eliza appraisingly. "Shut her up and tie her to my wagon…and here," he handed Bob the free papers. "Pin these to his shirt. There aren't any free niggers in Missouri." He gave Henry a final stony look then walked into the camp.

James Dawson climbed from his horse, pulled a knife from the waistband of his trousers and cut the rope tethering the still wailing Eliza to Henry. He helped her to her feet.

"You heard your pa, James. Shut that bitch up," Bob said impatiently.

James let go of Eliza and she ran the few steps to Henry. Her hands were still tied and she could do no more than push her body up against his. James retrieved a neck-cloth from his saddle bag then pulled Eliza away from Henry by her upper arm. *"NOOOO!"* she screamed, twisting around and kicking at James. A small group of men from the camp had gathered to see what all the fuss was about and a pair stepped forward and subdued Eliza while James gagged her with his neck-cloth. Henry, meanwhile, was struggling fruitlessly against his tether trying to get to her.

"Let's get this done," Bob said. "Some of ya'll give me a hand over there." He mounted his horse and spurred it forward into the camp. The horse moved too fast for Henry to keep up and he fell and hit the ground face first, cutting his cheek open on a jagged rock. He struggled to keep his head raised up as he was jounced over the wagon-rutted road. A few men stopped what they were doing and ran alongside him, kicking him. Another man ran up and hit him in the back of the head with a cast iron cook pan. White light exploded behind Henry's eyes and he bit his tongue. The metal taste of blood filled his mouth. The assailant called out: "Did ya hear that? Sounded like a dang church bell on Sunday mornin'. That nigger's head's as hard as a rock." He was dragged several hundred feet to a huge oak at the road's edge. The old tree had a thick limb that jutted straight out from the trunk about twelve feet up and spanned nearly the entire width of the road.

There were six people hanging from the tree limb.

Even with the blood from his cut face blinding one of his eyes, Henry saw more than he could bear: five men and one small boy; all slaves. The flickering of the campfires made them look as if they were alive and engaged in some sort of macabre dance. The boy, who couldn't have been more than five, was naked. His face was a rictus of torment.

Henry panicked and began to struggle violently. Bob jumped off of his horse and began fashioning a slipknot on a coil of rope. Three men pulled Henry to his feet; one of them gut-punched him, knocking out his wind. Bob heaved the end of the rope in the air but it fell short of the limb and tumbled to the ground. He gathered it back up and threw it again, this time it sailed over the limb a few feet from the lynched boy.

"Bring 'im over here," Bob ordered. The men dragged Henry, still gasping for breath, underneath the dead slaves. Bob slipped the noose over Henry's head and pulled it tight.

"No! We're…free…we're *free,"* Henry wheezed and began throwing his shoulders back and forth. Bob was already on his horse and moving; Henry was jerked into the air, his windpipe suddenly closed by the weight of his body. He kicked his feet wildly and began spinning in circles. He saw the other hanged slaves as he turned. He saw the boy, his tortured features stared at nothing. He heard the taunts and laughs of the men below him.

Suddenly he was falling; the laughs turned to shouts of surprise. He hit the ground with a strangled cry, his knees buckled with the impact and he landed on his back. Cool night air rushed into his burning throat. He looked up and saw several men running toward him. Acting purely on the instinct to survive, Henry rolled over on his side and forced himself to his feet. He ran for the side of the road as fast as his legs would move. Two men—one of which didn't look older than fourteen—were running at a diagonal to Henry's path in an attempt to cut him off before he reached the side of the road and the woods beyond.

Just before Henry reached the trees, the older of the two tripped and fell.

Henry, with his hands still tied behind his back and on a collision course with the second, bent down and twisted his upper body slightly to the right just before slamming into him at an all-out run. He heard a snapping sound as his shoulder impacted with the man/ boy's chest and sent him flying into the brambles of the roadside. Rifle and pistol shots rang out among the shouts and Henry both heard and felt something zing past his left ear as he plowed through the underbrush. He ran blindly, the darkness growing thicker as he gained distance from the campfires. Tree branches whipped and scratched his face and the din of the chase was so close behind that he could hear the labored breath of his pursuers in between their shouted curses.

"If I fall, I'm dead, if I fall I'm dead, if I fall I'm dead, repeated over and over in Henry's mind like a chant.

There was the crash of someone falling, right on his heels. Then cries: "SON OF A *BITCH!* OWWW, GODDAMN! Help here, boys! Help here, now! Busted my damn leg I think!"

Then Henry was alone. There were a few more shouts, growing more and more distant. Then nothing.

He kept running.

A few minutes later he finally did fall. He rolled onto his back and lay there, his chest heaving, until he caught his breath. He listened for the sounds of pursuit and heard none. Then it hit him: *Eliza.*

His shame was immediate and deep. "I left her there," he said aloud. "Oh, Lord, I ran away and left her." Henry began to sob; "I have to go back...I have to go—" Suddenly he heard a branch break—not very far off. He tried to hold his breath but his chest wouldn't stop hitching. After a moment he gained control and listened silently. A minute passed. Footsteps; moving slow. Two of them. One was nearly right on top of him and another was off a ways in the direction he'd come from.

The one farther away spoke: "Come on, Frank, we ain't going to find him. I can't see hardly a thing. We're going to get lost, is what we're going to do. Besides, what that boy do so wrong as to get himself hung, anyway?"

"You don't be talking like that, Ned. Mister Dawson's giving the orders, and he isn't going to be happy if that nigger gets away. Besides, I thought I heard something."

"Well it ain't *our* fault. He'll be mad at Bob, not us. Bob was supposed to be doing the hanging. And that nigger's probably halfway to Kansas by now. You know how they can run."

"Bob needs to check he isn't using a rotten rope next time he's fixing to hang someone."

The man—Frank—stopped less than four feet from Henry. After what seemed like an eternity, he said, "Fine, then, let's go back," and started away.

Henry stayed where he was long after he could no longer hear the men walking through the brush. The moon was higher and a little of its light now filtered through the trees. Henry's hands had fallen asleep. He rolled onto his side and tried to get up. It wasn't as easy this time without the aid of fear but he managed it after a couple of attempts. He scanned the ground for a rock to cut the rope with. It was hard to see. Walking slowly, back in the general direction of the men's camp, he finally came across a pumpkin-sized rock which had split in half. Henry kicked the pieces apart and dropped to his knees in front of the larger of the two. Twisting his body around so he could get his wrists positioned over the rock he began running the rope back and forth on the split edge. It was a lot more difficult than he expected. The rope was tough and the scant moonlight provided little to see by. After several minutes he was finally free. He sat down and massaged his wrists. A shallow cut from the rock's edge trickled blood. Henry didn't even notice. He was thinking about Eliza.

The decision to try to free Eliza wasn't really a decision at all. He was simply compelled to do it. He still couldn't shake his feeling of cowardice for running away but he realized there was nothing he could have done for Eliza had he stayed. He would have been shot, or more likely subdued and hanged a second time. Now at least, he thought there could be a chance of freeing her when the men were off their guard. That meant he had to wait. He hoped they would assume he'd kept running and was miles away by now.

He found a large patch of mayapple in a shallow depression which was partially surrounded by a stand of oaks. He decided to lay up for the remainder of the night and most of the following day, figuring he'd try to creep up on the camp at dusk. With any luck he'd be able to spot Eliza, then wait until the men fell asleep before making his move.

It was the longest twenty hours of his life.

He lay awake in the mayapple until the early hours of the morning. He imagined every possible savagery Eliza could be enduring, and he alternated between crying for her and seething with hate for all things white. Finally, shortly before sunrise, he slept. The sleep, however, was fitful and filled with dreams of Eliza. Eliza, lying naked in the road, surrounded by men, and screaming his name over and over. He tried to run to her but couldn't. It was as if the very air had come alive and was pushing back at him with invisible hands. It was like trying to run under water.

He awoke before midday drenched in sweat, the echo of Eliza's screams still ringing in his ears. His mouth felt like it was full of cotton and his tongue throbbed dully with his heartbeat. He spent the hours running possible outcomes through his head. He'd been a plantation slave his entire life, not a fighter. Outside of John Brown teaching him to defend himself, he'd never even been in a fistfight with another man. He hoped he could be brave when it came to it. For Eliza.

2

The camp was gone.

Henry reached the road just before sunset. He hit upon it a little too far south and had to backtrack a half mile before coming to the place where the camp had been. There was no question of it being the right spot; the bodies still hung above the road, swaying slowly back and forth. The thick limb of the oak creaked ominously from the combined weight of the corpses.

Standing at the roadside, Henry stared indecisively into the deepening shadows. After some inner debate, he took off at run, southward on the road, back toward the deadfall where he and Eliza had made their makeshift camp.

He found the deadfall with little trouble but was both winded from the run and light-headed from dehydration by the time he reached it. He cursed himself again for not discovering that the road was so close when he'd chosen the deadfall as a their camp. Everything was still there, minus the small bundle of food, which had been dragged several feet away and ripped open, the contents eaten. The small jug of molasses, however, was untouched. He pulled the stopper and poured the thick liquid into his mouth before packing up their possessions, slinging them over his shoulder and heading for the river.

It was a good clip, and it took Henry the better part of an hour to reach the river. He felt selfish for using up the time, but knew his body needed the water. When he arrived he hastily dropped his and Eliza's things and slid down the grassy bank to the water. Wading out to his waist, he bent over and drank by double handfuls until he had his fill. He touched the cut on his face; it didn't feel very deep. *Now I'll have a scar on both sides of my face,* he thought as he washed the dried blood away. Afterward, he clambered back up the bank and retrieved the empty molasses jug, then returned to the river and filled it. It didn't hold much, but he knew he'd be thankful for it later.

Feeling refreshed from the water and molasses, Henry made his way back to the road, alternately running and walking. When he arrived back at the oak with the hanged slaves he didn't waste any time. The ropes were tied off to a pair of smaller trees at the roadside. Henry stood under them and fished his knife out of the grain sack he'd been keeping his belongings in.

One by one he cut the ropes. The bodies made sickening thumps when they hit the road. Fighting back the urge to vomit he cut the last one and stowed the knife back in the sack. He was grateful for the darkness.

He began dragging the bodies off the road and into the brush. When he got to the boy he started to weep. "I'm sorry I can't stay and give you a proper burial," he said to the boy as he laid him next to the others. "I have to see to Eliza now."

Henry ran northbound on the road. He was painfully aware that he was following men on horseback, and he knew that if they didn't stop for more than a night at a time, he'd never catch up to them on foot. Even being burdened with the wagons wouldn't slow them enough. He pushed the thought away and concentrated on running.

It didn't take long for him to begin flagging. He stopped briefly and drank half of the water in the molasses jug. He was more hungry than thirsty now, and he considered mixing the small amount of flour in Eliza's bag with the remaining water. He decided to wait until daybreak and continued on instead.

A stitch in Henry's side forced him to stop again two hours later. He'd been keeping a steady pace between a fast walk and a run when he first felt it. It wasn't bothersome right away, but it steadily grew deeper and more painful the longer he ran. Finally, already slowed to a sort of bent shuffle, he stopped and rested.

The rest of the night passed. Henry ran when he could, but mostly he walked. His thoughts were fatigue-induced jumbles, bordering on delirium. His mind jumped seamlessly from one memory to another. He remembered the first time he and Eliza had made love. He was fifteen, she was seventeen. It happened after Master Abbott's bible reading one Sunday. All Abbott's slaves were allowed the afternoons to themselves on Sundays. They still had to work the morning, as Abbott didn't feel the Christian day of rest applied to negroes. He gave them Sunday afternoons *"Out of the goodness of his heart."*

They were both over-eager that first time, and the act had been clumsy yet wonderful beyond words. He remembered how Eliza had suffered for a week afterward with a rash and blisters from the poison ivy she'd lain in. For the next two years they'd made love nearly every Sunday afternoon.

3

When the sun rose Henry moved off the road and into the woods. He kept moving parallel with the road, stopping to look and listen every time he heard something—real or imagined. Finally, in the early afternoon, he simply couldn't go any farther. He was in an area where the trees were thinner and the underbrush was taller so he just sat down. He would be out of sight to casual passersby—if there were any—and he was too spent to search around for a better location.

He opened Eliza's bag intending to get the small sack of flour. Her coat was on top. He wondered if she'd been cold the previous two nights. The nights were getting cooler. He began weeping again. He pulled her coat from the bag and held it against his face. The lining smelled so strongly of Eliza it caused him to let out a cry of anguish. He pushed the coat forcefully into his face, dampening his cries. After awhile the tears subsided; he lowered the coat. A runner of snot was smeared on the inside of the collar. He wiped it off on his own filthy and worn-out shirt, vaguely noticing the free papers that were somehow still pinned there.

He dumped a small amount of water into the flour sack and began kneading it. Thick, milky liquid seeped through the weave of the fabric and dripped from between his fingers. He tilted his head back, squeezed the pasty batter into his mouth, then chased it down with the remainder of his water. Curling up on the ground with Eliza's coat cradled in his arms, Henry slept.

The sound of horses on the road dragged him out of a deep and dreamless sleep. He sat up, disoriented, just in time to see ten or more riders heading north at a gallop. He ducked back down, but the caution was needless; the riders were past before he'd completed the motion.

From the position of the sun, Henry guessed it was three hours before sunset. He cursed himself for sleeping so long. His head and legs ached. After stowing Eliza's coat back in her bag, he stood, the muscles in his legs protesting. He began walking, resuming his northward course through the woods, parallel with the road. He'd make better time on the road, but knew it would be safer to stay off of it until dark.

After his over-worked muscles loosened up, he began jogging through the underbrush. As with the flight from his captors of three nights prior, the calloused bottoms of his feet barely registered the thorns, twigs, and stones they trod over. In all his twenty years, Henry's feet had never touched a pair of shoes.

He found Eliza the next morning.

Exhausted and dehydrated, Henry nearly passed her by—would have, in fact, had he not heard her labored and wheezy breathing some ten feet from the roadside. The sun had been up for over an hour. He was no longer running, but walking drunkenly and mumbling to himself. He'd fallen several times during the night.

The sound came from his right. He stopped and listened. Suddenly every nerve in his body was alert. He sprang to the roadside and into the brush; Eliza was there, splayed out on her back with one scratched and bleeding leg sticking up in the air. It was caught up in the branches of a scrubby hazelnut shrub. She was naked from the waist down, her dress torn off at the midline. It appeared to Henry as if she'd been tossed there from the road. Her left cheek was severely bruised, and the eye was so blackened it was completely closed from the swelling.

He picked her up, gently, and carried her a little further from the road. "Oh, Henry…I knew you'd…find me," she said weakly as he squatted and laid her down in a small patch of woods grass. He dropped her bag, retrieved her coat and carefully put it under her head.

"I'm here with you now, Eliza. I'm here. I'll look after you just like you looked after me when we was children an' I took that first whippin, from Master Townley," he said, fighting tears.

"Henry, I'm snake bit," she said, lifting her arm up and reaching for him. Henry took her hand and cupped it in both of his.

"Where, Eliza?" He began looking over her battered body. "Where are you bit a—?" He saw it before the words were completely out of his mouth. Her left leg—the one that hadn't been stuck in the hazelnut—was so swollen it had split open from her knee to her ankle. Blood and bright yellow pus oozed sluggishly from the wound.

She began to cry. The wheezy sound of her breathing turned to a high-pitched whistling every time she drew a breath. "I don't want to die, Henry."

Henry's heart broke. He leaned over her and hugged her to him, stroking her hair, hot tears running freely down his face.

"We'll find us some help. Come on now." He removed her second dress from her bag—a faded blue flower print that had belonged to the late Missus Cromwell, which Eliza called "*her best*"—and carefully worked it over her head without even trying to remove the remainder of the dress she was wearing. Once done, he put her coat back in her bag, re-shouldered everything, and lifted her again.

No longer fearing discovery but hoping for it, he resumed walking northeast on the road. Eliza had passed out or fallen asleep. He hadn't seen a single house since he'd set out after her but he knew there had to be some along the road somewhere.

After about an hour Eliza woke and began moaning softly. "Henry, I can't…it hurts. You have to stop."

"We have to keep going, Eliza."

"Henry, please."

"Just for little while, then."

He laid her down at the roadside, then sat down next to her with his legs splayed out in front of him. He lifted her head and slid over slightly so he could let her rest it in his lap. Minutes later, Eliza was dead.

Henry cradled her head and howled with grief; his sense of loss so immense as to be immeasurable. His body shook uncontrollably with the sobs as he cried her name over and over. *"Eliza...Eliza... Eliza..."*

4

Still sitting at the roadside with Eliza's head in his lap six hours later, Henry didn't even look up when the rider halted his horse in front of him.

"Well, you look like you've been through it. That your wife?" the man asked, looking down at Henry with clear sympathy. Henry didn't move.

"You hear me, son?"

Henry raised his head, then nodded slowly. "We never had no preacher."

"You a runaway?"

"No, sir."

The man measured Henry silently. His face, baked by the sun and creased with age, was thoughtful. Henry let his head drop back down.

"What happened to her?" The man asked finally, nodding toward Eliza.

Henry slowly lifted his head again. "Some men took her. They tried to hang me but the rope broke and I ran. I followed them, but it was too late. She was snake bit." He turned his attention back to Eliza and began stroking her hair.

"These men, were there a lot of them? Thirty or forty, all on horseback, with a couple of wagons?"

Henry nodded without looking up.

The man grunted as if Henry had affirmed something he already knew. "Local militia, least that's what they call themselves. They're no better than the ones they're supposed to be fighting—perhaps worse...who do you belong to?"

"I'm free, sir."

"I suppose you can prove that."

Henry heard Emmet Dawson's voice, *"Pin these to his shirt. There aren't any free niggers in Missouri."* He looked down at his shirt, still moving slowly as if in a daze. The free papers were there, pinned underneath his left breast. They were dirty, crumpled, and torn. He pulled them off and stared at them a moment before looking up and holding them out toward the man on the horse.

The man waved his hand. "I don't need to see them. You might want to take better care of them, though. Unless you're just planning to sit there until someone else who wants to hang you comes along. My guess is it won't be too long."

"Yessir, I reckon you're right."

"Well, a man's got to decide things for himself. You have any skills?"

"I can do some carpentering."

"My name's Macklin, James Macklin. Folks just call me Red, mostly, though most of the red's turned gray now. I'm just outside of Lawrence—that's Kansas in case you don't know. Could be I'd have some work for you—paying work—if you can make it there. Though, I don't see your chances are that good—being honest. Just stay away from Fort Scott if you make it across the line. You might find some help in some of the outlying farms, but if you go into to town you'll be hanged, like as not."

The man took one of the three canteens slung from his saddle and dropped it at Henry's feet. "I'm sorry I can't do more for you."

Henry looked at the canteen, then at the man on the horse. Tears began welling in his eyes. "My name is Henry, sir."

"God be with you, Henry." The man glanced at Eliza again before spurring his horse and riding away.

Henry leaned forward and hooked the canteen's strap with his forefinger and dragged the canteen close enough to pick it up. He pulled the stopper and drank deeply. There was a moment just as he was lowering the canteen where he thought he was going to be sick. He fought it back and after a few moments the feeling passed. He stared down the road in the direction the man had gone—the same direction Henry had come from—and wondered how far Lawrence was, and if the man had meant what he said about having paying work. He looked at the canteen, then down at Eliza. "I guess I can't stay with you. I thought I could…I thought seeing it's my fault you're…I shouldn't have run off. I shouldn't oughta left you.

Now I'm all mixed up inside. Mayhap being...being dead with you would be better than going on livin' without you." Henry broke into fresh sobs as he hugged Eliza's stiffening body to him.

After a time, the tears dried up. He stood, his taxed muscles screamed. A light breeze blew his free papers across the road. He retrieved them and put them in his sack. Then, with a heavy sigh that was nearly a sob, he slung the canteen over his shoulder, carefully picked up Eliza's body, and walked into the woods.

It was late afternoon before Henry had dug a hole he felt was deep enough to bury Eliza in. He'd carried her nearly a mile into the woods when he came across a small pond. Up until then he was unsure of what he was looking for—he'd simply been walking—but when he saw the pond he stopped immediately; he knew it was the place.

Taking turns using his knife to loosen the soil, then scooping it out with his hands, he spent the next two hours digging the grave. Once satisfied, he rinsed out the small cloth sack that had held the flour in the pond. He set to washing Eliza: first her arms and face, then, pulling up her dress, he began on her legs. He walked the short distance to the pond several times to rinse the cloth. Fresh tears of grief fell as he worked, but a different emotion crept in as he reached Eliza's upper legs. A stream of blood, which had dried to a dark maroon, began around her anus and vagina and trailed down her inner thigh all the way to her knee. Emmet Dawson's face burned in Henry's mind. He gritted his teeth together and clenched his fist around the makeshift washcloth, his eyes gleaming with hate.

He laid Eliza in the grave. He knew he'd be unable to cover her face with dirt so he spread her coat out over her. That done, he put her drawstring bag neatly beside her and began filling the grave in with the dark soil.

It was almost sunset by the time Henry found enough rocks to cover the grave, and he was feeling lightheaded with hunger. Standing over his work, he wrung his hands together. He was aware that he was inadequate for what was required next.

"I'm not good with words; not like you were. You know how you were always having to correct me and all. Words for times like this are best left to preachers and to those who know God's book a sight better than I do. But If'n...*If* you can hear me, Eliza, I want to say I'm sorry...I'm sorry for letting you die, and...and," Henry's voice broke. "...and I'll miss you every day...I love you and I hope God's there waiting for you...and I hope you'll be waiting for me whenever I get there...I guess that's all."

5

Henry had been following the river eastward for five nights when he came upon the lone man's camp under a massive birch overlooking the river. He was hollow-eyed and gaunt, having eaten nothing in nearly ten days except for the flour paste, a few earthworms and two small crawfish he'd managed to catch in a creek where it joined with the river. The previous night he passed by a house built right on the river. The light spilling from the windows was warm and inviting. He stopped a safe distance away and considered knocking on the door and begging the occupants for something to eat. In the end he dismissed the idea as foolish and moved on.

He'd cursed himself early on for leaving the thread and bit of twine in Eliza's bag and burying it with her. He could have used it for snares. Having nothing to make snares with, he tried deadfall traps instead. He set several up every morning before he slept for the day, but all of them had been empty in the evening when he checked them.

It was a little before dusk and he was walking through the woods, ten yards or so from the river bank. The man was seated on a rock in front of a campfire, cooking some meat he'd spitted on a stick. He was singing softly to himself. There was a horse tethered to a nearby bush. The aroma of the searing meat was maddening. Henry hunkered behind some brush and peered around at the man. He was sitting at profile to Henry, and Henry's blood froze in his veins.

The man was Emmet Dawson.

Only he wasn't.

The man was around the same age as Emmet Dawson—mid-forties or thereabouts—and wore a similar beard, but the resemblance stopped there.

Henry looked around. He set down his things and quietly backtracked to where an arm-sized branch lay on the ground. He picked it up. From the weight he didn't think it was pithy. He crept back toward the camp.

The man caught movement when Henry was still ten feet away. He turned to see Henry walking toward him with the branch held like a club.

"What are you aiming to do with that, boy?" the man asked, his eyes darting.

"I'm hungry, I just need some food. Then I'll be on my way," Henry answered, closing the distance. The man smiled reassuringly. "Suurrre thing, c'mon in. I've got plenty to spare. Why don't you just put that stick...*down*." He wheeled on the last word, bringing up a pistol and aiming it at Henry. Henry lunged forward, swinging the branch in a wide arc and connecting solidly with the side of the man's head. The pistol went off but the shot went wild. The man crumpled to the ground, a trickle of blood ran from his ear.

Henry dropped the branch and looked down at the unconscious man, then at the pistol. He glanced around apprehensively, then squatted and picked it up. It was heavier than he expected. Next he pulled the stick with the chunk of meat skewered on it out of the fire where it had fallen when the man pulled the pistol. The meat was covered in ash. Henry didn't notice. He went at the meat greedily, dropping the pistol when he discovered he'd need two hands.

He didn't get very far. The first few barely chewed pieces he swallowed came right back up in a rush of hot, yellow stomach bile. He spit a couple of times, then forced himself to slow down. He took three smaller bites and chewed them thoroughly before swallowing. The meat stayed down the second time, though grudgingly.

The man groaned and Henry froze, watching him for any sign of movement. The man remained still, and the sound was not repeated. Realization of what he'd just done filled Henry with shame, and on the heels of that, there was fear for his life. He picked up the pistol, but it slipped from his greasy hand. He wiped the hand on his trousers, then transferred the spitted meat to that hand and wiped the other. He snatched up the pistol and hurried back to where he'd left his things.

He stowed the grain sack with his few belongings in it, the pistol, and the meat, in the saddlebags slung over the horse. He hastily removed the man's bedroll and a battered canteen and dropped them on the ground. Henry had never ridden a horse before, but he'd helped saddle them times beyond count and he had a good sense of how things worked. He untied the reins; the nervous horse chuffed and stamped. He gently stroked the horse's cheek and whispered some soft words of encouragement. After a couple of false starts he was able to get mounted.

The horse wouldn't move. Henry clicked his tongue, bounced up and down, and shook the reins. The horse simply stood there. Finally, willing himself to calm down, he pictured Lawrence Townley, his old overseer, mounted and riding. Townley was a skilled horseman. He spent as much time at the plantation on horseback as he did on foot. Henry jerked his legs against the animal's flanks, and the horse started forward.

He was now a horse thief, if not a murderer.

6

He regained his strength quickly; the man whose horse he'd stolen had a fair supply of dried beans, salt pork, and cornmeal stored in his saddlebags. He'd obviously been planning to be travelling for awhile. There was also another chunk of beef like the one the man had been eating when Henry came upon him. It was fresh so Henry had eaten it first.

He'd lost count of the days since he'd found Eliza. He was pretty sure it had been ten, but it could have been eleven or twelve—or nine. His thoughts were crowded and conflicted: could he have saved Eliza if he hadn't run away the night they tried to hang him? What if he had ran to her instead? Could he have freed her and escaped into the woods with her? He knew in his heart that he would likely have been shot or recaptured before he ever reached her. But what if he *had* reached her? Would she be with him now instead of being buried in a shallow and unmarked grave in the Missouri woods?

He also tried not to think about the man he'd hit with the branch, but his conscience wouldn't cooperate. He'd left another man in exactly the same predicament that he himself had been in: alone, on foot, with no food. *But it's not the same,* Henry told himself. *I passed two houses within five miles of where I left him. That man could stop for help; I couldn't.* His logic was cold comfort.

He travelled by day because he was too afraid to trust the horse through the woody terrain in the dark, even though during that first night the horse seemed unperturbed by the darkness or the terrain. But Henry was nervous, especially because he no longer had a fat moon to see by. The land finally opened up after two days of slow riding along the river. The trees slowly began giving way to grass and scrub. But since the area appeared sparsely populated, he continued on by day. He hadn't seen another soul since leaving the man by the river, and he made sure to keep a good distance away from the few homesteads he came across.

The Kansas/Missouri border came and went; he had no way of knowing. When he finally came to the wide and well-beaten road, he stopped the horse and dismounted. He stared south, then north. The landscape had become wide and, to Henry at least, nearly featureless. There was a surplus of brush and grass, but not nearly as many trees as there were in Osceola and Samuel Cromwell's place at Lawson's Bend.

The openness made him feel apprehensive, and he was aware of how he must look—like a runaway slave on a stolen horse. He wasn't as afraid as he had previously been, however. Part of him couldn't shake the feeling that he really didn't deserve to live without Eliza.

There was a decent pair of wool trousers in the saddlebags, and he had changed into them the previous day. They were too short in the legs and too wide at the hips, but still looked a far cry better than the ones he'd been wearing. These he discarded along with the torn and bloodstained shirt he'd had on since leaving Samuel Cromwell's farm. He'd thought about setting the horse loose and continuing on foot, but he couldn't bring himself to do it. He felt safer with the horse, and the pistol, which he had taken to wearing in the waistband of his trousers even though he didn't know how to shoot or load it.

At last he decided to follow the road north. He had no idea whether Lawrence was north or south, but north felt right to him. Sooner or later he would have to ask someone if he was going the right way.

Sooner turned out to be two hours later, just after noon. He spied the dust from the lone wagon long before it reached him.

A knot formed in Henry's gut when the wagon (which was travelling south) neared him. He stopped the horse and resisted the urge to put his hand on the pistol's grip. Instead he lifted a hand to the oncoming wagon. The wagon's driver reined in the four horse team alongside Henry. There was a second man seated next to the driver; he was eyeing Henry with open suspicion. Henry looked to the driver. "Excuse me, sir, could you tell me how to get to Lawrence… Kansas?"

"That's a fine animal," the driver said, ignoring Henry's question. "Where'd you get it?"

"I worked for him," Henry replied.

"That so? Well, I reckon it ain't completely unheard of for uuhh, *free* negro to own a horse of his own. I'm guessing you're one of them, then."

"Yessir, that's right…Lawrence, Kansas?"

"Although you do look a sight young. Did you lose your shirt?"

"You're *in* Kansas, boy." The second man spoke up. "Lawrence is up that way, round-about ninety miles. You just keep on the way you're going, you'll get there. Let's get moving, Lee. My backside's hollering at me to get off this damn thing."

"Thank you," Henry said and urged the horse on.

Once Henry was out of earshot the wagon driver turned to the other man. "What in the hell, Frank? That nigger's a goddamn horse thief, sure as shit draws flies."

"He was also carrying a revolver—had it stuffed down his pants, but he wasn't hidin' it."

"Well, if you'd keep your hands on that shotgun like you're supposed to when we're working we could have—"

"Done what, Lee? The line don't pay me to be regulating on horse thieves or no runaway niggers—especially with all the fighting going on. I'm not sticking my nose in all this business just to get it cut off by one side or the other. We'll stop at the sheriff's when we get to Fort Scott, tell them what we saw, and get back to work so we can go home."

"Could be there's a reward out for him."

"Ain't worth the trouble if there is. Now are you going to move this thing or do I have to shove you off and do the driving myself?"

7

Henry stopped to eat from the dwindling supply of food about three hours later. There was a small stand of trees a few hundred yards northeast of the road and headed for them. Once there he tied the horse to a scrub oak and removed a few pieces of dried meat from the saddle bag. The afternoon was hot and he rubbed his forehead; the skin felt sunburned and he wished for a hat. He turned to sit in the shade of a larger tree, and that's when he saw the dust cloud coming from the south—*fast*.

Fear clamped down on Henry's innards. Somehow he knew these men were after him. He jammed the dried meat back in the saddle bag, untied the horse, and climbed back in the saddle. He looked south; his heart sunk. There was a freshly beaten path through the grass leading from where he'd exited the road to the very spot where he now sat atop the big mare. He looked from the path to the riders and knew there was nowhere for him to hide.

Henry gripped the reins as tight as he could and pushed the horse eastward. The landscape whizzed past as the horse galloped, all-out. Henry stole glances over his shoulder, but the sun was at his back and the glare blinded him. Eventually the horse started tiring and he had to let her slow to a walk.

Gazing west twenty minutes later with his eyes squinted down to slits, Henry could see no sign of the riders and began doubting what he'd seen. What if the dust cloud had been stirred up by the wind? *But there was no wind.* Then he saw it again. It was farther away than the first time he'd spotted it, but it was there—a dusty break in the shimmering ground heat of the horizon. It was riders and they were heading in his direction. He yanked on the reins and urged the horse to continue east. He resisted his desire to push the animal and let her settle into a steady trot instead. He didn't stop until sundown.

Just before dark he came to a nearly dry creek. There were a few stagnant pools, and he let the horse drink. The canteen James "Red" Macklin had given him was getting low, but not low enough for him to risk filling it with the musty smelling water.

He hoped it didn't make the horse sick. "I dragged you into a heap of trouble and things jes keep going from bad to worse, don't they?" he said to the mare as he removed the saddle for the night.

He made a meal of some dried meat, and ate it unenthusiastically while keeping his eye on the west. He saw no sign of pursuit in the twilight. A wave of hopelessness washed over him as he lay his head on the saddle. He kept the pistol close.

He awoke with a start. It was still dark. He realized he'd fallen asleep without tying up the horse. Jumping to his feet he clicked his tongue and called out softly. "Come over here now, girl. *Click, click, click.* Come on, now." He listened intently: nothing. He tried again: "*Click, click, click*, come now, girl." Feeling the first tinges of panic he began walking in an ever-widening circle around the area, calling out, then listening; calling out, then listening. A short time later he realized that he could see. It would be dawn soon. He walked back to where he'd slept and ate a small amount of the salt pork and washed it down with a swallow of water. The faint glow slowly brightened, and he saw the mare about a hundred feet off, grazing. He ran over to her and led her back. "I must have walked right past you three times," he said, shaking his head. He saddled her immediately and was on the move before the sun showed fully on the horizon.

Four hours later he stopped and scanned the west. The riders were there and they had closed the distance from the previous afternoon by half. He guessed that if he stopped they would catch up with him within an hour. He really had no way of knowing for certain, though. He was a twenty-year-old plantation slave, not a tracker.

He rode on, urging the horse back up to a gallop. The horse tired more quickly this time, but Henry pushed her harder, pulsing his legs and leaning forward, yelling *Go, Go!*

What happened next, happened in a blink. At one moment Henry was seated solidly in the saddle, and the next he was tumbling through the air. He landed hard, his left leg hitting first with a loud snap before he turned end over end through grass and scrub. He lifted his head. The horse was lying several yards away, he could hear her breathing heavily. The world doubled, trebled, then went dark.

Sometime later, several shadows moved over Henry's battered body.

Four

1

Commandant's office, United States Military Academy, West Point, New York. April 6 1865.

No need to linger in the doorway. Please sit, Cadet Elliot," Commandant Black said without looking up from his work. John Elliot looked around the room nervously before stepping forward, removing his cap, and taking a seat in the large, leather-backed chair facing the commandant's desk.

After what seemed like an absurd amount of time to the young cadet, Commandant Black set aside his pen and eyed him from across the expanse of the spacious but tidy desk.

"I've known your father for well over twenty years. He is a dear man, and I have a great respect for him. Thus I find myself in a rather uncomfortable position. Due to your, ahh, alleged impropriety, Mister Jonathon Hanfield has requested that you be immediately expelled from this academy. He has even gone so far as to demand your arrest. Now, while Mister Hanfield holds no authority within these walls, he remains a very, very influential man." Commandant Black paused, thoughtfully running his hand over his long but neatly trimmed beard before reaching out and removing a cigar from the humidor on his desk. He smelled the cigar, running it slowly under his nose with his eyes closed before placing it neatly in front of him without lighting it. He turned his attention back to John.

"It was expected that you would be among the top of your class and receive a respectable post near your family upon your graduation. That, however, is now impossible. It's true, in fact, that were you another, you'd currently be sitting under lock and key ruminating upon your unseemly lack of self-control. And I would be finishing several very important letters instead of being burdened with the distasteful task of meting out justice based solely on politics: the politics of friendship, the politics of rectitude, and the politics of power and influence. Therefore, serving the best interests of all involved, you are being dismissed from this academy with a full military commission and rank of first lieutenant. This is an unprecedented maneuver and

I trust you will not squander the opportunity. You have forty-eight hours to attend to your affairs, then you will see Captain Brewer regarding transport to Fort Laramie in the Dakota Territory. Upon your arrival, you will report to Colonel Picton. Word has already been sent to him. You will be assisting the colonel in training recruited Confederate prisoners and aiding him with the Indian situation. Do you have anything you would like to say Cade— *Lieutenant* Elliot?"

"Sir, what if I wish to reject your generous offer and go home?"

"This is not an offer, Lieutenant. Is there anything else?"

John had been managing to hold Commandant Black's gaze, but now dropped his eyes.

"No, sir."

"Then you are dismissed."

John stood, saluted, then turned and walked to the door.

"And, Lieutenant?" Commandant Black queried just as John was grasping the doorknob.

He turned around. "Sir?"

"You will not discuss this matter outside the confines of your family. If you are not in Captain Brewer's office at noon the day after tomorrow, you will be found, tried as a deserter, and hanged. Good day."

"Yes, sir. Good day, sir."

2

John stared dejectedly through the window and watched the almost featureless Missouri countryside speed past. The train would take him as far as St. Joseph at the Kansas border where he would hook up with a group of wagons delivering supplies to Fort Laramie.

His first instinct had been to run—exactly what Commandant Black had warned him against. He envisioned he and Clara making for Texas, or perhaps California. He believed he could convince her to go with him.

But then what?

He would be a deserter from the army, and Clara's father would stop at nothing to find her. Jonathon Hanfield might even take his anger out on John's father, something that John couldn't bear. No, he would have to wait, and hope that time or providence would light a way for he and Clara. A dark part of him hoped Jonathon Hanfield would die. He knew it was a selfish and malign thought, but he couldn't shake it.

His own father, who had expressed equal measures of disbelief and outrage at what he called Jonathon Hanfield's *"Second-hand revenge"* was unable to sway Commandant Black to reverse his decision. "It was fortunate that I was even able to mediate on your son's behalf. This will all blow over given proper time, George," Commandant Black told John's father over whiskey in the commandant's study. "And, after it has, I will arrange another post for John—through the proper channels, of course. One that is closer to you. You must understand, however, that his service in the west must be exemplary and he must leave off this ridiculous and ill-fated romance with Clara Hanfield." He rubbed at his rapidly balding head. "What in god's name was he thinking?"

John's father ignored the question. "How long, Henry?"

"I think four years should be sufficient. Possibly sooner if the young Miss Hanfield succeeds in wedding someone more to her father's liking. Meanwhile, perhaps John will prove himself to be the adept leader all of his instructors at the academy believed him to be, and you will have the honor of welcoming home a captain. He should be viewing this as fortuitous. The unrest in the territories will provide opportunities for him to make a name for himself."

"I still can't believe—"

"That Jonathon Hanfield can somehow influence the Superintendent of the United States Military Academy and in turn the Commandant of Cadets? Don't be naive, George. You of all people know how far his influence extends. And please keep in mind that your son's foolishness is to blame here. Now, I appreciate the distance you have travelled on short notice, but I have a council, if you'll excuse me. It appears a cadet was caught stealing laudanum from the infirmary." Henry Black set down his not-quite-empty glass, then looked seriously at his longtime friend. "Did you know about it, George?"

George Elliot was silent. It was answer enough for the commandant.

The following morning a travel-weary George Elliot was preparing to board a steamship for his return to Manhattan. John stood beside him at the mooring.

"You'll be at least twenty-three when I see you next," George Elliot said, looking at his son. "I don't know what your mother would have made of this if she—"

"She would have wanted me to marry Clara. No matter the consequences."

"You're right, of course. But a woman doesn't always think with her head. They make decisions of the heart. Which is why men have both the right and responsibility to the run of things."

"What if we chose to marry anyway?"

George Elliot, who was both shorter and slimmer than his tall and stoutly built son nonetheless grabbed John by his wool military coat and gave him a brisk shake.

"Don't even *think* it. Jonathon Hanfield would have you stripped of your commission and dragged before a judge on some groundless charge you could never be prosecuted over, only to publically humiliate me and tarnish the Elliot name. He already claims that you attempted to violate Clara. He also says there was a witness."

John ignored this. "You stood up to him once."

"That was a long time ago and I was a headstrong young man. I—*we,* have too much to lose now and the truth of the matter is he could crush us now, if he truly set himself to it."

"I love her," John said simply.

"I know you do, Son. But it was a foolish endeavor from the beginning—not only yours, but mine. I actually let myself believe that Hanfield might put aside his petty grudge for the happiness of his daughter. So who was the bigger fool?"

"I don't believe that being in love with someone— *anyone*— makes a person a fool."

"Perhaps you'll have a better understanding with the passage of time."

I certainly hope not, John thought bitterly.

3

"We'll be in St. Joseph in about ten minutes, sir," the conductor said as he passed John's seat. John gave a nod without turning from the window. He heard the conductor repeat the notification a few times as he moved through the car. After a few moments he opened his satchel on the seat next to him and took an inventory, mostly to be doing something. It was just before eleven a.m..

Although a far cry from New York, St. Joseph Missouri was bigger, busier, and more modern looking than John had imagined it. Riverboats dotted the Missouri River, and Fort Smith stood sentinel on a nearby hilltop.

The day was cool but clear. Several men and one old woman exited the train along with John, but he was the only soldier. He stood on the splintered wood platform and looked down the length of the train, wondering when his horse would be offloaded. A lone man in animal skin clothing sat upon a split-rail fence that ran perpendicular to the station. His hair was long and hung in greasy strings nearly to his chest. He was smoking a misshapen cigar. The man afforded John a short nod, then stood. "Lieutenant Elliot?"

"Yes?"

"Sergeant Campbell wanted me to take you straight to the wagons instead of the fort. He's in a rush to get moving," the man said without giving his name.

"I'm waiting for my horse, Mister...?"

"Raines."

"Well, I don't want to trouble you, Mister Raines. You can just direct me, and I'll join Sergeant Campbell as soon as I'm able."

The man walked over and pointed roughly north. "See that church steeple? Go left just past it and follow the street till the end. Talk to Howard Clutterbuck—he'll be the one flying that idiot flag with the skull on it over his barge. If he has a line, don't wait, just go right on up. Army gets served first."

"Sounds easy enough. Thank you, Mister Raines."

The man grunted "Welcome," and headed up the platform in the direction he'd pointed.

4

The northwest end of St. Joseph was more how he'd envisioned a city on the edge of the frontier. Well-kept brick and wood buildings gave way to dusty looking tents, and merchants peddled every imaginable ware from crudely built shanties resembling over-sized New York newspaper stands. The smell of livestock was overpowering.

And wagons.

John couldn't even begin to count the number of wagons. People of all sorts milled everywhere: traders, soldiers, emigrants, gamblers.

John spotted the tattered *Jolly Roger* right away. It hung from a crooked branch tied to the railing of a large, flat-bottomed river barge. A wagon was being pushed up on the barge, and John rode up behind. "That horse going to be still?" asked a fat man in a derby hat.

"I'll mind him," John answered as he walked the horse up.

The fifteen supply wagons were hitched and ready when John arrived on the west bank of the Missouri. His horse, which he had purchased on a whim in Hannibal, was restless and jumpy after the river crossing. It gave a short buck and nearly threw him as he approached the line of wagons. This raised a chuckle from the small group of men surrounding them. It was a motley group of about twenty-five: a few in uniform, most not. One of them was the man who'd been sitting in front of the train station when John had arrived. There was also a negro with a thick scar on his face, standing alone several feet away from the other men. He was the only one among them who didn't appear soiled and unkempt. He regarded John impassively.

As John dismounted, two men in cavalry uniforms exited what looked like a small livery. They spotted John, then spoke a few words together. One of them turned and walked to the group of men by the wagons, the other approached John.

"Lieutenant Elliot?" he inquired, then almost as an afterthought, he saluted. He was a short and burly man of about thirty with a strawberry colored beard.

John returned the salute; it was only the third one he'd received since prematurely becoming an officer, and he felt like an imposter.

"I'm Sergeant Campbell, sir. I was notified you'd be travelling with us just yesterday…I'm sorry for the hurry, but we received word that another two companies of galvanized volunteers are being sent up from a prisoner camp in Illinois, and frankly, sir, they don't equip these southerners very well. With all of the comings and goings here lately we're running short of just about everything as it is. This supply run was patched together on short notice mostly because we needed boots. The wagons aren't nearly fully loaded so we'll make good time, anyway."

"I understand. I'm prepared to be underway immediately. I would like to unburden my horse of some of my belongings…"

"Henry?" the sergeant said. "Would you please find a place in your wagon for the lieutenant's property."

5

Less than an hour later they were on their way. John chose to ride his new stud for awhile, he was proud of the acquisition. The big, high spirited horse was the only thing to bring a smile to his face since his summons to Commandant Black's office.

The fabled prairie spread out before him, golden and as seemingly as wide as the sea. He thought it was beautiful in its fashion, but he also knew right away that he could never feel at home in the open, desolate looking country. To him it somehow felt like loneliness.

He rode up next to the wagon being driven by Sergeant Campbell. He had a million questions he wanted to ask, but he also didn't want to appear naive.

"How go things at the fort, Sergeant?"

"Busy as a hive of bees, Lieutenant, sir. Most of us have been sent from elsewhere now that the war's finally winding down—I've been here seven months, and that makes me a veteran as far as the regular army goes. My father did some trapping on the Yellowstone and Platte, and I guess they thought I'd take to the country like he did. I like it well enough, but I can't say I wouldn't rather be back in Illinois. Anyhow, we're trying to put things together like a proper military post. Damn volunteers got the place in shambles—army's been mustering some of them out, but some are staying on for awhile on account of the Indians. Fighting may be done with the secessionists, but it's looking like there's going to be more of it up here. Possibly a lot more. After what happened down at Big Sandy Creek, Indians have been causing more problems to settlers and folks on the trails."

"What happened at Big Sandy Creek?"

"I guess news is a little slow going out. Cavalry under Colonel Chivington cleaned out a Cheyenne camp. Killed most everyone there—women and children included. Who're you going to be serving under, sir?"

"Colonel Picton...*women and children?* Why? Did the Indians attack us, or the other way around?"

"Hmm. I haven't heard of him. And the answer to that question depends on who you ask."

"What if I was to ask you?"

The sergeant, who'd been facing forward, minding the team while conversing, spared a look at John. "I'd say we're taking a lot of what don't belong to us, sir. And in light of that I don't see it matters much—who attacked who, I mean. What would you do if a bunch of folks came and started putting up fences where you usually hunted for your supper?"

"It's my understanding, Sergeant, that the treaties with the Indians provides ample land for them as well as other provisions for their welfare."

"Begging your pardon, sir, that sort of thing may look fine on a few sheets of paper, but if one side don't keep up their end of the bargain, and the other side doesn't really understand the bargain in the first place, it all spells trouble to me. Of course, I'm just a sergeant, and one that don't know how to keep his opinions to himself most times at that."

"And is it your opinion that the United States government has broken the treaties it's made with the local indigenous?"

"I'm not saying that exactly, sir."

"You can speak plainly, Sergeant," John said with a rueful laugh. "Not very long ago I was a cadet at the military academy still a year away from graduation. I was hoping for eventual placement that didn't take me too far from my home and…and someone I cared about. I've yet to form an opinion on any of the politics of my new posting."

"Well, sir, I haven't been here long enough to say for certain, and these matters are better left to more educated folks, but I think we've put the Indians in a position to where they almost have to fight us. I mean, sir, it's a big country, but it isn't *that* big."

"It certainly looks big from where I'm sitting. The prairie stretches the imagination. I would think there is plenty of room for all of us."

"It's getting smaller all the time, sir."

6

They made camp just before dark, about eighteen miles from St. Joseph. The men went about their duties as a matter of course. John tried to stay out of the way and made busy seeing to his mount. Randall Flemington, a private, and the only other regular soldier among them approached him as he was removing the saddle.

"Excuse me, sir?" The thin and rather timid looking private inquired tentatively.

"Yes, Private…" John began, looking at the other man questioningly while still holding the saddle.

"Flemington, sir. Randall Flemington. Ahh, sir, Henry will take care of your horse for you."

"That won't be necessary," he said, carrying the saddle over to a nearby wagon and setting it on top of the tarped load of supplies.

"Well, sir. That's what he's getting paid for."

John glanced over at Henry, who was leading a pair of horses he'd just unhitched from a wagon toward the place where the rest of the horses were tied.

"He looks like he has enough work to earn his pay, Private. I'll manage my own animal."

"Yes, sir, Lieutenant. Aubrey Gibbs should have some chow ready shortly."

When John was finished tending to his horse he walked over to where most of the men were gathered around two campfires.

"Join me over here, Lieutenant," Sergeant Campbell called from where he was seated on a small wooden stool. He gestured toward an identical stool to his right. John took the offered seat.

"Private Flemington, please fetch the lieutenant some supper."

The private set down his own half-finished plate and walked over to where a big-bellied man with a beard nearly to his waist was stirring a large cook-pot over a third fire.

"Army's sending out officers younger and younger. The lieutenant's face is as smooth as a babe's backside," said a man sitting on his bedroll wearing a filthy, red union suit and patched wool trousers. This prompted a chuckle from the other men around the fire.

"This man is an officer of the United States Cavalry, Mister Hardin," Sergeant Campbell said sternly. "Your contract requires that you address him as a subordinate. You will apologize to the lieutenant at once."

"Beggin' the lieutenant's pardon. I was just foolin' a bit."

"No offense taken, Mister Hardin," John said amicably. Then he leaned forward slightly and eyed the man levelly. "I assure you that my age is not a shortcoming, nor should you ever equate it with weakness."

"Well a'course not," the man answered, looking discomposed.

"Sir?" Private Flemington said, holding out a plate of what looked like some sort of stew and a thick slice of bread. John looked up at him and took the plate.

"Thank you," he said.

The stew tasted as bland as it looked, but the bread was obviously fresh—probably baked that morning. He used it to sop up every drop of the flavorless liquid. Bland or not, he was famished.

"Excuse me, Lieutenant. I was laying out some feed for the horses and was wondering if you might want me to tether your horse with the others?" Henry said, coming up behind him.

"Yes, thank you. It's Henry, isn't it?" John said, setting down his plate and standing.

"That's right," Henry said, tossing the grain sack he was carrying from one shoulder to the other.

"Well, Henry, I could use a stretch after the long train trip and the ride today. I'll walk him over, you just show me where you want him."

"Today was a short travelling day. The sergeant will want to make thirty miles or better tomorrow."

"It's been awhile since I spent all day in the saddle; since I was a boy." John untied his horse from the wagon he'd left it by and followed Henry to the far end of their camp. There was a rope line tied between two wagons and the seventy some-odd horses were tethered there.

"That's a fine looking animal," Henry said.

"He is indeed," John agreed, and ran his hand down the horse's flank. "Private Flemington tells me you're a scout. Forgive me, but I am curious as to how you came upon such a profession."

"I lived with the Cheyenne…for a time."

"And how would *you* describe them? The stories back in New York are…conflicting."

"I really need to finish up here so I can get some supper."

"Yes, of course. Thank you, Henry." John walked back toward the campfires, sparing a thoughtful look over his shoulder at Henry.

"I never would have thought there would be a colored scout out here," John said, sitting back down next to Sergeant Campbell.

"He's the only one I know of, and I don't expect he'll be doing anymore scouting for the U.S. Army."

"Why is that?"

"Henry's been scouting for Colonel Watt up in the Nebraska Territory for the last few months. He only found out about Big Sandy Creek a few hours before we set out for Fort Laramie. He wasn't very happy, and he's made it clear he'll be moving on once we get back to the fort. It's unfortunate for the army. He's a reliable scout and Indian interpreter, a good trapper, and a crack shot with a rifle, too. You'll appreciate the game he brings in on this trip."

"Can I assume he had associations with the Indians who were killed?"

"He doesn't talk about it much, but I know he lived with Chief Black Kettle and his clan of Cheyenne a few years back. It was Black Kettle's band and some others that was at Big Sandy Creek."

"Was this Black Kettle killed?"

"No, he's alive. I heard his wife was shot. If it's true, I haven't heard whether or not she survived."

"Should have killed every damned one of them," Raines, the man who'd been sitting on the fence at the train station, said from across the fire. There was a murmur of agreement from the men, most of whom were already lying on their bedrolls around the fire.

"Unarmed men, women and children?" Henry spoke up from the shadows. He was leaning up against the nearest wagon. He had a plate of stew in his hand.

Raines pointed the stick he'd been whittling on at Henry. "I know you're cozy with the red sons of bitches, but those savages been raiding innocent folks from here to Kansas; stealing horses and livestock and all. Those savages even been carryin' off women and babes—eatin' 'em, I hear."

"Let's not forget that family down in Colorado Territory," another man added.

"The Hungates." This was Private Flemington.

"That's right. The Hungates," Raines concurred, waving his stick in Henry's direction. "What do you say to *that,* injun lover?"

"I say I won't speak to ignorance," Henry said, setting his still full plate down on the wagon and walking away.

"You calling me ignorant, you black son-of-a-bitch?" the man called after him.

"I suggest you leave-off now," John admonished with as much authority as he could muster.

The man regarded John from across the dwindling fire. Finally, he said: "Yes, sir," and tipped an exaggerated salute in John's direction. Then he lay back on his bedroll muttering under his breath. *"Fucking army pup…"*

7

The news of President Lincoln's assassination, relayed to them via a lone rider bound for Fort Laramie, came on April eighteenth. The reaction of the men was mixed and the first couple of evenings following the news there was much animated conversation around the campfire.

Otherwise, the rest of the weeks long journey was largely uneventful. There was a brief stopover at Fort Kearny—which John discovered was little more than a few mud hovels and a parade ground—where they were joined by three soldiers bound for Fort Laramie. They were forced to negotiate a few isolated patches of remaining snow, but outside of some sweat and cursing at the heavily laden wagons, the men all agreed it was a relatively easy go. John slowly became accustomed to the openness of the country, and spent his days learning what he could of life around Fort Laramie and of the Indians. He found it difficult to separate the wheat from the chaff in regards to information about the Indians, however, and decided he'd just have to wait and find out for himself. The men were largely settlers and teamsters, and most of them held the Indians in low regard. He attempted to canvas Henry on several occasions and was met with cordial yet clipped answers. At night he wrote letters to Clara he knew he'd never send, and conversed with Sergeant Campbell, who he'd come to like and respect.

The supply caravan arrived at Fort Laramie on the seventh of May, shortly after noon. As had become his habit when not riding his horse, John was seated on the wagon driven by Sergeant Campbell. Like St. Joseph, John wasn't sure of what he was expecting, but it wasn't what he was seeing. It looked more like a small town constructed on a bend in the river than it did a military fort. Rows of infantry tents, wagons by the score as well as several small Indian camps were scattered around the area. Indian women and children approached the wagon with their hands out, saying, *"Náháéána, náháéána."*

"Move away, savages," one of the wagon drivers shouted at them.

John looked down at them with a mixture of pity and fascination. He didn't understand the language, but what they wanted was obvious. He reached into his coat and removed a small sack which contained some beef jerky and a few pieces of hard candy. He tossed it to a girl of about ten.

"They'll be following you all over the territory now, Lieutenant. You hand out to 'em once, they come to expect it," one of the men called from behind him.

"Mind your team, Mister Pearson," Sergeant Campbell responded from his seat beside John.

Henry, whose wagon was at the end of the convoy, silently took several small, cloth bundles from the floorboard by his feet and tossed them on the ground as he passed.

8

The men scattered almost immediately with few goodbyes. John wanted to say a farewell to Henry, but soon after entering the fort, Henry was nowhere to be found.

Sergeant Campbell had a harried looking corporal locate Colonel Picton while he gave John a brief rundown on the fort's essential amenities. A short time later, the corporal returned with instructions as to where John was to be quartered, along with an invitation to meet with Colonel Picton in one hour. John shook hands with Sergeant Campbell—who assured him he would have his horse cared for—and followed the corporal to his quarters.

His housing turned out to be a large tent with a cot and makeshift desk as its only furnishings. He wondered why he hadn't been housed in the officer's quarters. Before they entered, the corporal pointed to an even larger tent some hundred feet away, and identified it as Colonel Picton's.

"Can I get you anything, Lieutenant?"

"Some coffee, if some can be had."

"I'll have some brought around."

The coffee never arrived and at just before two o'clock John walked from his tent to the one the corporal had said belonged to
Colonel Picton. There was no guard outside, and after a moment's deliberation John opened the tent flap slightly, and peered in. There was a man dressed in gray trousers and a red flannel shirt standing bent over a wide, plank table, his back to John. He appeared to be looking at maps.

"Colonel Picton?" John asked doubtfully.

"You're punctual; a good quality. Come in," the man said without turning. John entered the somewhat smoky tent and lingered in the entry. After a moment the man—presumably Colonel Picton— walked over to a brass clad steamer trunk, lifted the lid, and removed a bottle and two glasses. He poured without a word, then stepped toward John.

"I came by this whiskey not long after Shiloh. Some Confederate deserters were transporting twenty bottles of it, along with other plundered goods, aboard a farm wagon. We confiscated everything, of course, and hanged the thieves. An unpleasant but necessary punishment befitting the crime." He held one of the glasses up and admired it for a moment before handing it to John. "This is the last bottle, and I fear I'll never taste a finer whiskey." He took a sip with his eyes closed, savoring it, before slowly lowering his glass. "Sit down, please."

There were several chairs lined up on the far side of the plank table (which took up most of the tent) and John chose one at the end. He looked up at Colonel Picton expectantly.

The man was of average height and build with brown shoulder-length hair and a short, neatly trimmed beard. He was an unremarkable man, by John's reckoning, save for his eyes, which were a stunning hazel that glowed like gold. He ran his free hand lightly over one of the many maps on the table, then turned his attention back to John.

"Do you treasure our republic?"

"Yes, sir," John answered.

"You will not address me as *sir*. You will call me Frank. Or if that is too informal for your sensibilities, you can address me as Mister Picton. I will call you John. Also, after we conclude our conference here today, you will begin wearing non-military clothing and will not don your uniform for the duration of your service under my command. Our undertaking will require us to keep the United States Government well out of scrutiny. The men who will be serving under us are discharged soldiers, mustered-out volunteers, and ex-Confederate prisoners of war; all technically citizens, who are, therefore, not beholden to military guidelines. This is a…*privateer* undertaking by concerned patriots. The men will be paid twice the regular army wage and, for the sake of some semblance of military order, will still address you and I as *sir*. You…well, you were to serve under me in a entirely different capacity until I received this letter ten days ago." He tapped a sheet of paper on the table with his finger. "Under normal circumstances I would simply have you reassigned elsewhere, but these are not *normal circumstances*. The fact that you received your commission through questionable channels only complicates matters. So, I am under obligation to make use of you." He drained his whiskey, set his glass on the table, and picked up a different sheet of paper and a leather billfold.

"These are your discharge papers; awaiting only your signature. This will stand until our task is satisfactorily completed. Afterward, you will be reinstated at the rank of Captain, and be posted to the location of your choosing. This I promise you as a gentleman." He handed the paper to John along with the billfold. "As soon as you sign the discharge, the five hundred dollars in that billfold will be yours, and there will be another five hundred when we are finished."

"With respect, sir—*Mister Picton*, I don't understand what you're talking about," John said, setting the paper and the billfold on the table in front of him by his untouched whiskey.

"John, would you agree that the Confederacy is—*was,* a threat to our nation?" He took a seat next to John and gazed at him earnestly.

"Yes, of course."

"There is another threat. One that could divide this republic every bit as much as the southern secession if we don't act swiftly. This nation's prosperity and growth is being challenged by those ungrateful red-skinned savages out there. We offer them agreeable terms; we take them in and generously share the fruits of our labor with them. At this very moment they are cooking with wheat flour that was farmed and milled by white men. They're hunting with rifles we gifted to them to make their hunting easier, and they're wrapped in blankets manufactured by white workers. All we've asked in return is to be able to live peaceably on this land that God has ordained us to dwell in." He stood and paced the length of the tent, then turned and leveled a finger at John.

"But the red man is not peaceable. Not at all. Most particularly the Sioux and Cheyenne. Long before the first white man ventured west, the Indians were making war on each other. The Sioux drove the weaker tribes away from their hunting grounds, murdering the men and boys, and taking women and young girls captive to use as breeding stock to strengthen their numbers. More recently, the Cheyenne and Arapaho have aligned themselves with the Sioux, and together they've been raiding innocent settlers and attacking emigrants on the trails. For the last year they've rampaged through the countryside, murdering entire families only to steal a few head of livestock—they're abducting women and carrying them off to face God only knows what horrors. Two months ago, somewhere near a thousand braves attacked Camp Rankin and, after indiscriminately killing soldier and citizen, burned most of the town to the ground." He stood on the opposite side of the table from John and placed his hands flat on the wood, leaning over until his face was just inches away from John's. His golden eyes blazed and his voice was thick and full of emotion. "They *skinned* some of their victims, John. Good and decent God-fearing people whose only crime had been the desire to make a better life for themselves."

"I still don't understand why my resignation is required—"

Frank Picton raised one hand and slammed it back down on the table. *"THESE SAVAGES MUST BE BROKEN OR ERADICATED!"* He stared at John intently. Then, straightening up and seeming to gain his composure, he picked up his empty glass—glancing briefly at John's still full one—and walked slowly to his trunk to pour himself another two fingers of the confiscated whiskey. He continued: "This is what we've been tasked with, John—as patriotic *citizens,* not soldiers. The policy-makers of the east and their constituents are weary of war, and have no stomach for what needs to be done. Congress bickers back and forth and patriotic men like Colonel Chivington, who justifiably moved against a renegade Cheyenne camp this last winter are used as scapegoats to appease wealthy bleeding-hearts who've never experienced the brutal and inhuman nature of these uncivilized devils. So I've been instructed by certain unnamed parties from the office of the now deceased president—may God rest his soul—to hunt down and kill all hostile enemies. And I've been empowered to do so without the encumbrances of political and military constraints. We will appear to be nothing more than a local militia protecting what is ours.

"Do you understand *now*?"

"May I see the letter?" John asked.

Picton picked it up and handed it to him without a word.

As per our discussion, the west must be opened.

Please proceed with haste, Colonel.

John looked up at Picton incredulously. "This is hardly an official order."

"Your naiveté exceeds what can be excused by your tender years, John. Allow me to simplify: this is a covert affair. You will sign the discharge and assist me as you were instructed to do by Henry Black, or you will leave my tent, Fort Laramie—and the territories for all I'm concerned—and return east where you belong. You're an untried young officer with no field experience, and whether you stay or go means nothing to me. I was ordered to utilize you, that is all. If you have a grievance, I'm sure General Moonlight will be around sometime in the next several days and you can bring it up with him. I don't expect him to be very sympathetic, however. He knows what these savages are capable of and supports this endeavor to the fullest."

"How long before I'm posted closer to New York?" John asked, thinking of Clara.

"We intend to pursue hostile bands through the coming months of good weather. We've hired some Pawnee scouts—they'll do anything to see Sioux killed—and there's a nigger who's supposed to know this territory like the back of his hand. A claim I find dubious but hard to dispute. We're going to fight these redskins the same way they fight us: we'll travel light, hit them and run like that bushwhacking murderer Bloody Bill did to our boys down in Kansas and Missouri. I've got better than forty freed confederate prisoners camped out here— Missouri bushwhackers every one of them—in addition to forty of my own men, who are hand-picked veteran fighters. We'll push the wagon-burners hard until winter, and, if we can, we'll surprise them at some of their winter camps when the snow flies and chase down more next spring. By mid-summer they'll be broken, scattered, or dead. You should be having Christmas dinner with your family next year."

"You're going to accomplish all of this with eighty men?"

"In the future I will ask that you do not question me. For now, suffice it to say there will be more men when required. For the present, we will use stealth and the skill of our fighting men to accomplish things that marching regiments of soldiers could not. I will explain my strategy further, in good time."

"I met the scout...the colored one. He worked on the supply caravan I came in with. I think he moved out right after we arrived." John downed his whiskey and reached across the table for an inkwell and pen.

9
New York, New York. April 10 1865.
"How dare you have a hand in facilitating this…this *outrage*." Jonathon Hanfield shouted at his cowering wife as she shrunk down into one of the parlor's four wingbacked chairs. He towered over her, spittle flying from his lips as he bellowed.

"*You;* helping our daughter slink around backdoors like a common trollop. And I have to discover this through a witless kitchen maid? How long has this been going on under my very nose?" He leaned down and grabbed her chin, squeezing painfully. He raised her head toward him.

"Speak, woman, and I had better hear the truth."

Louisa Hanfield averted her eyes and attempted to turn her head, but her husband held her fast, moving his face within inches of hers. Angry red splotches had risen on his normally pasty features. He lowered his voice, his tone menacing.

"You have ten seconds before I welt your backside so severely you will not sit for a month."

"We—" she began, her voice cracking. "We thought once he graduated and received his commission, you would see what a fine young man he is, and…and, warm up to him."

"Warm up to him?" he said softly, his anger turning to incredulousness. She could smell cigars and sweet brandy on his breath.

"Warm up to him," he repeated, releasing her face with a little shove before straightening up and walking to the window. Staring out at the street below and speaking calmly, he said: "You do realize that this *fine young man's* father nearly brought ruin down on this house with his ramshackle fleet of worthless ships, his tireless ambition, and his damnable *pride?* I tendered a more than generous offer for those splintery vessels of his. Had it not been for Senator Dickinson's intervention on my behalf in securing the government contracts that should have been mine by right, I would have been reduced to running coal barges on the river instead of owning one of the most profitable fleets on the eastern seaboard."

He turned from the window and faced his wife.

"And you would repay all of the comforts and luxury I have bestowed upon you through my hard work by embarrassing me? By allowing my only daughter to be courted by my most hated enemy's son without my knowledge or consent?" He moved toward the door. When he reached it, he turned and pointed a finger at his wife.

"You will be leaving in the morning to visit with your gib-faced sister in Pennsylvania until I send for you. By the time you return our daughter will have completed her schooling and will be engaged to a suitable young man of my choosing. As far as the young Mister Elliot is concerned, he will be fighting hostiles in the west before month's end. Take heart, I had requested that he be court-martialed and hanged."

He turned back toward the door and spoke over his shoulder as he walked through, "You will not see Clara before you leave. I have arranged for her to pay a visit to the Davenports tonight."

10

Louisa Hanfield watched her husband of nineteen years walk out of the parlor. She listened to his footfalls fade until she heard the familiar sound of the heavy, oak door to his study closing. She could picture him standing in front of his bar and pouring a glass of brandy while examining his stately features in the mirror above the mantle. She did not love him. She had never loved him. The marriage hadn't been arranged, exactly, but it was the nearest thing. She'd been relentlessly driven into it by her father, and he hadn't been a man to be refused.

She supposed that was why she'd hidden Clara's relationship with John Elliot from her own husband, who was so much like her father in so many ways: a driven, sometimes cruel man who accepted nothing less than absolute subservience from his family.

She fell asleep weeping silently.

11

Clara Hanfield listened to the clatter of the horse's hooves on the cobbles and the occasional muttered words of encouragement from the driver while gloomily watching pedestrians as they hurried about their business. She hated the city; it was all ambition on one side and desperation on the other. It also stank. She missed the tranquility and fresh air of the farmhouse at Cornwall where she and her parents frequently wintered. Her father had grown up in the modest farmhouse, and inherited it when his own father died the year before Clara was born. Jonathon Hanfield never seemed happy during their stays, however, and he had not accompanied Clara and her mother to the house in three years. Her mother once told her in confidence that he was ashamed of his simple roots.

Cornwall was also closer to West Point—and John. She imagined him squatting down next to her, his wild shock of straw-colored hair blowing in the icy evening breeze while he tossed stones into the lake…

"I should go and see your father," he said, tossing a final stone and turning to her.

"That's a terrible idea," she replied, smiling faintly. She leaned back on the small square of oilcloth he'd laid on the partially snow covered ground for her and gazed up at him, searching his face. She couldn't decide whether or not he was being serious.

"Oh," he said, "and why is that? What happened between our fathers was a long time ago. And I am not my father. I should think yours would appreciate a man with courage enough to stand before him and speak plainly of his love for you."

"So you love me, then?"

"You know I do."

"If that is true, then you will trust me when I tell you that my father will not see your declaration of love for his daughter as courage, but will look at it as arrogance." She reached up and took his hand. "Please wait a little longer. Once you receive your commission—and coming from the top of your class—my mother will convince my father to allow us to marry."

"So I'm to marry you, then?" He was smiling wryly.

She gave him a shove, causing him to lose his balance and fall sideways into the damp grass. She stood, glaring down at him with mock indignation. "Perhaps one of my other suitors would show more enthusiasm at the prospect, John Elliot."

He reached a hand up to her. "Help me up."

She took his hand and let out a startled laugh as he pulled her down on top of him. He put both of his hands gently to the sides of her face.

"I would have no choice but to kill him and any other unworthy would-be husband seeking your affections."

He kissed her.

"There aren't really any other suitors...are there?"

Now she was the one with the wry smile. "That's for me to know. Kiss me some more and I may tell you."

12

"We've arrived, Miss Hanfield."

Clara was startled awake by the driver, Mister Peyton, or Clayton—she couldn't remember which—peering into the buggy. He wasn't her regular driver. Her father only used him on the rare occasions Miles Penbrook was unavailable.

"Thank you," she said, wondering vaguely why her father had suddenly decided to have her call on the Davenports. Lilith Davenport was Clara's best friend, but she would normally send a note along if she wanted Clara to pay her a visit. Lilith's father oversaw a good portion of Jonathon Hanfield's business and was his oldest and dearest friend. Lilith and Clara were born exactly eight weeks apart; Lilith in March, and Clara in May. They were seventeen.

She stepped out of the buggy and strode up the walkway to the familiar red brick house. The front door opened before she reached it and she saw Nathan Peck, the Davenport's aging butler, standing expectantly in the doorway. The driver handed her bag to the butler without a word before tipping his hat to Clara and hurrying back down the walk. The butler looked after the driver distrustfully.

"Good afternoon, Miss Hanfield. I trust your ride over was uneventful?" Nathan inquired, standing aside so Clara could enter.

"It was fine, Nathan. Thank you."

"Miss Davenport is in the garden room. Shall I escort you?"

Clara laughed. "No, thank you. I believe I can find my own way."

"Of course you can. I will bring along some refreshments shortly."

The Davenport's garden room was located at the rear of the sprawling house, and was constructed entirely of mullioned glass. Lilith, who was as short and portly as Clara was tall and slender, was seated at a small, ornately carved wooden table that was the room's only furnishing. Exotic looking plants hung from brass hooks throughout the room, giving off a damp, earthy smell that always made Clara think of early spring, regardless of the season.

"Is there a piece of gossip so urgent that you couldn't take time for an invita—" Clara began.

Lilith looked up from her book as Clara approached the table; the look on her face was one of guarded sympathy. The smile Clara was wearing when she entered the room began to falter.

"What's the matter?" she asked, stopping in front of the table. She looked down at Lilith with concern.

"Did your father tell you why he sent you here?"

"He just said, 'You're going to visit the Davenports for the weekend.' He didn't seem as though he was in the temper for questions, and I was excited for the visit so I didn't ask. I assumed you were having a dinner…"

Lilith stood and put her hands on Clara's shoulders, looking up at her earnestly. "He found out about you and John." She looked past Clara at the open door, then lowered her voice. "I overheard my father talking to my mother. You're father had John expelled. They sent him to *Indian territory.*"

"Oh, my. *No!* How could he have discovered—*Lillian.*"

Lillian Holt was a kitchen helper; she posted letters to John from Clara, and received letters for Clara from John at her family's house on the lower side.

Clara and Lillian had known each other for the better part of their lives, and were as close to friends as propriety would allow. Lillian's mother and father both worked at the Hanfield's home. Her father was both the head groundskeeper and head carpenter. Her mother worked as a cook in the kitchen. Lillian began helping in the kitchen when she was ten.

Clara pulled away from Lilith and paced across the room. After a moment she turned back, her face pinched with anger. "I must get home at once. Can you have Nathan arrange for a buggy?"

"But your father—"

"Damn my father, Lilith!" She shouted suddenly. *"Please."*

Lilith started, looking chagrined. "Yes. Yes, of course. I'll locate Nathan."

13

It was dark by the time Clara returned home. She'd pressed the Davenport's driver (who was already nervous due to the declared urgency of her errand) repeatedly to hurry. The streets were busy, however, and he decided getting her home in one piece was more important than whatever business prompted her sudden departure from the Davenport's.

"Leave my things at the door," she called over her shoulder as she nimbly exited the still rolling buggy.

"Yes, Miss Hanfield," the driver replied after her, but she was already halfway to the front door.

Clara stormed through the door and into the dimly lit foyer.

"Father?" she called out with barely contained anger. "Mother?"

She strode into the room, glancing up to the second floor landing that overlooked the foyer before turning in the direction of her father's study. She could see light from beneath the door. She was starting toward the study when she heard her mother speak from above her.

"Do you know you sound just like him when you're angry?"

Clara stopped and wheeled, startled. Her mother was sitting in the shadows at the top of the open staircase.

"Did you know of this?" Clara asked.

"Yes."

"And you chose not to tell me? Why?"

"Darling, I…" her mother rose and began descending the stairs. "…I'm sorry, I couldn't tell you—"

"Because *I* forbade it." Jonathon Hanfield stated matter-of-factly, stepping out of his study behind them. He stopped just outside of the open door and puffed at his cigar—something Clara had never seen him do in the house, save for the confines of his study.

"I forbade it, and knowing your mother as I do, knew she would be utterly incapable of keeping silent." He gestured toward Clara with his cigar. "Which is why I sent you to the Davenport's. Tomorrow morning your lovely mother will be on her way to Pennsylvania and, had you stayed where you were supposed to, you would be none-the-wiser when you left for Vermont next week. Certainly your go-between would have been unable to enlighten you, as I released the entire Holt family from my service this morning along with a substantially greater severance than they deserved. I have no doubt they were well aware—the girl's mother, most certainly—of their sneaking daughter's clandestine forays into the postal business." He pulled a thick stack of envelopes bound together with a ribbon from his smoking jacket and waved them in the air.

"You let them go?" Clara said, looking across the room at her father with disbelief. "This is horrible. How will they live? How could you do this?…You've gone through my things?" Another question suddenly stole her attention and her eyes narrowed.

"What do you mean, Vermont?"

"I was saving this as a surprise, but I suppose the cat is out of the bag, so to speak. I am sending you to one of the country's finest schools for young ladies. You will leave next week, summer with them, then complete your schooling and be home for Christmas."

"I will *not!*" Clara shouted angrily before covering her mouth with her hand, shocked at her own impertinence.

Jonathon Hanfield closed the distance between them in three quick strides and slapped Clara open-handed on the mouth. Louisa let out a cry and raced down the stairs. When she reached them, Jonathon shoved her in the chest without taking his eyes from Clara. Louisa went sprawling to the polished marble floor, where she lay crying.

"Go to your room, Louisa," he said dismissively, still not looking away from Clara, who was holding a hand to her reddening face. There was a small trickle of blood leaking from the corner of her mouth.

Randall, the Hanfield's *Man About The House*—who most people would call a butler—rushed into the room through the servant's door. He was carrying a lamp in one hand and a kitchen stove faggot in the other.

Jonathon looked over Clara's shoulder: "Everything is fine, Randall. A family matter."

Randall stood there, his eyes darting to Louisa, who was still lying on the floor, sobbing, then to Clara, where they lingered. After a moment he gave Jonathon a short nod and returned through the servant's door.

Jonathon turned and kneeled next to his wife, offering his hand. She took it, and he helped her to her feet. "You go to your room now, Louisa. I'll have Randall bring you a glass of sherry." Louisa cast a sympathetic look toward Clara, but obeyed her husband and walked up the stairs.

Jonathon returned his attention to Clara.

"And you will do as you are told; now as always. In time you will see that every decision I've made has been with your best interests in mind. Truly, Clara, eventually you will thank me for this. The rotten apple never falls far from the tree, and I will be in my grave before I see my daughter with an *Elliot.*" Jonathon turned and started back toward his study. "I'll send Phebe up to draw you a bath."

14

Clara was fuming. She strode across the room, ripped down her bed canopies, and threw them on the floor. She paced her room furiously, kicking at the expensive silk canopies and cursing her father under her breath. She began opening her dresser drawers; they had obviously been rifled through. The polished walnut box she'd been keeping John's letters in was missing. This upset her even more. The box had been a gift from John.

Thirty minutes later, just as she was regaining some of her composure, there was a knock at her door. Clara opened it and stood aside. It was Phebe, one of the family's housemaids. Phebe had been employed by the Hanfields since before Clara was born. She stood at the door looking unsure; she was carrying a large copper pot full of steaming water.

"Please come in, Phebe, before you scald yourself," Clara said. Phebe gave her a hesitant smile then looked over her shoulder and nodded her head. Two other girls, both about Clara's age followed Phebe into the room. They were also carrying pots of hot water, which they dumped into a large copper bathing tub. Phebe then drew some cold water from a siphon that ran from a storage cistern in the attic. Jonathon Hanfield frequently boasted to his contemporaries about this and other modern conveniences he'd had fitted in the house.

After Phebe was satisfied with the water temperature she shooed the two girls off and gathered up the canopies. "Can I get anything else for you, Miss Hanfield? Some tea?"

Clara looked at the canopies, feeling ashamed of her tantrum. "No, thank you, Phebe," she said. Her father had taught her at a young age that she wasn't to apologize to the house staff. Until now, she'd never thought much about it. Until now, she'd never had reason to.

Phebe turned to leave.

"Phebe?"

The older woman stopped and turned back, "Yes, Miss Hanfield?"

"I'm sorry about soiling the canopies. It was childish of me and needlessly made more work for you."

"Oh, don't you worry about that, Miss Hanfield. Everybody gets in a temper at one time or another. I just hope you feel better."

"Thank you, Phebe. Goodnight."

"Goodnight, Miss Hanfield."

Clara lowered herself into the steaming water and laid her head back on a cushion placed over the thick rim of the tub. She let the heat do its work, slowly relaxing her taut muscles and conflicted mind. The ancient maple outside her window creaked rhythmically in the light breeze, lulling her into a semi-doze. When the water cooled, she stood, the chill room causing her skin to break out in goose-flesh. She didn't notice. Water ran to the floor in steady runnels as she walked to her vanity, where she stood motionless in front of the mirror. Soon a large puddle formed around her feet. Her father's great love of the sea was born at fifteen, when he'd secured an apprenticeship on a trading schooner. Later in life he became fond of saying that water was the great renewer. Clara thought this profound, particularly coming from a man who rarely spoke in the philosophical.

She reached around and took the length of her hair and wrung it out. The pitch black locks stood as her only resemblance to her father. The rest: small breasts, wide hips, strongly built legs, were all her mother. She rubbed her belly thoughtfully for a moment.

She knew what she had to do.

15

Three days later, on the morning she was to depart to her new school, Clara was up long before dawn. She lit a candle and padded quietly past her parents' room—her mother had left for Pennsylvania two mornings before as decreed by her father—and down the stairs. Her father's study was locked, but she knew he kept a key on top of the molding over the door. She stood on her toes and reached her hand up, sliding it across the moulding until her fingers touched the key. She slid the key into the lock and turned it; the snick of the tumblers seemed exceptionally loud in the early morning silence. Opening the door slowly, she glanced over her shoulder toward the stairs. She was terrified of being caught.

Once in the study she hurried to the oversized writing bureau and opened the roll-top. Holding the candle close to the interior, she felt along the bottom, pushing aside her father's pen rack and other writing paraphernalia until she found the small depression. She pushed it as she'd seen her father do many times when she was still young enough to sit on his lap, and with a click the secret panel opened. The compartment was fairly large: about four inches deep by a foot square; it was full of money.

Clara scooped up several handfuls of the notes and set them aside. She then closed the compartment and did her best to arrange her father's desk the way it had been. She set the candle down and removed a beaded reticule from her nightgown and stuffed the money inside. With one last look at the arrangement of the desk, she shut the roll-top, hurried out of the study, and returned to her room.

16

Miles Penbrook arrived with the coach at eight a.m. as instructed. Randall Eastman, who'd been waiting with Clara's luggage on the front porch, picked up the trunk and two travelling bags and walked to meet the coach. Miles, who wasn't a whole lot younger than Randall's fifty-eight years, climbed down to assist him.

"Looks like those joints aren't bothering you very much this morning," Miles said, taking one end of the trunk and helping to lift it up onto the coach."

"No. Not very much," Randall agreed.

"Miss Hanfield's off to school, is she?"

"Yes, she is," Randall replied, a troubled expression crossing his once handsome but now careworn features.

"Clara!" Jonathon Hanfield called up the stairs. "Miles is waiting."

Clara stood in her doorway looking into the bedroom she'd spent her entire life in. It was the last time she'd ever see it.

She walked past her father without a word, but paused and waited for him at the front door. He kissed her on the cheek, which she endured with a polite smile.

He held her at arm's length: "You are a picture of beauty. Is that the dress and reticule I bought you last Easter?"

"Yes."

He ran his hand lightly down the sleeve of her dress, and over the handbag which she had looped about her wrist. Clara tensed.

He dropped his hands. "I realize you're still distressed, but you'll eventually see the wisdom in the decisions I've made on your behalf."

Clara managed a strained smile and gave a short nod. He opened the front door.

"I'll visit in the summer," he said, and walked her to the coach.

Randall was already sitting inside when Clara climbed in. He was to accompany Clara to the train station and see her safely off.

"Good morning, Miss Hanfield," he said, offering his hand to help her to the seat.

"Good morning, Randall," she said, ignoring the hand and taking the seat across from him.

It was four miles to the train station and Clara rode in silence, waiting until they were nearly there before leaning out of the coach and asking Miles to stop.

The street was busy—very busy. It took a moment for Miles to locate a place to halt the small, two horse coach. Once safely stopped, he climbed down and opened the coach's door.

"What is it, Miss Hanfield?"

"I want you to take me to West Point."

"West...*West Point*? I beg your pardon, Miss Hanfield, but I'm supposed to get you to the train station by nine-thirty. Your father will be furious with me if you miss your train. What in the world would you want to go to West Point for, anyway? I mean, if you'll pardon me asking."

"To see where the Elliot boy was sent off to," Randall said matter-of-factly.

"The Elliot boy?" Miles echoed, sounding nonplussed.

Clara gaped at Randall.

"I apologize, Miss Hanfield," Randall said, wringing his hands together in a childlike gesture. "But I overheard everything the night Mister Hanfield struck you. And truth be told, I already knew about your courtship with the Elliot boy—well, I guess he's not such a boy anymore..." he trailed off.

"Who else knew about it?" Clara demanded.

Randall averted his eyes.

"Randall!"

"Phebe...and Sarah...I suppose most of the house staff."

"And after all of this time he just now found out," she mused.

"Well, *I* didn't know anything about it, and I don't *want* to know anything about it. It's none of my business," Miles said, sounding agitated. "Now, Miss Hanfield, we really should be getting to the station."

"I'm not going to the station, Miles. And if you won't take me to West Point, then please stand aside and let me out. I'm going, with or without your help."

"Miss Hanfield, *please*. You can't be walking about the city alone. And you have to understand, we can't just parade ourselves upstate on a whim. I mean, the snow's probably about gone, but I don't know what the road looks like, and we'll have to change horses at least once...and what about an escort? The roads aren't safe and there is a war going on. How about we go back and speak with Mister Hanfield?"

Clara got up and began to push past Miles.

"Miss Hanfield, no. Please. I'll take you to West Point," Miles said as he moved out of her way. Clara ducked back into the coach and sat down.

"Miles, allow me," Randall said. "You can hire a cab to take you back to the Hanfield's. I'll drive Miss Hanfield to West Point."

"Nooo, sir. I'm responsible for this coach. It's one of a kind and was built special for Mister Hanfield. If anyone is driving it to West Point, it's going to be me."

Miles climbed back up onto the coach's elegantly built driver's box muttering something about foolishness and hating ferries. Still talking to himself, he worked his way back into traffic.

There was an hour delay awaiting the ferry at the river crossing. Clara and Randall both paced around nervously while they waited: Clara because she was in a hurry to be out of the city, and Randall because he was worried about Clara. Once aboard, the crossing went quickly and they were soon on their way. Clara remained mostly silent, outside of commenting on something or other she saw along the road. Randall bit his lip nervously, afraid to ask her the questions that troubled him.

The trip took most of the day, and it was early evening before they arrived at West Point. Miles' concerns had proved unfounded: the road was in fine condition, and was busy with spring traders. The fancy coach garnered some curious looks, but nothing more. They stopped at an inn which boasted an impressive stable around midday. The three ate a lunch sullied by a somewhat uncomfortable silence while the inn's hostler traded the tired pair of horses for two fresh ones. The hostler pledged to Miles that the Hanfield's horses were in good hands, and that they'd be well rested and ready the following day when the travelers returned for them.

The military academy itself was a rambling network of buildings built on a sharp bend in the Hudson river. Miles waved down the driver of an ice wagon who was passing in the opposite direction and asked where the hotel was located. The teamster pointed to a three-story building with a high porch. Miles thanked him and urged the horses forward.

Clara and Randall went inside and secured adjoining rooms, while Miles saw to the horses. They assured the man at the desk that they could handle their own baggage. Randall escorted Clara to her room, then turned to go down for her things.

"I'm going to have a baby," she blurted suddenly, still standing in the doorway. Randall turned around slowly. He looked at her with naked sympathy. Clara began to cry.

"Oh, Miss Hanfield...are you certain?"

"Yes."

"Why don't you go in and sit down. I'll bring up your things, then we'll sort this out."

Clara nodded her head, then went into the room and shut the door.

The rooms were located on the second floor, and Randall took the stairs slowly. This was only partially due to his arthritic joints. He was actually in fine condition for a man of his age, outside of the arthritis. A lifetime of chopping stove wood and carrying water buckets had seen to that. His mind, however, was reeling with Clara's revelation and all the possible ramifications that went along with it.

"We're in real trouble here, Randall," Miles said as Randall stepped out onto the hotel's porch. He was sitting on a bench that ran the length of the porch, smoking a battered wooden pipe.

"Help me with Miss Hanfield's things," Randall said. Miles stood and followed Randall down the steps.

"Well, did she tell you what was going on?" Miles asked as they grasped a handle of Clara's trunk and lifted it off of the compartment on the rear of the coach.

Randall stopped and gazed across the trunk at Miles. "Yes, she has, but I can't tell you what it is. She'll have to do that, if she wants to. You get the horses stabled and join us back here. We'll be having tea in the dining room."

"Well, I hope it was worth us losing our jobs."

"You lost your job the minute she asked you to stop the coach. Come on, let's get this upstairs."

The dining room was empty save for a woman of about thirty who was sitting alone and reading a book. Randall ordered tea for three.

"Miles should be returning from the stable soon. Should I have him take his tea outside while we discuss your plans?" Randall asked softly.

"No, I've put him—both of you—in a terrible position with my father. Now that it's too late, I wish I could take it back. Unfortunately, like so many other things, I can't. I should have hired a coach and left you and Miles in New York. My father still would have been angry with you, but now…I'm sorry for acting so selfishly. You both deserve the truth."

Miles entered the dining room thirty minutes later.

"Your tea is cold," Randall said as Miles took a seat at the small round table.

"Never cared much for it anyway."

Clara plunged forward before she lost her far from inconsiderable nerve.

"I'm going to have a child. I had you bring me here so I could find out where John was sent. He doesn't know.

Miles glanced at Randall, then turned back to Clara with a look of open contempt.

"Miss Hanfield, you've ruined your life and mine along with it. I can't abide this—*any of it.*"

With that, he stood and walked out.

Randall reached over and patted Clara's hand reassuringly. "You stay here, I'll go talk with him."

Randall found Miles back on the porch bench, refilling his pipe.

"You forget your place, Miles."

"My *place?*" Miles glanced at the door then lowered his voice. "I have no place, thanks to that spoiled little whore. I'll be lucky if I'm not brought up on charges."

Randall advanced. "How dare you speak that way about Miss Hanfield."

Miles set down his pipe and stood up, toe to toe with Randall. "I'm speaking the truth, nothing less. She's bringing scandal to a fine family. I'll take you two back to New York in the morning—I have a coach and two horses to return—then good riddance to her, and to you as well if you're going to get between her and Mister Hanfield."

"Mister Hanfield is a tyrant and a despicable man. For fifteen years I've endured his degradations for the sake of that young woman in there. Go back to the tavern and speak under your breath about scandal with your motley crew of mudsill friends. I'm going to look out for Miss Hanfield, whatever the cost."

"She's not your daughter, Randall."

85

The statement stung. Randall pulled a small sheaf of bills from the inside pocket of his coat, separated some, and held them out to Miles. "This will more than pay for your room and meals. I won't be quartered with you."

Miles looked at the bills for a moment, then took them with a shrug. He sat back down and resumed refilling his pipe.

Randall walked back inside the hotel, his head hanging, deep in thought. Two years before beginning employment with the Hanfields, his own daughter—who was twelve at the time—took a fever and died, along with his wife and four-year-old son. They'd lived in a small cottage on the estate of his previous employer. Afterward, he tried to continue working for the family as they'd been good to him over the years. In the end, though, he found he simply couldn't bear the memories.

He moved into a small boarding house and lived off of money he'd saved for the next eighteen months. Finally becoming restless, he'd interviewed with Jonathon Hanfield. He was well aware of the shipping tycoon's reputation for being difficult, but Randall felt he was up to the task.

Missus Hanfield had introduced him to the two-year-old Clara, and Randall had fallen for her at once. He learned that he still had love to give, and in his opinion he could never have found a more deserving recipient.

Clara was no longer seated at the table; she was talking to the same man (presumably the proprietor) who checked them in. She was holding out an envelope, and the man was nodding his head and smiling, although to Randall he appeared put-upon. Knowing Clara as well as he did, Randall chose to leave her to her business. He sat back down and sipped his cold tea.

A short time later Clara returned to the table. "Mister Cranston was taken aback by my irregular request. Apparently it's not every day that an unannounced visitor requires correspondence be delivered to a cadet. I explained to him that I was a relative and must get a message of family importance delivered right away. Now I'm I liar *and* a thief."

"Thief? I'm sorry, perhaps it's time you explained everything to me because I have no idea what you're talking about."

"Where is Miles?"

Randall lowered his eyes and shook his head slowly.

"I understand. I saw the way he looked at me; the way *I* would have looked at me not very long ago. I know it's only the first of many such looks. I also knew that you would never look at me that way.

"Of course I wouldn't."

"I've sent a message to William Drayton. He's John's closest friend here at the academy. I've never met him, but John speaks well of him. I'm hoping he knows where John was sent. My father claims he was posted in the territories. He never said where. If he knew at all, he wouldn't want me to.

As soon as I find out, I'm going to join him."

"Miss Hanfield, it's a hard life out west. What will you do for money? And are you sure Mister Elliot will live up to his fatherly duties? What about your father? He's not likely to let this go. He could make things very difficult for the two of you, not to mention Mister Elliot's father."

"I took over three thousand dollars from my father's study. I've justified this by considering it the only inheritance I will ever claim from him." She paused, running the tip of her finger around the rim of her empty teacup. "John loves me. I know this in my heart. He's kind, truly. A quality I feel is lacking in most men; present company excluded, of course. He'll be a good husband and a fine father. As far as my own father is concerned, he will be consumed with how others will view this. I believe his fear of scandal will override his need for control and revenge. I think he will be content—as content as someone such as him can be—if I simply stay away. He would only have had me sent away anyway, and my child would have been taken from me. I will never, ever allow that."

"What about your mother?"

"She, of all people, will understand."

"I'll escort you wherever you need to go."

"Thank you, Randall, but I've demanded too much of you already. Miles was right about me ruining his life—and yours. All I could think about this morning was getting away. It was the selfish act of an overindulged child and I'll never forgive myself. I'll manage on my own." Clara smiled ruefully. "I am my father's daughter, after all."

"What's done is done, Miss Hanfield, and no one's life has been ruined. This is merely a bend in the road. I'm afraid I wouldn't be able to sleep nights not knowing whether or not you reached your destination, though. I will have to insist that you allow me to escort you. You can pay me the sum of fifty dollars, if it will make you feel better."

Clara regarded Randall from across the table. His sincerity was undeniable. Here was a face that was as familiar as her own parents'; a face that was quick to smile and rarely displayed anger. It was a face that had comforted her through the small injuries and heartaches of childhood and adolescence. It was the face of the man she had always wished was her father.

Clara smiled and offered her hand. "I accept your offer, sir."

17

It was shortly before ten o'clock the following morning when there was a tentative knock on Clara's door. She'd just come up from breakfasting with Randall in the dining room. Miles didn't join them, but had long since had the horses hitched and ready to go. Unbeknownst to Clara, he'd threatened to leave them if they weren't ready to leave by nine. Randall, however, had convinced him to stay with another five dollars from his dwindling supply of cash.

Clara thanked the young woman who delivered the note, and closed the door.

Dearest Clara,

I am sorry I cannot visit you personally as I know your need must be urgent to have brought you here to the academy. In regards to John, his whereabouts are a matter of some debate among the cadets and most of the officers are being quite closed-mouthed about the affair. None of the cadets (including this one) have been made privy to any of the details leading up to his departure. I say most of the officers as there is one (who I shall leave unnamed) who has informed me that John is on his way to Fort Laramie in the Dakota Territory. I believe this information to be reliable as the officer in question is very fond of John.

I am troubled as to why you are here and I pray all is well.

Yours truly,
William

18

Clara and Randall devised their plan during the coach ride back. They agreed it was likely that Jonathon Hanfield would already have half of the city searching for them and that they should get as far from New York as they could, as quickly as possible. Clara gave Miles one hundred dollars (omitting the fact that she'd stolen it from her father) and apologized to him for the trouble she'd caused. His response to the apology was mumbled and noncommittal, but he took the money. It was dark when Miles left them at the train station in New Jersey. Randall—stating his name as George Randolph—purchased two tickets that would take them to points west by way of Philadelphia. The train departed at eight-fifteen p.m.

Five

1

Somewhere in Kansas, October 22nd 1861.

Henry opened his eyes. He stared up into the cloudless sky, disorientated. He was lying on his back and moving backwards. The world spun and grayed as he tried to lift his head. He lay back for a moment until the feeling passed. His whole body ached, but his left leg was bright fire. He looked down at his feet. His leg was bent at an unnatural angle midway between his knee and his ankle. Seeing his leg that way made him queasy, and he threw up on himself. There was an exclamation in a language he didn't understand, and he looked up, startled. The sudden movement of his head made the world spin more violently. He fought the urge to vomit again. Two men on horseback were following close behind him. One was pointing at Henry and speaking to the other. They were Indians. He'd never seen one himself, but knew that's what these men were. One was shirtless, and the other wore something ornamental over his chest and torso. It was constructed of beads—probably bone—and resembled a washboard to Henry.

They aren't really red at all, he thought as he looked back down at his legs. He was lying on an animal hide that was laid over a frame of thick branches. He was being dragged through the grass and scrub on it. The two riders behind him were pulling similar devices with their horses.

He slept.

Pain jarred him awake. He screamed. There were men—*Indians*—standing over him, and someone was pulling on his leg. He tried to struggle free, but his right arm wouldn't move and hands were pushing on his chest. The pain in his leg was unbearable; the leg-puller pulled again and Henry screamed a second time. Someone shoved a stick in his mouth. Henry passed out.

He was being dragged behind a horse again. For how long? Hours? Days? Pain shot up his leg as he was jounced over the uneven ground. The sun was hot on his face…

2
Colorado Territory, October 29th 1861

He awoke; his leg throbbed dully. He was inside a tent made of animal skins. The tent was bigger than Henry and Eliza's little house had been, and it tapered to a near point at the top where it was open to the sky. Smoke drifted lazily out of the hole. The quality of the light coming from the hole told Henry that it was either dawn or evening.

There was a small fire burning in the middle of the tent just to Henry's left. He attempted to push himself up to a sitting position so he could see more, but when he tried he found that he still couldn't move his right arm. He threw off the hide that was covering him and saw that his arm was being held fast against his body with thin strips of hide. He was completely naked. His left leg was splinted with smooth sticks that were held in place with more strips of hide, and there was some sort of poultice tied to his right knee. He began trying to untie the strips holding his arm in place. The arm didn't appear injured, and outside of some pain in his shoulder when he flexed his hand, it seemed fine.

"Hová'aháne!" a man spoke urgently from behind him. The speaker came into view on Henry's right and hunkered next to him. He took Henry's left wrist gently but firmly and pulled Henry's hand away from the knotted thongs. "Névé'nėheševe," he said soothingly before letting go of Henry's wrist.

"Why is my arm tied?" Henry asked. "Do you understand me?"

The man simply smiled. He was quite a bit older than Henry. His long, black hair was streaked with gray, and his brown eyes were so dark as to appear almost black. After a moment he pulled the buffalo hide back over Henry's body up to his chest, said a few more words Henry couldn't understand, then stood and left.

Henry twisted his head and looked after the man as he exited the tent. The pain in his leg was making it hard to concentrate. He also felt pain on his scalp and inspected the area with his fingers. There was a good-sized lump near the crown and he winced when he touched it. *Knocked my head pretty good,* he thought.

He wasn't afraid. It was obvious the Indians wanted to help him—had most likely saved his life. *Why* was the real question. He wondered if they were the ones following him all along, or if they'd rescued him from his pursuers.

The tent opened, and the man returned along with three other men and two women. He squatted next to Henry, put a hand behind Henry's head, and lifted gently while holding a horn cup to Henry's lips. Henry hadn't realized how thirsty he was until the water hit his mouth. He gulped it down as fast as he could swallow, water running down his chin. The man chuckled, and there was some subdued conversation from the people behind him.

Henry looked up at the people, then back at the man in front of him. He tapped his chest with his finger. "I'm Henry...*Henry.*"

The man smiled and nodded. He put a hand to flat on his own chest. "Mo'ohnee'ėstse."

"Ma-oh—"

"Mo'ohnee'ėstse," the man repeated.

Henry got it pretty close.

For the next several days he was nursed by the Indians. Mo'ohnee'ėstse and a woman, who Henry reckoned was his wife, brought Henry food and water and helped him outside to do his necessary. Mo'ohnee'ėstse was patient with him and quick to understand the things Henry was trying to convey. He even seemed to understand some English. At one point Henry wanted his *(stolen)* trousers, and Mo'ohnee'ėstse had brought them, cut off the left leg from the knee down, and helped Henry into them. Others came and went; some brought food—meat, mostly—some just stood and looked at him, speaking softly to one another. He wondered if they'd ever seen someone like him before.

He awoke from a doze with sunlight from the open tent flap shining on his face. Mo'ohnee'ėstse entered, followed by another Indian—one of the men who'd stood in the tent on previous occasions, silently observing Henry. He appeared to be a little older than Mo'ohnee'ėstse, and was dressed in a white muslin shirt and deerskin trousers. His long hair was woven into two braids. A third man filed in behind them.

A white man.

The man was fiftyish and stoutly built. He looked at Henry curiously, then at the Indian in the muslin shirt. The Indian nodded slightly and the man sat down cross-legged in front of Henry.

Henry eyed the man warily.

"My name's William Bent," the man said. "You look a little worse for wear…Henry, is it?"

"Yessir, that's right. I was thrown from a horse."

"That's what I was told. Standing Elk," he nodded toward Mo'ohnee'ėstse, "had to put the animal out of its misery. It's probably been dried and eaten by now. I hope you weren't too partial to it."

Henry glanced at Mo'ohnee'ėstse.

"You're his guest—and the guest of Chief Black Kettle." This time he gestured with an open hand to the man in the muslin shirt, who nodded at Henry. "Standing Elk claims your destiny and his are entwined. He says he dreamed of a great warrior. He says he saw *a dark man with the spirit of a bear,* and that the man had a scar on his face and would bring great medicine to his people. He says he's supposed to be this man's guide in this world. Of course, there was a time I'd be inclined to dismiss talk like that as superstitious nonsense by folks that don't know any better, but I've spent a long time among these people—my sons are half Cheyenne—and I've seen enough to know sometimes there's more to this life than meets the eye. Besides, who am I to scoff at another man's beliefs? There was also a time I'd be inclined to question what a colored man would be doing in the middle of Kansas carrying a twenty dollar pistol, lying next to a dead horse, with a posse chasing after him."

He eyed Henry speculatively for a moment before continuing. "These men seem to think you have some value…do you?"

Henry thought of the man by the river, and of his failure to save Eliza.

"I don't know, sir."

"I respect an honest answer. A man like you could do worse than living with the Cheyenne. They're fine people: fair and generous. Standing Elk and his hunting party saved your life; I guess you know that. If they hadn't been following a group of Pawnee that ran off with some of their horses, they never would have come across you. The men who were chasing you turned around when they spotted the Cheyenne. You must not have been very important to them."

Bent glanced back at Black Kettle before continuing.

"Anyhow, I have to be on my way. Black Kettle just wanted me to have a look at you. You'll meet my children eventually; two of my sons are about your age." He stood and looked down at Henry. "Gifts are meaningful to the Cheyenne—*very meaningful*. Standing Elk was admiring that Colt pistol of yours. Good luck to you, Henry."

"Mister Bent?"

"Yes?"

"Can you ask Mo'ohn—*Standing Elk,* why my arm is tied to my body?"

"You dislocated your shoulder. You have to let everything heal up or it'll keep coming out of place. You rest now and let them take care of you."

3

Henry spent the next twenty months with Standing Elk and the Cheyenne. As suggested by William Bent, he gifted the pistol to Standing Elk. In return, Standing Elk and his only wife, Walking Woman, gave Henry the lodge he had convalesced in, four buffalo hides, a pair of doeskin trousers, and a gray mare to replace the horse Henry had lost. Henry had mixed feelings about the whole affair, as the pistol wasn't really his to give, and the horse had never belonged to him either.

For the first time in his life Henry was surrounded by people who accepted him as nothing less or more than they saw themselves. Granted, there was a sort of hierarchy within the band, but it was subtle and of no comparison to Henry's life of masters, overseers, and foremen. Henry learned that respect was earned among the Cheyenne, not purchased or given as a birthright. His heart ached daily for Eliza, and he wondered what she would have made of the Indians.

At the beginning the Indians' attitude toward Henry ran the gamut from simple curiosity, to awe, to indifference. All respected Standing Elk's dream, and therefore treated Henry kindly. Most went out of their way to teach him things. The better part of them had never seen a person of African descent, and marveled over things like the way Henry's hair grew in tight curls. His scars, both on his face and his back were also of great interest. Stories began among the children (and even some adults) that Henry was a great warrior of his people. Black Kettle and some of the elders (including Standing Elk), however, knew that a goodish number of whites were in the habit of keeping people of Henry's race as slaves.

His leg slowly healed, and Henry made himself as useful around the camp as he could. He felt strange not having a job to do, but impressed the Cheyenne with his willingness to work hard at whatever task he undertook. He earned some of his own respect with his skill at trapping small game. Henry had learned a unique snare design from John Brown that rarely failed to capture anything that wandered into it. With low food stores almost a constant, the extra game helped greatly.

During his stay Henry also discovered both a knack, and an affinity for horses. He spent a great deal of time on the gray mare and would ride off by himself, sometimes for days at a time. The area surrounding the camp was virtually treeless for miles, and Henry never really got used to it. If there was anything he missed about Missouri, it was the trees. The closest thing to real woods was over forty miles away. So he'd ride to them. Occasionally Standing Elk or Spotted Paw—a young brave who Henry had befriended—would join him. Mostly though, he would go by himself. He enjoyed sitting alone and reading out of one of the books William Bent had given him. He read as much as he could, and always thought of Eliza when he did.

That first winter Henry and Standing Elk could be seen together often; the great Cheyenne medicine man and the freed slave. Standing Elk taught Henry much herb lore, as well as how to make and use a bow, tan hides, and track animals. Walking Woman made Henry a fine doeskin tunic, fitting of a Cheyenne. Over time, Henry learned their language. Standing Elk, Spotted Paw and William Bent's son Robert took time to instruct him. That, along with the simple day to day interactions, accelerated his learning. Henry taught Standing Elk more English as well, although Standing Elk took the instruction grudgingly. He referred to English as the *language of lies* and preferred not to speak it. Henry had the idea that Standing Elk knew more English than he let on, though. For Henry, understanding the language of the Cheyenne was easier by far than understanding the Cheyenne themselves. Their collective point of view was dramatically different than anything Henry was accustomed to. In the beginning this made it difficult for him to extract the meanings and intentions from the words that were spoken. The Cheyenne simply didn't perceive the world like he did.

"You carry a heavy heart," Standing Elk said to Henry matter-of-factly one day when the two were walking by the small creek that ran by the camp. He spoke the language of the Cheyenne.

It was late spring and the creek was high. The clear water babbled and gurgled over it's bed of stones. Henry picked up a few off of the grassy bank and began tossing them thoughtfully into the fast moving water. In the eight months Henry had been with the Cheyenne, no one had inquired about his past. He figured this was Standing Elk's polite way of asking.

They sat together by the creek for the next several hours. Henry told his story the best he could; he left nothing out. He wept when he recounted finding Eliza dying in the brush, and couldn't meet Standing Elk's eyes when he told of how he stole the man's belongings by the river, including the pistol he'd given Standing Elk. He used Standing Elk's language as much as his still-limited understanding of it would allow. Learning single words and meanings had been easy. Learning how to string sounds together along with all of the other subtleties needed to make *conversation* was much more difficult. When he got stuck he used English words he knew Standing Elk understood.

When Henry was finished, Standing Elk was silent for a long time. He stared across the creek at the horizon. The westering sun set the distant mountains ablaze with orange fire. Finally he spoke, in English. "We do not always see meanings for what is in our path. The white man makes…peósané…*hate*, grow in the hearts of all others he touches. I battle with this. I do not want this hate. The same hate is in your heart. We must defeat this hate." He stood, looked down at Henry, and added in Cheyenne: "Now we smoke."

The Cheyenne didn't include Henry in certain aspects of tribal living. He was excluded from many ceremonies, and all of the council meetings that Standing Elk attended in Black Kettle's lodge. These meetings occasionally included leaders from other Indian tribes such as the Arapaho and Sioux. Other times, Standing Elk travelled with Black Kettle to Fort Wise, where councils were sometimes held with white leaders. It was once a trading post owned by William Bent, who leased it to the U.S. military the year before Henry's arrival. The fort was located in the southeast of the Colorado Territory. The Cheyenne camp itself—the first of two camp locations Henry lived at during his time with the Cheyenne—was a day's ride north of the fort. Henry accompanied them once, along with some others from the camp, but the trip wasn't for a parley with the bluecoats. It was only to collect food and sundries that were promised to the Cheyenne in the Treaty of Fort Wise. When they arrived at the fort, less than half of what they were promised was awaiting them and the steers they were supposed to receive were scrawny and ill. Black Kettle wouldn't take the sickly steers, and through an army interpreter admonished the bluecoat captain in charge of the allocation to eat them himself.

The 1861 treaty, which Black Kettle and other chiefs signed early that year, relinquished all but a small portion of their previous lands to the U.S. government. Black Kettle had signed the treaty believing that his refusal would bring all out war between the Cheyenne and the bluecoats and, ultimately, the annihilation of his people. He believed the whites were too strong and numerous to be resisted, and that peace for his people could only be obtained through acquiescence. Other Indian chiefs refused to sign the treaty and ridiculed Black Kettle for being weak. Once, not long before Henry left the camp and began scouting and interpreting for the army, Standing Elk confided in Henry that he agreed with the other chiefs. Standing Elk never said that he thought Black Kettle was weak, though. Just wrong.

Henry was allowed on a hunt during his first spring with the Cheyenne. His leg was completely healed, although he still walked with a limp. Some of the braves were reluctant to bring him along, but in the end respect for Standing Elk's dream of Henry being sent to them by the Great Spirit won over, and he was included.

As it was when Standing Elk found Henry lying in the Kansas scrub, the hunting party travelled well out of their treaty-designated hunting grounds. It wasn't a calculated breach; the Cheyenne didn't operate that way. It was simply go where the game was, or face the possibility of starvation. Unlike the hunt when Henry was found, however, this one went smoothly. They didn't have to chase stolen horses over a hundred miles, and they didn't return to camp with pemmican made from a few small deer and one unfortunate horse. This time they came across a small herd of buffalo on the second day out, about fifty miles from the Cheyenne camp. They killed several of the animals, and transported the meat back to camp on the same type of *travois* that they'd transported Henry on. Henry was only a spectator during that first hunt, but did his share of dressing the slaughtered animals. Two months later he was permitted to participate and even made a kill; one of only six on that particular hunt.

4

On one of his many solo outings to the woods, Henry was riding along the Arikaree River. He came across an old woman with her foot caught in a beaver trap. He'd heard her crying weakly as he passed not twenty feet away. He stopped the mare, dismounted, and limped back to where she was lying in some tall grass several feet from the river. The trap, which was old and caked with rust and dirt, was clamped firmly on the middle of her foot. *Must have been here a long, long time*, Henry thought, looking at the trap. Standing Elk once told him that the whites had killed off most of the beaver in the time when Standing Elk's own father had still walked in this world.

"I'm going to free you, Mother," Henry said, kneeling by the woman. She was severely dehydrated, and alternated between weeping and mumbling nonsense in Cheyenne. He grasped the old trap and pulled it apart. The rusty trap squealed in protest and the woman let out a short but piercing scream before fainting. Henry examined her foot; it was swollen and misshapen, the area around where the trap's jaws had been was bruised to a near black. Henry guessed most of the bones in her foot were broken. He retrieved his canteen and a small scrap of cloth he used for washing and began to wet the woman's sun-cracked lips and face. She awoke and whispered, "Néá'eše, néá'eše," over and over.

"You're welcome, Mother," Henry said.

After gently picking her up and carrying her to the shade of a nearby tree, Henry began fashioning a travois much like the one he himself had been carried on the previous fall. Not knowing where she came from, only that she was Cheyenne, Henry decided to take her back to Black Kettle's camp. Once there, Standing Elk and Walking Woman tended to her. At first Standing Elk thought she would die. He thought her wounds would poison her body. But she survived. A short time later she was using the very crutch Henry had used while his leg healed; Henry simply cut it shorter.

It turned out she'd been with Black Kettle's band previously. She departed with her son and thirty others after Black Kettle signed the Treaty of Fort Wise. Like many other Cheyenne, her son and a handful of braves were unhappy with Black Kettle for signing the treaty. They claimed that every time the whites made a new treaty, the Cheyenne and other tribes were forced to live and hunt only where the whites allowed them to. They also claimed the whites always made big promises but never kept them—a claim Henry had seen validated when the army shorted the Cheyennes' rations and attempted to give Black Kettle sick beef.

A few weeks prior to Henry finding her by the river, the woman's son and several other men had joined with a band of Cheyenne warriors called *Dog Men*, who were bent on making war with the whites. That left the old woman alone with seven other women, five children, and two old men (her husband had been killed ten years before while on a buffalo hunt). Black Kettle finally sent some braves to bring them back to his camp where they could be looked after.

5

On a May morning in 1863, two years almost to the day before Henry would meet the newly commissioned Lieutenant John Elliot on a supply caravan headed for Fort Laramie, William Bent arrived at the camp looking for Henry.

Henry was working on building a combination drying rack/meat smoker. It was trickier than it should have been because wood to use for framing was scarce. He'd managed to scrounge a few broken lodge poles, and was busy splitting them with a hammer and stone wedges when William and another man came up behind him.

"You're a clever man," William said to Henry's back.

Henry straightened up and turned. "Thank you," he said, glancing at the stranger in the army uniform. He waited for William to say more.

"I have someone I'd like you to meet. His name's Captain Fitchner; United States Calvary. He's delivering a personal dispatch to Major Wynkoop. The Major's on patrol somewhere up the Platte. The Captain needs a scout."

Henry looked at the Captain. "I've only been up that way once. You're better off with someone else, a Pawnee, I reckon." Henry suggested a Pawnee, knowing that none of the Cheyenne braves would accompany the bluecoat Captain.

"I'm more interested in an interpreter than a scout. We should have no trouble locating Major Wynkoop. After delivering the dispatch I've been ordered to locate the Cheyenne chief Morning Star and discuss other matters with him. Mister Bent tells me you speak and understand their language."

Henry raised his eyebrows and shifted his gaze to William Bent, who cocked his head slightly toward the Captain as if to say: *Talk to him, not me.*

Captain Fitchner pressed on: "The job pays five dollars a week," he said proudly.

Henry looked at the captain levelly, then let his eyes pass over the Indian camp and its seventy plus lodges with their conical tops pointing skyward. "I'm much obliged for the offer, Captain. I'll have to think on it some."

The captain was visibly disappointed. "We're heading out in two days."

"A couple hours should do it," Henry said.

"My men and I will wait just outside of camp for your decision." He nodded at William Bent and walked away.

"The captain was doubtful when I explained to him you were a negro," Bent said.

"I reckon he would be."

"Anyhow, when he came to me I thought you might be interested."

"I'm interested. I've been wondering for awhile if I shouldn't be moving on, try to earn myself a living. I just—"

"Need to talk with Standing Elk first?"

Henry nodded.

"Well, I'll be at the fort. See me there before you leave, if you decide to do it. I have a few things I can outfit you with."

"I will. Thank you."

Henry watched William Bent walk off to where his horse was tied, shooing off some children who were admiring his saddle and rifle scabbard.

He found Standing Elk mending a woman's finger. She'd cut it deeply making deer hide thongs. Henry stood aside patiently while Standing Elk finished. When he was, Henry told him of the captain's inquiry.

"Perhaps this is your path," he said in English—he spoke it more often since Henry had come to live with them. Sometimes Henry and Standing Elk would go back and forth between languages so seamlessly that neither of them noticed they were doing it.

Standing Elk smiled vaguely. "Now your purpose for coming to us may be shown, though it's curious that it should be through the white man." Standing Elk reached out and gripped Henry's upper arm. "Beware him. Few are good. They are possessed by their desires and will bite an open hand like a wounded dog. They value only these things on which they can place value."

"I have no trust in white men," Henry said. "Except William Bent, I reckon."

Henry was up and on his way to the fort before the sun rose. Standing Elk, Walking Woman, Spotted Paw, and Black Kettle all visited Henry the previous night. They presented him with gifts: a fine beaded pipe with an elk horn bowl from Black Kettle, a pair of new moccasins from Standing Elk and Walking Woman, and a bone handled knife from Spotted Paw. This last meant a great deal to Henry, as he knew the knife was a prized possession to Spotted Paw. Henry wished he could tell Spotted Paw to keep his knife, but he'd lived with the Cheyenne long enough to know that if someone offered a gift, you accepted it.

He rode the gray mare bareback; more because he'd become accustomed to it than to follow the Indian way. He'd buried the stolen saddle soon after his leg had healed enough to allow him to dig the hole. He knew he would never feel right using it. As he was putting it in the hole he noticed for the first time the man's initials engraved on the skirt: *A. Hoyt.*

Captain Fitchner wasn't expecting him until the following morning, so Henry kept a leisurely pace. His intention was to camp about five miles north of the fort, and ride in at first light. He would see William Bent before departing with the soldiers.

6

William Bent was standing beside a loaded buckboard when Henry arrived at the fort. Henry dismounted and tied the mare to the wagon.

"Morning, Henry," William said, setting down the feedbag he was carrying and walking around the back of the wagon.

"Morning," Henry returned.

William lifted the tarp covering the rear part of the wagon. Henry looked at the saddle and saddlebags, then at William Bent.

"There's a shirt—should fit you—tobacco, jerky, salt, and a few other essentials in the saddlebags." Then he reached under the tarp and brought out a rifle.

"And this," he said, handing the rifle to Henry, "is a *Spencer* rifle. It's beautiful, isn't it? It's a repeater. It takes cartridges—seven of them. Look, you load them right here." He showed Henry how to load the Spencer.

"I—" Henry began

"These aren't gifts…well, they're mostly not. I billed the army for the saddle and saddlebags. Captain Fitchner wasn't too happy about it, but interpreters come dear right now so I told him you'd have to have a proper saddle. It's not new, but it's a good one. The saddlebags are new. My guess is the captain paid for them himself. Probably could have pushed them for higher wages if you weren't a negro—no offense, you understand. The wages are damn good regardless. You can settle up with me for the essentials and the cartridges later. The rifle is yours."

Henry took back the rifle and held it at arm's length, examining it. "This is really something. I'm indebted to you."

"No, you're not. I haven't had the time to know you, but Black Kettle, Standing Elk, and my boys speak well of you—the highest, as matter of fact—and I'll feel better knowing someone is along who has the Cheyenne's interests at heart. Living here has changed my views on more things than I can count…anyway, you enjoy that rifle."

Two hours later Henry departed with Captain Fitchner and twenty-seven Colorado volunteers. It was the first of several such expeditions for Henry between the spring of 1863, and the spring of 1865.

Six

1

Clara entered the dimly lit mercantile with Randall right behind her. They'd just arrived in St. Joseph via riverboat and Clara was already anxious to find someone to take them to Fort Laramie. There was a bald man with thick, gray sideburns weighing slabs of bacon at the store's counter. He looked up as Clara and Randall approached.

"Excuse me," Clara said. "We're seeking transport to Fort Laramie."

The man looked past Clara to Randall with his eyebrows raised. Randall held his gaze briefly, then turned and walked back to the front of the store. They'd set their baggage on the porch, and he wanted to keep an eye on it. The store was located away from the bustling and somewhat desperate looking riverfront, but he didn't want to take chances. He also knew that Clara preferred to handle things herself. The storekeeper, taking the hint, turned back to Clara.

"None of the wagon trains will be leaving until the first week of May, provided the weather holds out. Have to wait for the grass to grow enough for the livestock, you see. You can wait and go along with someone then." He recited this as if speaking to a child.

"Our business is urgent. Perhaps a privateer?"

The man continued in the same patronizing tone. "I reckon one could be had, that is if you have the currency. But it's not so simple as that, Missus…?"

"Miss Randolph; Clara Randolph."

"Right, *Miss Randolph*. As I was saying, you can hire a wagon and driver, but you're going to need some protection as well. It's not safe travelling by ones and twos, and the cavalry aren't out along this stretch in any numbers yet. The Indians are riled up over some doings over'n Colorado and they been up to dickens. And also, if you got livestock you're gonna need feed cause like I said, there ain't much grass yet."

"We don't have any livestock, but we have enough *currency*, Mister…?"

"Smith."

"Mister Smith, if you'd be kind enough to help us hire a reputable teamster and the proper escorts, we'd be inclined to outfit ourselves here at your store—assuming you are the owner, of course."

The man puffed up appreciatively. "I am."

"Can I also assume you own the livery next door?"

"You can."

"Good. We will also need two horses—the best you have—along with bridles and saddles, grain, and whatever else you feel we will require for the journey."

Smith regarded Clara from across the counter. After a moment he turned and called out, *"Robert!"* Clara followed his gaze to a door-sized opening in the wall of merchandise behind the counter. Soon, a boy of about fourteen stepped through the opening.

"Yes, sir?"

"Go down to the Golden Star and see if Stephen Billings or Vance Lipton is around. Tell them we got a Miss Randolph and…" he turned to Clara.

"My father, George Randolph," Clara said.

"And her father. They want to go to Fort Laramie, no livestock."

"As soon as possible," Clara added.

"Of course. As soon as possible. Go on, boy."

"Yes, sir." The boy hurried away.

"Might be awhile. You can go see Nero out back. He'll show you the horses."

The boy, presumably the storekeeper's son, returned thirty minutes later with a short, burly man that looked to be in his mid-thirties. He had a long, auburn colored beard, and the red-rimmed eyes of a long time drinker. Clara and Randall had moved their belongings (with Smith's permission) inside the store. They were standing at a large, oblong shaped corral looking at the horses Smith had to offer. Clara knew how to ride, but otherwise didn't know a great deal about horses. Randall, though far from an expert, knew a little more. He thought that all of the horses were poor examples of the noble species but he nonetheless had Nero—Smith's elderly negro stableman—cut out two buckskin geldings.

"Good choices, sir." Nero said, as he led the horses out of the corral and toward the stable.

The burly man approached Clara and Randall as they moved to follow the stableman.

He addressed Randall. "Name's Vance Lipton. I'm told you're needin' a wagon and escort to Laramie?"

Randall extended his hand. "Pleased to meet you, Mister Lipton. I'm George Randolph, this is my daughter, Clara."

Vance Lipton nodded at Clara and said "Ma'am," before continuing.

"I can get you to Fort Laramie. The only problem is most of the experienced men hereabouts are already hired out to the folks getting ready to set out next month. It's too bad, there was a small supply wagon train for the army headed out of here not ten days ago. You could have travelled with them…I'll find the men, but it's going to cost. "

Clara's eyes lit up, but she kept silent. She wondered if John was with them.

"Mister Lipton?" Clara queried. "How long will it take to get to Fort Laramie?"

"Well, if we're not bringing too much along and you don't mind long days, we can be there well this side of three weeks." He turned back to Randall. "Now about payment—"

"We will pay you one hundred dollars, Mister Lipton," Clara said. "For your services and use of your wagon. Fifty dollars now, and the remainder when we arrive at Fort Laramie. We'll also pay twenty-five dollars each to the men you employ."

Lipton looked questioningly at Randall, as if awaiting confirmation of what he was hearing.

"My daughter speaks for me in all matters, Mister Lipton. You'll find she is quite capable. If you'll excuse me, I'll just see how the groom is faring with our horses."

2

Clara and Randall had acquired simpler clothing more suited to the frontier while they were in St. Louis. Everything else they needed they purchased at Smith's Mercantile. Smith happily walked them through the store, loading purchases onto a small, pull-behind wagon. Clara bought herself two books for the trail, and a straw bonnet that she thought was ugly but practical. She purchased Randall a wide-brimmed felt hat that mirrored what other men were wearing. At Smith's suggestion, they also purchased a Henry repeating rifle and one hundred cartridges for forty-five dollars.

They left their purchases at the mercantile and found a suitable restaurant and hotel. The agreement was to meet Vance Lipton at Smith's at nine a.m. to load the wagon. Clara was so excited at the prospect of seeing John that she barely slept.

Lipton was at Smith's Mercantile at eight a.m. along with his long time friend, Beckett Longstreet, and two new men. The first was Beckett's niece's husband, James Rickman, who was just home from the war and needed paying work. The other was Rickman's friend from the army, Elias Spearse. The story was that Spearse had saved Rickman's life in the battle at Backbone Mountain in Arkansas. Beckett always considered James Rickman shiftless, and he normally wouldn't have hired him to clean chamber pots. Fortunately for Rickman, though, Beckett was partial to his only niece. She'd all but begged Beckett to take her husband on. As for Spearse, he was staying at the Rickman's small spread outside of St. Joseph. He was originally from Ohio, but that's really all Beckett knew about him.

Ordinarily, Vance would have made the run to Fort Laramie with just Beckett Longstreet. But after the incident with the Indians at Big Sandy Creek there'd been reports of attacks on settlers and travelers. Vance didn't want to take any chances. Besides, the old fellow and his willful daughter obviously had no problem affording the extra precautions. Robert Smith, the shrewd storekeeper, told Vance that he'd sold the old man and his daughter one of those new Henry rifles along with the other supplies. He and Beckett both had Springfields, and James Rickman carried a Sharps. Rickman's sidekick had showed up with an old Enfield that looked like it might explode in his face if he actually fired it, but he had a newer revolver that would come in handy if the worst did happen and they ended up in close fighting. Vance knew that if they made a show of the rifles as they travelled they'd be safe from anything but a large war party. He always brought two extra ponies and some whiskey in case things got sticky. He'd rather give the Indians a few gifts than fight with them.

Clara and Randall arrived promptly at nine. Their new horses were already saddled and ready although Vance expected both of them to ride in the wagon most of the time. Clara was dressed in a simple, tan colored riding habit, and Randall wore brown denim work trousers with a gray cotton shirt and wool coat. He jokingly referred to the ensemble as his peasant attire.

They ferried across the river an hour later; the same ferry John Elliot had used to cross only a handful of days before. Its tattered and ridiculous looking Jolly Roger flapped jauntily in the breeze.

3

While Clara and Randall were eating their first supper on the trail, an impossibly tall and big-boned man arrived on the six o'clock train. He stood, picked up his straw hat, and fastidiously brushed off his tailored linen suit before walking to the end of the car and exiting the train. Like many from the east, he'd expected St. Joseph to be smaller. Once his horse was offloaded he asked the station man where a good hotel room could be had.

His name was Theo Brandt. He'd been sent by Jonathon Hanfield to retrieve his daughter Clara *by any means necessary.* Hanfield was also going through his contacts in the army, but he felt more comfortable sending Theo to manage things. Hanfield also wanted Randall Eastman *left for the carrion-eaters,* if at all possible. Theo had already seen to it that the Hanfield's driver, Miles Penbrook, had been left lying in a rubbish heap behind his favorite tavern with his throat cut. *For the rats,* Theo thought. *Aren't they considered carrion eaters? If not, they should be. Damn rats will eat the eyeballs, tongue, and testicles of a man before his body is cold.*

Once checked into his room he removed his suit, neatly folded it, and changed into a pair of brown wool trousers and a simple, blue chambray shirt—items he'd also had tailored, as finding clothing for a man his size was difficult. On top of his unique size, he was also extremely fussy about how his clothing fit him.

Theo had been managing "unpleasant tasks" for Jonathon Hanfield for years. He wasn't a hired strong-arm, or a killer; he was a problem solver. Occasionally a killing was necessary in order to solve a problem. And although he certainly possessed the physique for it, and felt no aversion to it, Theo Brandt had never committed murder himself. He simply coordinated things.

Once changed, Theo left the room and rode down by the river. It was nearly dark, but the area was well lit and alive with activity. His mouth puckered with distaste as he chose the largest and liveliest looking saloon.

It took Theo two hours of buying drinks and asking questions before finding what he was looking for in the form of four ex-Confederate militia men from central Missouri. Two of the men were brothers—twins, though not identical—named Wayne and George Beaderman. The young twins shared pale complexions and orange freckles that completely covered their foreheads, faces and necks, but that's where the similarities stopped. Wayne had jet black hair and a hefty build. George had hair that matched his freckles and was so slight of build as to look sickly. They claimed to be expert trackers. A claim endorsed by the other two men—a father and son.

The father's name was Emmet Dawson.

"So let me be clear, Mister Brandt," Emmet said, setting his whiskey glass on the table. "The extent of our responsibility to you will be to accompany you to Fort Laramie, assist you in locating this unfortunate young woman, then see the two of you safely back here and aboard an eastbound train. In the event we fail to locate this young woman, or if the army has already found her, you will still be bound to the agreed upon sum?"

Theo looked fixedly at Emmet. "Miss Hanfield's father wishes that her captor never have the opportunity to harm her again."

"We'll fix him, Mister," Wayne Beaderman blurted. "There's nothing lower than a man who'll take from a woman what don't belong to him."

Theo ignored him and continued to address Emmet. "There will be an extra three hundred dollars if Randall Eastman doesn't live to stand trial." He laid several gold pieces on the table. "This should cover your provisioning and the rest of your evening's drinks. See you at the river, say eight a.m.?"

Emmet Dawson made the gold pieces disappear.

4

Riding atop the wagon next to Vance Lipton, Randall Eastman stared across the plain at the small grove of trees. It wasn't that he found the trees particularly interesting, it was because they were all he had to look at in the bland, unchanging countryside. Clara was behind him in the shade of the wagon's canopy, trying to read one of the books she'd purchased in St. Louis. After another particularly rough jounce of the wagon, she gave it up and set the book aside. She looked out of the slit in the canvas between Vance and Randall. Unlike John Elliot, Clara thought the plain was one of the most beautiful places she'd ever seen. Its openness gave her a feeling of freedom, and the air smelled clean and earthy. Perhaps she and John would make a home somewhere out here.

It was just past noon. They were six days out from St. Joseph and making excellent time according to Vance Lipton. "Easy going compared to a fully-loaded wagon train," he'd said.

While Clara looked out at the frontier and daydreamed about her future with John and their child, Elias Spearse was watching James Rickman out of the corner of his eye, waiting for the signal. Both he and James were riding in the rear, behind the wagon and the small string of horses tethered to it.

The plan was simple: Rickman would ride up behind the old man—Beckett, was his name—who was on vanguard, while Spearse rode up and disarmed the other two on the wagon. Rickman made him promise not to shoot anyone, but Spearse was reserving the right to do so at his own discretion if the situation warranted it. Spearse wasn't worried about the easterner; the old man was sort of a dandy—work clothes or no—and handled his new rifle as clumsily as a virgin handled his first whore. Vance Lipton, on the other hand, was clearly a man to be reckoned with. They would have to be careful.

The moment came: Rickman nodded at Spearse and spurred his horse forward. Spearse did the same, drawing his Colt Navy revolver with his free hand.

"Stop the wagon," Spearse said, coming up behind Vance Lipton.

Vance looked over his left shoulder at Spearse, then over his right one at Rickman who had his rifle pointed at Beckett's back. He stopped the wagon.

"Set the rifle down, Mister Randolph," Spearse said, without taking his eyes off of Vance. "Then both of you climb down and sit on the ground over here...get out of the wagon, Miss Randolph."

Vance ignored Spearse and looked back at Rickman, who had dismounted and was marching a bewildered looking Beckett past the front of the wagon and around the team of horses. "What the hell is this, James?" Vance asked tightly.

"You just be quiet and get down off there, Vance. Elias and me are taking the money we know these two are carrying. This don't have nothing to do with you." He followed Beckett around the front of the wagon and shoved the older man roughly to the ground. "Now you stay there, you old shit."

"This is how you treat folks trying to help you," Beckett said, looking up at Rickman.

Rickman barked a laugh. "Help me? You done nothing but run me down since I married that ungrateful bitch niece of yours."

"Run you down? Cause I thought with you being a married man you might want to do some work and make a living?"

"Enough of that," Spearse said, still not turning from Vance. "Now you get off that wagon or I swear I'll kill you."

Randall stepped off of the wagon and began walking around the front of the team just as Vance dropped the reins, snatched up Randall's rifle, and leaped off the wagon behind him. Spearse fired the pistol just as Vance disappeared behind the wagon. The shot went wide and caught one of the lead horses in the flank. The team spooked and took off. Clara screamed, and Randall, who had ducked down when the shot was fired, was kicked by one of the horses as it passed. He fell to the ground, narrowly missing getting run over by the wagon and the string of horses tied behind it. Spearse aimed the pistol, waiting for the wagon to pass so that he had a clear shot at Vance. When it did, Vance was already crouched with the Henry aimed. He adjusted the rifle minutely when Spearse came into view and fired just as Spearse pulled the trigger on the Colt.

Vance's shot took Spearse in the neck, knocking him from his horse. Spearse's bullet hit Vance in the pelvis, shattering the bone before exiting just above his buttocks.

With Rickman's attention turned to the action, Beckett stood and rushed him, tackling him to the ground. Rickman lost his grip on his rifle with the impact, and it went tumbling through the scrub. Rickman was smaller than Beckett but was also nearly half his age. He easily overpowered the older man, and ended up sitting on Beckett's chest with his knees pinning his arms, immobilizing them. Beckett gasped for breath under Rickman's weight.

"You old shi—" Whatever Rickman was about to say was cut off when Randall swung Rickman's own rifle by the barrel in a wide, sweeping arc. The hardwood stock cracked his skull and killed him almost instantly.

Randall didn't wait to assess the damage; he tore off after the overturned wagon screaming Clara's name.

The wagon didn't make it far. The team ran less than a hundred yards before the lame horse collapsed. The lead horses over-compensated for the dead weight and veered left just as the wagon hit a natural depression. The wagon tipped over onto its side and, fortunately for the eight horses strung behind it, the iron ring they were tied to broke away from the back of the wagon. The team wasn't so lucky: aside from the one that was shot, one broke both of its front legs, and the others were tangled in the rigging, unable to free themselves.

Clara's first instinct was to jump, but she was afraid she'd be trampled by the string of horses running behind. She was looking out the back indecisively when the wagon went over. She was thrown onto the prairie along with the wagon's other contents and narrowly missed being trampled by the panicked horses anyway.

She'd hit hard, and her wind was knocked out. She struggled to her knees, disoriented. Horses were whinnying at each other. A man was screaming. She looked up; Randall was running toward her. She put her hands protectively over her stomach. *The baby,* she thought fearfully.

Randall blundered to his knees in front of her, wheezing.

"Oh, Miss Hanfield are you hurt?" he asked breathlessly, while reaching out and taking her scraped and cut hands.

She looked at him beseechingly. "No. But the baby—"

"You can't worry about that now. I'm sure the child will be fine," he said with more confidence than he felt. "Mister Lipton is shot...I think I may have killed Mister Rickman. Let me help you up. Perhaps we can help Mister Lipton. Are you sure you're not hurt?"

Clara nodded and let Randall help her to her feet. They hurried over to where Beckett was kneeling next to Vance. Vance's face was as pale as paste, but he was conscious and cursing.

"Damn, low, dirty, sons of bitches," he growled.

"Help me get him over to the wagon. We got to stop the bleeding," Beckett said.

Randall glanced over at James Rickman and Elias Spearse. Neither of the men were moving. Beckett struck him lightly on the leg. "There ain't nothing you can do for them, and I couldn't imagine why you want to anyhow. Now c'mon, let's get him over there. Miss Randolph, if you wouldn't mind picking up your father's and that scoundrel Rickman's rifles…"

Clara wasted no time and moved to retrieve the rifles. She picked up the Henry she'd purchased in St. Joseph, then went after the other one, which lay where Randall had dropped it after hitting Rickman with the stock. She gave Rickman's body a wide berth, though she couldn't help looking at him. The side of his head was caved in, and there was a great deal of blood. There was no doubt the man was dead. She hurried after Beckett and Randall, who were dragging Vance to the overturned wagon.

"Mister Randolph, cut that lead horse on the left free, then shoot the rest," Beckett said, after a quick glance at the injured and struggling horses. They'd laid Vance in the narrow shadow thrown by the wagon, and Beckett began pawing through the scattered cargo looking for suitable bandage material.

"I think this one's dead," Randall said, after taking the Henry from Clara and walking up to the horses.

"Shoot it anyway," Beckett said without looking up.

Clara set down the other rifle. "How can I help?" she asked Beckett.

"Here, take this," he said, tearing a cotton shirt in half and handing to her. He strode back to Vance.

Clara followed and knelt beside him. She flinched at the heavy report of the Henry rifle.

Beckett seemed not to notice. "Vance, you got to help us now. When I count to three, you roll over onto your side so we can get to the exit hole. Miss Randolph, you hold half that shirt tight over the front hole and half of it over the back one while I get this belt around him and cinch—"

The last of his words were lost as Randall fired the Henry again, but Clara understood what she needed to do.

Beckett looked at Vance: "You ready?" Vance nodded.

"One, two, thr—"

Vance screamed in pain and effort as he rolled to his side; Clara screamed in horror as Beckett fell on top of her with an arrow in his chest. *"INDIANS!"* Randall screamed from a few yards behind her.

Clara rolled out from under Beckett, who was struggling to his knees. He looked up at her and began to speak, but nothing came out except a gurgling sound and a great, gout of blood. He raised a hand toward her, then his eyes rolled back in his head, and he collapsed to the ground. She turned to the sound of high-pitched cries and pounding hooves, and saw what looked like twenty or more naked and painted men riding toward her.

"Run!" Vance croaked, swinging an arm weakly in her direction. Clara looked around frantically, her heart racing. She wheeled and ran around to the other side of the wagon and ducked down behind it.

A split second later, she thought of Randall. She stood back up. He was there, clambering over the dead horses, coming around to her side of the wagon.

"Randall!," she called.

He looked up at her, lost his footing, and fell. He crawled the rest of the way over the horses, then stood and ran toward her. Two arrows hit him almost simultaneously: one in the buttocks and one in the middle of his back. Inertia carried him the last several steps, and he collapsed almost at Clara's feet. Clara dropped next to him just as several of the riders reached them. Randall pushed himself up, looked at Clara regretfully, and started toward the first Indian to dismount. He picked up a nearby length of iron; it was part of the cooking tripod and the only thing within reach that might conceivably serve as a weapon. *What did I do with the rifle?* he thought bewilderedly.

The piece of iron might as well have been a feather. The young brave stepped forward and swung his war-club before Randall had even lifted it. The two-pound granite hammer hit him squarely on the left side of his head, and Clara heard a sickening crack. Randall fell to the ground.

The young brave stood indecisively over Randall. He'd wanted a scalp, but curiously the white man had almost no hair at all. He contemplated taking the scalp anyway, but the man was also old— very old. It would almost be like taking the scalp of a woman. He glanced around and saw Randall's Henry rifle. It was sticking up in between the two dead horses Randall had crawled over. The young brave raced after the prize before another could get it. The old man was all but forgotten.

Clara was cowering against the wagon as the brave walked away from Randall's unmoving body. Love for her lifelong servant and caretaker overcame her fear, and she ran to him. As she was kneeling beside him, she was suddenly yanked roughly backward by her braid. She landed on her back—*hard*—and unintentionally kicked Randall's face. Suddenly more angry than afraid, Clara reached her arms over her head and gripped her thick braid while simultaneously twisting her body. Her captor lost his grip and she scrambled to her feet. She sprinted away, but there was nowhere to go in the endless grassland. She saw trees not too far distant. *The river,* she thought, just as a hand clamped tightly on her arm.

Clara wheeled and swung, open handed, striking the brave solidly on his ear. This time he cried out, then doubled his effort and wrestled her to the ground. Thinking of the baby, Clara stopped struggling. She looked up; there were several more Indians standing over her. They were all naked except for some kind of animal skin breechcloth over their genitals. Some had feathers in their hair, and their faces were painted with blacks, whites, yellows, reds, and greens. They were things of nightmares. One of them was the one who struck Randall with the club. His face was painted solid black from his nose to his hairline. He was holding Randall's new rifle. They were pointing and laughing; not at Clara, but at the at the one who was now straddling her. He was rubbing his ear and looking up at the others ruefully. He wasn't any older than Clara. She began to weep.

5

The *Hotamétaneo'o,* or *Dog Men* had watched the wagon and its accompanying horsemen from across the river for two days. The group of twenty-four braves was led by Short Bull, one of the lesser Cheyenne chiefs. He'd contemplated attacking and taking the rifles, horses, and whatever food the whites carried, but the whites were displaying their rifles plainly and this made him cautious. His Dog Soldiers were out of powder for their three old muskets and Short Bull's own pistol. He knew they could still defeat them with weapons of the Cheyenne, but the whites were obviously prepared for battle, and he was reluctant to needlessly lose any of his braves. Many of his warriors were on a hunt in the north, and the remainder were at the camp with the women and children, three day's ride to the northwest. In the end he had contented himself with watching and waiting.

His prudence was rewarded when the whites began to fight amongst themselves. He quickly readied his warriors and waited for events to unfold. Once he saw that three of the whites were either injured or dead, he ordered two of his younger braves to chase down the white's fleeing horses while he and the rest of his Dog Soldiers attacked.

There was no battle: two of the whites were already dead, and another mortally injured. His warriors killed two old men and captured a young woman. They said she was spirited. He would take her with them. Perhaps she could be traded. There were rifles, pistols, shot, powder, and food. There was also whiskey, but Short Bull would not allow his warriors to take it. The white man's drink was poison to his people. The warriors he'd sent after the horses returned with six of them. Short Bull bid them each pick one since they missed the attack.

He bent over the dead white man's body and picked up the pistol lying next to it. It was a good pistol. He told his warriors to take everything they could carry.

6

Clara's emotions ran from terror to anger and back to terror again in mere moments. She was pulled to her feet by two of the braves and marched past Randall's body and the three dead horses that were still attached to the overturned wagon by their rigging. She was brought in front of a man who was older than the rest. The man wore animal skin leggings in addition to the breechcloth, and his face was painted with three simple white stripes which ran ear to ear. He was standing over Elias Spearse's body, intently examining Elias' pistol. He jammed the pistol into the hide thong that secured his breechcloth, crossed his arms, and looked appraisingly at Clara. He motioned with his hand and she was released.

"Please don't hurt me," Clara said, still weeping. "I have a baby."

The man, obviously their leader, continued to stare at her for a moment, then said something to one of the younger men. He spoke in a language Clara couldn't understand. The speech had a lot of *Teh* and *Hoh* sounds. When the man finished speaking, the brave removed a knife from a hide scabbard and started toward Clara.

"Wait!" She screamed and began to back away. "I have a baby. A *baby."* She rubbed at her belly, then made cradling and rocking motions with her hands. Two of the Indians restrained her.

The man stared at her curiously, then made the same strange hand motion he'd made before; she was again released. Clara thought frantically, then put both of her hands on her stomach and slowly moved them out about twelve inches. She quickly repeated the gesture: "Baby," she said. "I'm going to have a child."

Understanding dawned on the man's face. He looked over at the other men and smiled, then nodded, and pointed at Clara. *"Mé'eševotse,"* he said almost proudly before turning his attention back to the brave holding the knife and affording him an expectant look. The brave stepped forward again and grabbed a handful of the hem of Clara's dress. Clara screamed in panic and tried to move away again, but was again held fast. The brave quickly and neatly cut around the dress, leaving only a few inches below her waist.

He backed away and examined his work, pointing his knife at her drawers and chuckling before returning it to its scabbard.

The man who was called Short Bull walked a few yards and retrieved his horse. He led it over to a frightened and confused Clara, who was standing cross-legged in an attempt to keep the open-crotched drawers closed. Without preamble he picked her up as if she weighed nothing and set her on the bareback horse. He said something to the men and they all laughed. Then he climbed up behind Clara and urged the horse away.

Seven

1

John stumbled away from the mutilated bodies and vomited in the dust of the dooryard. The small house and outbuilding were burned to the ground. Frank Picton looked after him, his expression was stony.

"I've no doubt you completely understand now, if you didn't before. Straighten up and wipe your face. If you've no stomach for war, then you're of no use to me. I'll not have the men see you mewling and puking. If you're to lead them, they must respect you. We'll ride back to camp and send some men back to give these poor souls a proper burial."

John wiped his mouth and looked back at the bodies: two men, one woman, three children. All were stripped and scalped. The men had their penises and testicles cut off. He walked back and picked up his hat—which had fallen off when he stumbled away from the corpses—and dusted it off. Frank Picton was already mounted and starting away.

John had ridden out of Fort Laramie six days after his disturbing and perplexing meeting with Frank Picton, along with seventy men. There should have been eighty, but ten of the galvanized volunteers—freed Confederate prisoners who swore allegiance to the United States—slipped out shortly after reaching the fort. *So much for allegiance,* John thought.

Word came to Picton of an Indian raid on a settler's place about sixty miles southeast of the fort near the Platte River. Two brothers, both former trappers, had been trying to set up a new trading stop to serve the increasing demands of emigrants and settlers. An army courier hoping for a replacement for his injured horse had discovered the mutilated bodies of the brothers and their families. He left them where they lie and limped his horse the rest of the way to Fort Laramie.

Picton was already planning to head south to hunt down Indian bands—*renegades,* he said—who were camped off of their treaty-designated lands, when Brevet General Moonlight forwarded the news of the attack to him. Picton ordered John to prepare the men to leave the next morning.

After making camp five miles northwest of the site of the raid and sending out two Pawnee scouts to circle the area (Henry was not to be found at the fort), Picton and John had ridden in to assess the situation.

Now, standing by his horse, he thought he *did* understand. There could be no acceptable reason for the murder of these people. Perhaps he'd been as naive as Frank Picton said he was. Wasn't this proof of everything the colonel—*Frank*—had told him? He took one final look at the children lying facedown in the ashes and dust, put on his hat, then followed Picton.

The next morning they headed southwest toward Colorado. One of the two Pawnee scouts told Picton in very broken English that the raiders had gone that way. He also thought they were Cheyenne *Hotamétaneo'o*—Dog Men, not Sioux. Picton stated bluntly that he didn't care what tribe the Indians were from. He only wanted to find and destroy them.

They traveled southwest for three days, the main body of the force several miles behind the vanguard consisting of the Pawnee scouts and seven ex-confederate militia men who were supposed to be seasoned bush fighters. There was some tension amongst the men—understandably in John's opinion. Only a short time ago these men would have been shooting at each other, not sharing beans, salted pork, and jugs of whiskey.

On the fourth day, shortly after noon, one of the men from the vanguard rode back and informed Picton that they'd discovered a small Indian camp about seven miles ahead. He said they weren't the Indians they were chasing; they were Cheyenne, but it didn't appear there were very many braves, and there were only two horses that they could see. He said that the Indians they were after almost had to have passed through the camp, though.

Picton made a show of consulting his map. "Perhaps their warriors are out hunting. Nevertheless, those Indians are not on lands designated to them by the treaty they signed. They are therefore trespassing on United States property without leave and are to be considered hostiles. John, please send five men back to the last water we passed. Tell them to set up camp and have them help Mister Paulson prepare for surgery. The

Pawnee scouts as well; we won't need them. The rest of us will attack the camp at dusk."

John rode to the rear of the men and located Richard Paulson. Paulson had been a veterinarian in Illinois before the war, and a surgeon during it. His wife died of typhoid while he was away. He'd served under Frank Picton and, having nothing to go home to, had followed Picton to Fort Laramie at Picton's request.

John relayed the message to Doctor Paulson, then picked out five men at random. He only knew a handful of the men's names, mostly the ones he'd been introduced to personally by Picton; men who'd served with him in the war.

"Can't you pick somebody else, Lieutenant? I didn't come to do camp work. I've put up with these prairie niggers long enough and I'm ready to shoot some more of them."

"Local volunteers?" John asked almost rhetorically.

"Yes, sir. I was with the Colorado First, then with Colonel Chivington at Big Sandy Creek.

"What's your name?"

"Rogers, sir."

"Well, Mister Rogers, if you can find someone who's willing to trade with you, you are welcome to come along."

"Yes, sir." Rogers started away.

"Mister Rogers?"

"Sir?"

"I expect five men in addition to Mister Paulson to set camp."

Rogers looked chagrined. "Yes, sir."

2

The camp was located next to a medium-sized stream. There were only about sixteen lodges in all. The surrounding area was completely treeless, and it would be nearly impossible to take the Indians by surprise unless they waited for darkness and crawled through the grass. Frank Picton, citing the clearly inferior numbers of the Indians, discarded the option out of hand.

After synchronizing watches with Picton, John and half of the men circled well around the camp—about a half mile—and situated themselves behind a gentle rise that would obscure the horses. The plan was for a straight cavalry charge with the two lines coming from opposite sides of the creek, closing into a circle as they approached to cut off escape.

John's heart was racing as he held the pocket watch and counted off the last minute before eight o'clock. He'd been preparing to be a soldier for three years, but there was nothing that could have readied him for the conflicting feelings of fear and excitement he now felt.

When the second hand passed the nine, John stuffed the watch into his pocket, drew his pistol, and spurred the big stallion forward.

It was a slaughter.

The people in the camp heard the horses while they were still far off. Seconds later they saw them; riders coming from both sides at a full gallop. There would have been plenty of time to react and defend themselves had there been warriors in the camp.

There weren't.

The camp was occupied by seventeen women, nine children, five old men, and two horses. All, including the horses, were survivors of Colonel Chivington's attack at Big Sandy Creek six months before. Four of the women's husbands had been killed there, and the rest— who'd been on a hunt during Chivington's attack—had departed with a mixed Cheyenne/Sioux/Arapaho war party in the aftermath. The women, along with their children and the five related old men, had broken off from Black Kettle's band because they no longer felt safe under the chief. The women had not seen their husbands since.

Picton's riders reached the camp first, and shot or sabered nearly half of the shocked and frightened Indians before John and his men reached the creek.

John's horse pounded through the creek and up the short embankment on the other side. The scene was chaos: Pistol and rifle shots cracked sharply over the arrhythmic thunder of hooves, and screams of fear and agony mingled with whoops of triumph and glee. One of the lodges caught fire and was billowing black smoke into the darkening sky. Someone burst from a lodge immediately to John's left, and he wheeled and fired the pistol, missed, and quickly fired again. The second shot hit the fleeing woman in the center of her back. She fell forward, the naked infant she was carrying flew from her hands and lay screaming in the dirt several feet in front of her motionless body.

John leaped off his still-moving horse. Riderless, the already frightened animal galloped off in a panic. John didn't even notice, he ran for the screaming child. He was less than ten feet away when a rider galloped past him close enough to brush his arm. He watched in horror as the man deliberately turned the horse and trampled both the woman and the infant.

Looking around dazedly, John recalled he'd been taught that stallions were poor battle horses. His was nowhere to be seen. He turned this way and that, the pistol in his hand held loosely at his side. There were dead and dying Indians everywhere. A man whose name he couldn't remember was walking from body to body, taking scalps and hanging the dripping prizes from his belt.

It was over. The whole affair had lasted mere minutes. The shots tapered to sporadic pops. He turned back toward the trampled mother and child; there was an old man standing over them. He wore only a breechcloth. His long, gray hair hung in stringy clumps about his face. He was staring at John reproachfully. John stared back, unable to look away. He wondered if the woman was the old man's daughter.

There was a sudden report from just behind John. The old man stumbled backward several steps. He stared down at his bleeding abdomen for several seconds before collapsing to the ground. John turned his head to see who had fired just as the shooter strode by him, holstering a pistol. It was the man who hadn't wanted to stay behind to set up camp. John was trying to remember his name… Rogers? *Yes, that was his name.*

Rogers looked down at the body of the old man, then at the woman and infant. The infant's crushed body was partially trampled *into* the dirt. He smiled at John.

"These two red-asses got a proper earth bath, eh, Lieutenant?"

John turned and walked away.

3

One of the men found John's horse a quarter mile downstream while looking for Indians who'd managed to run off. He didn't find any, nor did anyone else. He led the big bay back to the camp where John was sitting on his haunches, pretending to listen to Frank Picton recount his part in the *"battle"* to the handful of men who were closest to him. John rose, took the reins, and thanked him.

"Welcome, Lieutenant, sir." The man said in a thick southern drawl. "You ought to get yourse'f a geldin' ya know. Betta temperment."

John nodded distractedly. "I'll consider it."

"Suit yourse'f, sir."

Picton had the men pile everything in the camp onto the smoldering remains of the burned lodge. Then, when he deemed the re-kindled blaze hot enough, he had them throw on the bodies of the thirty-one Cheyenne. A few of the men grumbled about the pyre, calling it an invitation to any warparties that may be in the vicinity. Picton, overhearing some of the conversation simply said, "Gentlemen, aren't we here to fight Indians?"

By ten o'clock they were riding back to their own camp under the light of a waning moon. The men were passing a jug, the conversation was animated and cheerful. John, who was riding in front next to Frank Picton, was quiet. Sensing his mood, Picton said, "Don't allow this to weaken your resolve, John. Bitches make pups and pups grow into dogs. Those Indians were a hundred miles away from where they should have been, and the trail of the murdering bastards we're following led right to them.

They were guilty by proxy if not by action. Make no mistake. They were hostiles, every one."

John thought of the screaming baby.

They struck out with the sun the next morning and passed the still smoking remains of the Cheyenne camp before eight o'clock. The Pawnee scouts stopped and spent several minutes sifting through the grisly remains before moving on and rejoining the vanguard. No one was sure of what it was they were looking for, and none of the men asked. Their relationship with the Pawnee scouts was strictly one of necessity. They were Indians, after all, and were looked upon with suspicion and contempt.

At midday Frank Picton rode ahead with two men to meet up with the scouts while the rest of the men stopped to water the horses and eat a small meal. John was sitting on his bedroll a short distance from the group, attempting to write Clara another letter. For the first time since leaving West Point, however, the words simply wouldn't come. He carried in his saddlebags upwards of thirty letters he'd written to her since being sent west. On most occasions he could fill a sheet of paper in minutes.

But not today.

Through all of the events since that day in Commandant Black's office two months before, John continued to feel optimistic about the future. He believed that he and Clara being together was nothing short of preordained, and that ultimately they would triumph over their troubles. He wrote her letters knowing full well he couldn't mail them, but he knew she would have them eventually nonetheless. When all of this was behind them they would read them together and laugh over his awkward declarations of love and inept descriptions of life on the prairie.

Now, for the first time, John was plagued by self-doubt, and he wondered if he would even see Clara again.

"Can we have a word, Lieutenant?" The man who addressed him was not quite old enough to be his father. John grappled for his name.

"What can I do for you, Mister…Childs is it?"

"Childs, that's just right. Well...we're here to tell you that we didn't sign on for the likes of what happened last night. Mind you we ain't no injun lovers, and I'm not happy about goin' back on my word, but there wasn't a single fighting man among them reds in that camp, and killin' women and children just ain't right no matter what cause you think you have. Now Frank here," Childs cocked his head toward the man next to him, "wasn't even there on account of he was one of the ones you asked to stay back with the doctor. Us three, we just laid back some when we saw what the situation was. We don't intend to be a part of another one." He held out a small drawstring bag. "This is the money we were advanced; every cent. I had to add a dollar of my own on account of Quincy was short—spent some of his on one of them injun whores back at the fort. Anyway, we'd be obliged if you'd give it to Colonel Picton when he gets back."

John looked at the offered bag. "Why did you wait until he left?"

Childs looked at the other men, saw no help there, then looked at his feet. "We thought he might try and stop us."

"What makes you think I won't?"

"Well," he said, looking more uncomfortable by the moment, "beggin' your pardon, Lieutenant, I know you're an officer and all, but you're not much more than a boy—in deed *and* countenance. I saw you yesterday. Some others did as well. Your horse run off and you looked like a lost babe that didn't know where his mama was. These men won't follow you if you want to make trouble for us. My guess is you didn't like what happened anymore than we did."

"I see." John took the bag. "Mister Childs, none of you have been conscripted. You're free to go any time you wish."

Childs looked like he was about to say more, but didn't. Instead, he touched a finger to his sweat-stained hat and walked to his waiting horse. The other three men followed.

Later that afternoon John and the men caught up with Frank Picton where he was waiting along with the two men he'd taken with him. The three were sitting under the meager shade of a solitary tree. Picton was smoking a pipe and examining one of his ever-present maps.

"Our scouts seem to have lost our quarry. We'll camp here tonight. If they don't locate fresh sign by tomorrow, we'll head back up to the Platte and search for renegades elsewhere."

John told him about Childs and the other men. Picton was unconcerned. "It was inevitable. Why do you think they lost the war?"

4

The four men who'd refused to kill innocents rode back the way they'd come. They all agreed to forget the west and head back to Missouri after stopping at Fort Laramie to gather what supplies they could. Home, *where we should have gone in the first place,* Andrew Childs thought as the bleak and endless grassland rolled out before him. A silence fell over the group as they passed the Indian camp with its pile of charred corpses. They all tried not to look; they all did.

It was far too late by the time they heard the pounding of hooves behind them. They spurred their horses and made a gallant run for it, but were overtaken in minutes.

They were stripped naked, scalped, and dragged screaming behind horses running at a full gallop back to the remnants of the Cheyenne camp by the stream. There they were mutilated and left for the scavengers.

Eight

1

Henry found Standing Elk forty miles northeast of Fort Laramie. It wasn't the first place he looked, or even the second, but Henry considered himself fortunate anyway. There were many places Standing Elk could have been. In this particular spot there was a small, shallow lake which nearly dried up in the summer. Thousands of blue flowers bloomed around it for a very short period of time during the spring. Standing Elk claimed the dried blooms had healing properties, and he made a point to collect some every year.

What Henry didn't expect was the one hundred or more braves who were camped around the lake as well.

He rode in under watchful eyes on the same gray mare Standing Elk had gifted him four years earlier. Henry and the mare had seen a lot of miles together in the interim. After some deliberation he'd named her Harriet, after the woman who had raised him. He'd briefly considered naming her Eliza, but knowing that chances were pretty good he'd outlive the horse, he'd decided against it.

Henry spoke to a Northern Cheyenne brave he'd met on one of his scouting expeditions. The brave told Henry that Standing Elk could be found on the far side of the lake, where the flowers had not been trampled as badly. He also stopped and spoke to a Southern Cheyenne man named Flying Hawk, who was from Black Kettle's band, and about Henry's age. When Henry had still lived with the Cheyenne he'd taught Flying Hawk how to make snares, and Flying Hawk in turn showed Henry how to make fish traps in the stream.

"Mo'ohnee'ėstse said you would come," Flying Hawk stated solemnly.

Henry could only nod.

He rode the mare around the lake, keeping to the water's edge so as not to crush any of the delicate flowers. Standing Elk was there, bent over the flowers with a small, hide bag in his hand. He straightened up and watched Henry dismount and walk toward him. "I've been waiting for you," he said in

English as Henry approached. "The *Hotamétaneo'o* wished to leave, but I told them *Nótaxemâhta'sóoma* would be coming, and here you are. You must bring William Bent and the Soldier Chief—"

"I'm not a warrior."

"This is what they call you," Standing Elk said dismissively, then bent down and began picking flowers again.

"Tell me what happened," Henry said, switching to Cheyenne. He squatted and began picking flowers too.

Standing Elk told Henry what happened at Big Sandy Creek. How the Soldier Chief had told Chief Black Kettle and Chief Left Hand that the Indians were to live there. The Chiefs did as they were bidden, but then soldiers came and attacked the camp without cause. Standing Elk was away on a hunt with most of the other men when it happened. His wife, Walking Woman, was killed, and so was Henry's friend, Spotted Paw, who'd stayed behind because he'd fallen attempting to break a horse, but had broken his arm instead. Supposedly Spotted Paw had been shot four times and still killed three white soldiers and led several children to safety before dying of his wounds. The old Cheyenne Chief, Yellow Wolf, was killed as well. All together almost one hundred fifty Cheyenne and Arapahos died; mostly women, children and old men.

Standing Elk told the story matter-of-factly—which was his way—but Henry knew the loss of his wife and the others affected him deeply.

He also told Henry he'd participated in one of the attacks on the white soldiers during the previous months—that he could no longer tolerate them. They would have to go back to where they came from and take their people with them. Henry knew that would never happen, and he knew Standing Elk did as well.

For Henry, the hatred which had slowly been fading over the last four years tried to return. He suddenly wished that he was a warrior like the name Nótaxemâhta'sóoma implied. He didn't fully understand the word; it meant Shadow Warrior or possibly Spirit Warrior. He guessed the former as shadow could refer to his skin color. It didn't matter. He wasn't a warrior. He wasn't anyone. He was a man without a place, without a nation. He'd been accepted by the Cheyenne, even respected, though he was still unsure why. But he would never truly be one of them. And he would *never* belong with the whites, though there were some he could almost call friends; and one, years before, who had most likely saved his life with a few kind words and a canteen of water.

Standing Elk asked Henry in Cheyenne to bring William Bent and the Soldier Chief, Major Anthony, north to the Powder River to speak of returning all of the lands the whites had taken with their tricks and lies four winters before. He said that otherwise, he, along with the Dog Men and other Cheyenne, Arapaho, and Sioux warriors, would continue trying to force the whites out.

"I don't think Major Anthony is the Soldier Chief anymore. At least not the one you want. I'll bring William, though, if I can. He could be out east already for supplies.

Standing Elk said that he would wait with his relatives, the Northern Cheyenne, at the Powder River for William Bent. He also said he would ask that the other Indians not attack any more whites until then. He was doubtful he'd be listened to.

"They are growing more restless and angry." He flapped his hand toward the other side of the lake. "Short Bull took a white woman. I've spoken with her. She will have a child when the snows fall. He took her to show that he can take from the whites like they take from us."

Henry gazed across the shallow lake. "What's he going to do with her?"

"I do not know. I do not like these things. We need more flowers."

Henry suddenly felt uneasy. He'd heard stories of the Sioux taking women, but had never been witness to it. Short Bull was a Cheyenne; one of the Dog Men, and this was a white woman, not a squaw from a rival tribe. Henry met Short Bull once while scouting for some traders. He was proud and, like Standing Elk, a man of few words. Henry wanted to ask more questions but let it go. He'd known Standing Elk long enough to know when a conversation was finished.

He departed only three hours after he'd arrived. Normally he would have given Harriet a longer rest, but he knew Standing Elk wished him to hurry. Henry felt the underlying tension in his friend's outwardly calm demeanor. Standing Elk didn't even offer to smoke with him, which was a first.

The news of the abducted woman awoke something in Henry that had lain dormant for a long time. He made it less than a mile out of the camp before memories of Eliza consumed him. He stopped Harriet, stared up into the early afternoon sky, and began to weep. The tears began as a trickle, then Henry let out a wail of loneliness and despair so loud that it caused a crow roosting in a lone cottonwood to squawk indignantly and take flight. He began to sob uncontrollably.

The tears eventually subsided. Henry dismounted and walked Harriet over to the cottonwood the crow had recently vacated. He sat against the tree and looked out across the plain; it's lush green already showing the faintest signs of fading, foreshadowing the stark grays and browns that would soon dominate its vastness. A colorless mirror into his own emptiness.

2

Dusk.

Henry lay in the knee-high scrub looking through his field glasses at the Cheyenne camp by the lake. He'd purchased the valuable binoculars from a discharged Union soldier in St. Joseph for ten dollars—less than half of what they were worth. The soldier, who reeked of whiskey and was minus his left arm, claimed he'd taken them off of a fallen Confederate officer. Ten dollars was a lot of money, but Henry jumped at the chance to own the glasses. They had proven themselves useful on more than one occasion since.

He was searching for the abducted woman. He figured it would be easy as there were no lodges; the camp was only a temporary stopover for the constantly moving war party. Earlier, when he'd visited with Standing Elk, there'd been a large group of Oglala Sioux at the camp. This was Sioux land, after all, and the Cheyenne were only here by the Sioux's leave. Standing Elk had indicated that the Sioux had joined them in some of the retaliatory attacks after the affair at Big Sandy Creek. There was no sign of them now. Apparently the Sioux had moved out since Henry had departed earlier in the day. He guessed there were still sixty Cheyenne and a handful of Arapahos in the camp.

There was a large stand of mixed pine, cottonwood, and hackberry trees near the lake. It was the first place he looked and he wasn't let down.

The woman—the very *young* woman—was sitting against a tree on top of a blanket with her knees up to her chest and her arms wrapped around her legs. She looked to be about Eliza's age when… She also looked only partially dressed.

Pushing the thought away he lowered the field glasses, backed a little further into the scrub, and rolled over onto his back. He was overwrought with indecision. He considered trying to bargain with Short Bull for the woman but knew the inquiry would be viewed with suspicion. What would Henry want with the white woman, after all? Short Bull would be angry if he knew Henry intended to return her to the whites. Did the whites know she was captured? There was no way for him to know. Henry did know that if the army found out she was taken, and where she was, things could go badly for the Cheyenne. He also had Standing Elk to think about. He didn't want to shame his friend, to whom he owed his life. He thought William Bent would know what to do, but he didn't know where Bent was or how long it would take to locate him. If he'd gone east for supplies, which he was known to do this time of year, it would be a long time before Henry could bring him up to the Powder River. And what if Short Bull and his band of Dog Men separated from Standing Elk and the other Cheyenne warriors?

You already know what you're going to do, so why don't you just think about how you're going to do it and stop chewing over things that don't matter any?

He took his own advice and began to work on the problem.

Outside of some trees in the immediate vicinity, the southeast side of the lake—the side Henry had first arrived and then departed from—was wide open plain and a rider could be spotted a long way off. He'd circled well around the camp to some breaks a mile to the north of the lake. Then he was able to follow a creek—probably the one feeding the lake—that offered good cover. He tethered Harriet to a tree on the creek bank, then worked his way as close to the lake as he felt was safe. If the Indians were watching for an attack—which they most certainly were—they'd know this was the direction that it would most likely come from. They'd have posted lookouts and most likely there were some braves roaming the breaks; looking for game if nothing else. He decided to stay where he was until full dark. He'd just have to hope Harriet wasn't discovered in the meantime.

Over the last three and a half years the pain of Eliza's memory had receded. Occasionally there were days he didn't think of her at all. Now, lying on his back in the clump of scrub, waiting like he'd waited in another patch of brush years before, her voice came back to him.

"You're going to be a father. You're going to be the father of a free child," she said, smiling up at him and holding out a small hunk of the pork and the last of the stale bread. Henry ignored the offered food, and stood over her, his mouth agape. "You best close your mouth before something flies in it. I was going to tell you some days back but I wanted to be certain. Then Master Cromwell freed us, and—"

Henry fell to his knees and put his hands to the sides of her face. "Are you sure?"

"I just said I wanted to be certain, and I am."

"You don't look...I mean...when? How long?"

"In the spring."

"Well, we have some time to get settled, then."

She set the pork and bread down in her lap, put her hands over his, gripped them, and pulled him close. She kissed him softly.

"Did you find a good place for your snares?"

"Yess'm. You'll be eating rabbit this evening. Or mayhap squirrel."

"Good. Now do you want this?" She picked up the pork and bread.

"Yes, but I want somethin' else, first." He slid his hand up her dress.

"You can have whatever you want."

It was the last time.

3

Henry waited until well after midnight before working his way down toward the lake. He wept off and on during those hours. The tears were lurking just below the surface again, like they had in the weeks following Eliza's death. He fought them back the best he could and tried to devise a plan to free the woman. At moments, however, the similarities between the present and the past were just too overwhelming.

He only had two options: either create a distraction, or slip in and out quietly. He liked the former, but the only diversion that would have a chance of working would be running off their horses. He could probably do it, but the horses were on the southeast side of the lake, and the woman was on the northwest side. It was a small lake, but he would still lose any advantage of surprise and disorder by the time he reached the woman. There were two other snags as well: the battle-hardened horses may not spook easily, and the Cheyenne may already be on the lookout for Pawnee horse thieves.

He chose surreptitiousness, which came with its own risks.

Squatting in the dewy mix of grass and wildflowers, fifty feet from the stand of trees where he'd seen the woman, Henry tried to calm himself. If he were caught he would almost certainly be killed, and Standing Elk would be humiliated and lose much of his status. He had the Spencer rifle, but no intention of killing anyone. If it needed to be used, it would be stock forward.

The May moon was in its third quarter and there was enough light for Henry to see a little, but not so much that he felt exposed. He crept up slowly to the stand of trees.

She was there.

Looking at her long, black hair, she could easily have been an Indian woman, but her skin was so white that the faint whisper of moonlight gave it a pale, almost unearthly glow. She was lying on her side not fifteen feet away. She was facing Henry. There was a man sleeping on the other side of her: Short Bull, Henry assumed. Gazing into the stand of trees, he could see other sleepers scattered about. The nearest was less than twenty feet away. Henry stayed where he was, indecisive. He began wishing he would have tried running off the horses. He didn't see any way he could succeed in getting her away. Even if he were able to wake her without disturbing Short Bull—if it was Short Bull—could he then silently convince her to go with him? He considered leaving. He could ride back to Fort Laramie and tell whoever it was the army currently had in charge about the woman. They'd send someone, an officer, along with a company of cavalrymen. They could be here inside of a week...

He recalled what happened the last time he chose not to act right away. He saw Eliza, lying in the brush, beaten and bloody. Was their unborn child already dead inside her? Or did it survive as long as she did? Was there pain, or fear? The tears once again spilled down his face. He put down the Spencer—thinking of how, only moments before he'd pledged not to kill anyone—and pulled his hunting knife from its hide scabbard. Crawling slowly but deliberately he closed the distance between himself and the two sleeping figures.

He circled around slightly so he came at their heads. Short Bull was sleeping on his back; there was no doubt it was him. Henry reached out, and in one motion clamped his left hand tightly over Short Bull's mouth while simultaneously sawing at the Cheyenne chief's throat with the hunting knife in his right. He used all the force he could muster and cut nearly halfway through Short Bull's neck in three quick strokes. A gush of hot blood splashed all over Henry's hands and arms. Short Bull's back arched and his legs began kicking; the woman let out a breathless cry to his left. The strength ran out of Short Bull in mere seconds. Henry released him and looked at the woman. She was staring at him, but it was too dark to read her face. He scanned the other sleeping figures; there was no movement. He turned back and leaned toward her. She recoiled slightly but stayed where she was. Henry whispered, "Come with me, I'll get you somewhere safe."

The woman kept staring at him but didn't move. He was about to repeat what he'd said when she slowly raised her arm toward him. At first he didn't understand, then she raised her arm a little higher and he saw it. There was a strip of hide tied to her wrist. He reached out and hooked two fingers around the strip and followed it. The other end was tied to Short Bull's forearm.

Henry pulled his knife, slick with the dead chief's blood, and flicked the razor sharp blade across the thin strip of hide. "Come on," he whispered, and began crawling away.

She was following, he could hear her. He stopped and picked up the Spencer, then stood.

"Can you walk?" he whispered.

"Yes."

"Follow me. Watch my legs, not my back, and walk right where I walk."

He fought the urge to hurry and walked carefully back up the creek on shaky legs. Soon he was able to make out Harriet's shape silhouetted against the muted moonlight.

"What's your name?" Henry asked, as he squatted by the creek and began vigorously washing his hands and arms.

"Clara Hanfield. You killed him." Her voice was flat.

"Yes'm, I did." He stood and walked over to Harriet. "Come on, we have to get as far away from here as we can before they wake up. We'll have to ride together."

He untied the reins from the tree, climbed up and reached a hand down to her. Clara looked at the proffered hand for a moment before taking it and allowing Henry to pull her up behind him. She let out a short cry when she hit the saddle.

"Are you hurt?"

"No...yes, a little. Please, let's go.

"Hang on then."

Clara didn't move.

"Ma'am, you have to hold on or you'll fall off."

"Yes, of course. I know." She reached around his waist and clasped her hands together.

Nine

1

Randall awoke, but couldn't open his eyes. After a few moments of confusion he realized they *were* open.

He was blind.

He was lying on a thin and uncomfortable bed in a stuffy room. His head ached terribly, his ears were ringing, and he was so thirsty that his tongue felt swollen to twice its normal size. He raised a shaky hand to his head; it was bandaged. He remembered the painted young Indian swinging some sort of hammer at him. Then nothing.

Suddenly he sat bolt upright. His head throbbed sickeningly. *Clara.*

He lowered his head back down. "Hello?" he said, in a barely audible croak.

"Is anyone there?" a little louder this time.

"Hello?"

Footsteps. A door opened nearby.

"You're awake," a man's voice said amiably.

"Is Clara well?"

"Clara?"

"Yes, I was travelling with a young woman, Clara Hanfield. Is she here?"

"I don't recall anyone saying anything about a young woman. Clara you say?"

"*Yes*. Dear god, where is she? Where am I? Where is this place? I cannot see, I've been blinded."

"Sir, please try to calm yourself. You've taken quite a blow to the head. The arrow wounds were both superficial; the one in your back wasn't even an inch deep. But your skull's been fractured quite severely. As far as a woman is concerned, this is the first I've heard of one. You were the only one brought here. I was told there were four other men found with you. You were the only survivor."

"Someone must have seen her. May I please have some water?"

"I have some right here."

The owner of the voice walked next to the head of the bed. Randall could hear him pouring water, from a pitcher or some other receptacle.

"I'm going to lift your head."

"Are you a doctor?"

"Verily. Doctor Sam Evans, at your service. You're lucky I was here, friend. The resident sawbones apparently vanished one night this winter. He was last seen staggering around the parade grounds, drunk, and the next morning, he was gone. I was called out from Independence to see to the former commander's broken leg; he was thrown from his horse—drunk too, more like than not. The leg was rotten by the time I arrived and the good colonel died two weeks ago. Now, every time I plan to leave, something seems to require I stay. In this case, *you*."

He put a hand under Randall's neck and gently lifted his head. "Just a little now," he said, holding the tin cup to Randall's lips.

"Thank you."

"You're welcome. There is a possibility that in time your sight will come back. I've heard of it happening, although I wouldn't set your hopes on it.

"And I'll inform Major Brighton you're awake. Perhaps he knows something I don't and can shed some light on things for you. I'll bring you something to eat, as well. I'm sure you must be hungry. I hope you like beans."

"Is this Fort Laramie? How long have I been here?"

"You're at Fort Kearny, such as it is, and you've been here four days. A captain and eight men heading for Fort Laramie found you, and managed to right your wagon. They hitched up some of their own horses, removed the arrow from your back, broke the shaft off the one in your backside, then wrapped you in a blanket and put you inside. They used every inch of daylight and then some, not to mention wearing out their horses getting you here."

"I am indebted to them."

"Well, I'm sorry won't get a chance to tell them. They stayed two days then moved on."

After the doctor left, Randall worried over Clara. His head ached horribly and he was having trouble concentrating. Perhaps the doctor had a powder...

"Mister Eastman? Mister Eastman?"

The voice pulled Randall from his doze. Not the doctor. Someone else. He opened his eyes and had an unsettling moment when there was still darkness. Then he remembered he was blind.

"Who's there?"

"My name is Major Brighton, Mister Eastman—"

"How do you know my name?" Where is Clara?"

"You were identified three days ago by a man named Theo Brandt. Brandt is a representative of Mister Jonathon Hanfield from New York who, incidentally, telegraphed us some time ago requesting us to be on the lookout for you and his daughter. In addition to Mister Hanfield's telegraph we also received one from an angry New York senator.

"As far as Miss Hanfield's whereabouts we can only assume she was carried off by the Indians who attacked you."

"Oh my, Clara...what is being done? You *are* searching for her?"

"Mister Eastman, Mister Hanfield claims that you brought his daughter out here against her will. He's demanding you be tried and hanged. The senator's correspondence was not quite so bluntly stated, but amounts to nearly the same. I myself find the veracity of these charges questionable. There were several letters found among the items not taken by the Indians. They were addressed to one Lieutenant Elliot at Fort Laramie. I recall meeting the lieutenant only weeks ago, right here. I also recall him saying he was from New York. Mister Brandt was pompous, unhelpful, and downright evasive when I questioned him regarding Lieutenant Elliot's connection to Miss Hanfield. His welcome quickly wore thin, and he's since moved on. I've sent a telegraph to Fort Laramie inquiring about the lieutenant, but have yet to receive any word in return. If you are as concerned about Miss Hanfield as you appear, you'll explain all of this to me so I can best decide how to be of service to the missing young woman."

Major Brighton struck Randall as a man who was intelligent and fair-minded. He told him the entire story—omitting Clara's theft and maternal revelation—beginning with Jonathon Hanfield's fit of temper, and ending with the young Indian swinging the club.

The major listened intently, interrupting only occasionally to ask Randall to clarify something or to offer him a drink of water.

When Randall was finished, the major was silent for several minutes. Finally he spoke: "It's plain to see that no crime has been committed here—at least not by you. The murder of the four men and the apparent abduction of Miss Hanfield is another matter. The army doesn't mediate family affairs, Mister Eastman, and I'll not reduce this post to such picayune use unless I receive a direct order to do so. The doctor tells me you'll live, though you likely never see again. You're welcome to stay here while you mend. After that, other arrangements will have to be made. Perhaps you have relatives somewhere, well away from New York?"

"What about Clara?"

"I've sent out fifty men; all I can spare. Try to sleep, Mister Eastman. I'll keep you informed.

Ten

1

The scouts returned at a gallop. Picton signaled the men to halt, then waited for whatever word they carried. John, who'd been riding at the rear, rode up beside Picton.

"It appears they have news of some import," Picton said.

John remained silent.

The scouts reached them and reined in. One of the ex-Confederates spurred his horse forward until he was facing Picton and John.

"We got a war-party," he said breathlessly. "Or…well, could be a hunting party. I could see that Pawnee fella was scared, but I can't understand half of what he says…there was a bushel of 'em, to be sure. Indians…on horseback."

"Indians are less intelligent than niggers, Mister Blaylock. We are lucky our Pawnee friend can speak English as well as he does. Now, assuming we are speaking of more than sixty four pints of Indians, please tell me how many there were? Then you can tell me *where* they were along with any other pertinent details."

The men—excluding John—who were nearest to Picton, chuckled nervously.

"Well, sir, it looked to be about a hundred and fifty, possibly more, an' they were about fifteen miles west of here. They was heading west, same as us. The only reason we came on 'em is they's movin' slower than us. They had more than a few rifles."

"Thank you, Mister Blaylock. Rest your horses. In one hour we head north."

There was a murmur among the men. John looked at Picton but said nothing. Picton reached into his saddlebag and retrieved his map. After fighting the ever-present wind and consulting the flapping map for several minutes, he folded it and looked at John.

"It's a six day ride back to Fort Laramie. We'll resupply there, then head northwest, further up the Platte, then into Powder River country."

"We're not going after them, Colonel?" Bill Taylor, one of Picton's regular men asked.

"Of course not, Mister Taylor. We're not manned nor equipped for open battlefield forays, and we've no need for it. Have faith. We'll achieve our goals through stealth and patience."

"Yes, sir."

"John, please inform the men they have one hour."

John nodded and kicked his horse into motion.

2

Two days later they came to the top of a rise. It was midmorning and the day was shaping up to be unseasonably hot for the end of May. Below, grazing in the new spring grass, was a large herd of buffalo. John, who'd been silent and brooding since the massacre at the Indian camp, was momentarily awestruck. He smiled in spite of everything and looked to the man beside him. "How many do you think there are?"

"I don't know, Lieutenant. Biggest herd I ever seen. Ten thousand if there's one."

"Ten thousand," John mused.

"This is an opportunity for the men to hone their shooting skills while eliminating some of the savages' sustenance," Picton said, coming up alongside John. "Mister Taylor, take twenty-five men a half-mile along this crest, then string them out in a line. Take men with repeaters—that'll be Union men, mostly—and make sure they're fully loaded. John, here's an opportunity to show your fortitude. Take fifteen men—I understand some of those southerners can ride and shoot—and circle around the herd. Come up as slow as you can. When we start shooting they'll spook; you go at them hard; hoot and holler and keep on their flank so they have to run parallel with this hill. I'll stage the rest of the men right here. Mister Taylor, tell your men to shoot as many of those beasts as they can as they pass."

John canvassed the men looking for the ones who could ride and shoot well. "Don't come forward if you're not certain you can do it," he said. "I don't want to find any of you lying in the prairie grass with a broken neck." He found eleven who seemed confident in their abilities, and picked four more who were vouched for as good riders. He told the four to leave their rifles with men who were staying on the hillside with Picton.

"Why are we going to shoot the buffalo, Lieutenant?" one man asked. "The whole lot of us couldn't eat but one or two of them."

"We're not going to eat them. Buffalo are the Indians' main food supply, and we're going to eliminate some of them, although I don't think we can kill enough of them to make much of a difference."

"Ohhhh, so it's kind of like when we'd cut off a supply shipment during the war."

"Yes, kind of like that."

John led the men well around the herd. They were downwind, and he hoped to get reasonably close. He didn't know anything about hunting buffalo, and neither did Picton or anyone else among them as far as he knew. Downwind or not, the buffalo proved wary and began to move more deliberately when John and the men were still closing the distance. He motioned for the flanking men to move in closer to keep the animals to the edge of the shallow hillside. When he felt they were in as good of a position as possible for so large of a herd, he signaled Picton.

The men opened fire.

Things began as planned then quickly fell into chaos. The buffalo began running roughly northeast along the base of the hills and Picton's men easily shot them from above. After less than a minute, however, the herd abruptly turned northwest for no reason John could discern. He supposed afterward that the buffalo were more afraid of the rifle shots than they were of the men on horseback, although for him, the shots were utterly buried by the thundering of hoofs.

The buffalo stampeded straight at the formerly flanking horsemen as if they didn't even see them. Three of the lead riders never stood a chance and were trampled to death, horse and man. The rest were able to turn and a make run for it. One of the fleeing horses tripped. The rider, who had survived three major civil war battles, was trampled attempting to crawl out of the path of the herd.

The herd finally disappeared into the distance, leaving behind a swath of crushed and beaten prairie as wide as the Mississippi. Over one hundred fifty buffalo, along with three men and their horses, lay dead or dying.

"You allowed your men to get too close," Picton said, approaching John. "Learn from this. Hopefully you'll not make the same mistake a second time."

John was standing over the broken and bloody remains of one of the trampled riders.

"He was a southerner," Picton said. "Have his own tend to him. Gather the men. Tell them to butcher one of these animals. We're going to stay here for awhile. I'm sending the scouts out to follow that herd's back-trail. There's a good chance a herd of that size had Indians following it."

John turned away without a word.

3

Picton ended up being right. The scouts discovered a band of around eighty Arapahos less than five miles out the buffalo herd's back-trail.

"Let's prepare to move; quickly now," Picton said after the scouts returned with the news. "John, make haste. Those men have had ample time to bury the dead. Tell them to mount up."

They dropped down the opposite side of the hills and followed the base of them southeast. By late afternoon they were in position with only the low hills separating them from the Arapaho camp. One of the scouts led Picton, John, and five men to the crest where they could lay on their bellies and look down on the camp.

The camp was by a watershed where three streams joined together. John thought them to be tributaries to the south fork of the Platte River, but he wasn't certain. He'd looked over Picton's maps, but only briefly, two days before departing Fort Laramie. It appeared the Arapaho had either just arrived or were preparing to leave. There were several travois piled high with lodge poles and skins. He counted thirty-six men. The rest were women and children. Many of them were busy with a pair of skinned buffalo carcasses, and others were gathered together by the convergence of the streams. About twenty children were carrying sticks and chasing around a man covered in a buffalo hide. He ran around hunched over while the children pretended to stab him with the sticks. John imagined he could hear their laughter. He thought of the infant spilling from the arms of the woman he'd shot. The child who would never play buffalo hunter.

Picton nodded, then inched back down the hill until he could stand up and still be out of sight. John and the others followed. They'd almost reached the bottom of the hill when Picton turned to John and said: "I see no reason to wait. We'll have Taylor take the ten best sharpshooters and lay atop the hill. Then we'll divide the men: mine south, your's north. Taylor and his men open fire and we charge down the hill. They'll never—"

"No," John said. He stared at Picton levelly. "I don't know what it is you think you're doing, but this is neither just nor justice. We're not protecting anyone, and we're not at war with these people. This is murder and I'll have no further part in it." He turned and started away, but Picton reached out, grabbed his arm, and yanked him back.

"Of course it's murder, you pampered little pup," Picton hissed, his face only inches from John's. "You're even more naive than I first thought you to be. Did you really believe the seventy of us were going to roam the countryside engaging Indian war parties? *Frank Picton's seventy defeats five thousand bloodthirsty braves!* How poetic. You are right about one thing: we're not fighting a war, we are inciting one. Tell me something; do you have the slightest notion of how many Washington fortunes are invested in the western expansion? In railroads and gold mines, and telegraphs, and cattle, and other ventures beyond counting?…No? Of course you don't. We are going to finish what Colonel Chivington so ungracefully began. After we resupply we're riding north into Sioux country to inflame the filthy savages even further. Then, soon, perhaps by

this fall, when the heathens have lashed out sufficiently against more innocents, the public outrage will be such that they will be unable to decry the army for finally crushing the red vermin once and for all."

He sighed and released John's arm.

"The Indian and the white man will never be able to coexist. It's been proven, time and again. Treaties fail and only delay the inevitable outcome. This land is ours now. It was ordained by God. Mark my words, John, ten years from now the Indian warrior will be nothing more than a fireside story told to frighten disobedient children."

John started away and then turned back. "I'll expose this."

"To whom, John? You and I are only small players in a grander design."

"Do you expect me to believe that the murder of innocents has been *sanctioned* by our government because you showed me a scribbled note on a crumpled sheet of paper? We'll see."

He turned and walked through the men who'd gathered to listen. "This is nothing short of murder, and any man who wants no part of it may join me," he said.

"Afraid you'll lose your horse again, Lieutenant?" one man asked. There was muffled laughter.

Picton followed John to his horse. "Who do you think will listen to you?" he said, his voice not much more than a whisper. "Colonel Black? This has been out of that simpering bureaucrat's hands since the very day Jonathon Hanfield learned of you and his daughter. Oh, yes. I know all about you. You go ahead. You'll discover there are few ears to listen to a disgraced cadet who was so unfit for duty that he was discharged mere weeks after receiving a generously given commission. You are a coward, John. A coward attempting to conceal his yellow by self-righteously sighting high ideals as a pretext for fleeing in the face of danger."

John rummaged in his saddlebag and pulled out a wad of bills. He dropped them at Picton's feet and climbed onto his horse. "I may be a coward. But I'm not a mercenary."

4

John wished he'd studied Picton's maps more thoroughly. He was left with no choice but to return to Fort Laramie by the same route he'd travelled with Picton and the men. It was the long way around, but at least he was confident he could find his way. The alternative would have been to strike out blindly northward. Fort Laramie was only four days ride from where they killed the buffalo, according to Picton. However, with no maps and in unfamiliar country, finding the fort would be like finding a needle in a haystack.

Eleven

1

The sun was just rising over the horizon when Henry coaxed Harriet down into the rapidly drying wash. Only a small amount of water left over from spring rains still ran lazily down its center. He was taking a roundabout route to Fort Laramie in an attempt to make tracking him difficult. The Dog Men would not be happy about losing their chief.

Guilt gnawed at him. Over the years he'd often found himself thinking of the man by the river—A. Hoyt was the name engraved on the man's saddle. He wondered if Hoyt only pulled the gun because he was afraid; afraid of Henry; afraid of the ragged nigger stalking into his camp brandishing a tree branch and demanding food. Had he killed him? Was he a murderer? Now there was no question. He'd taken another man's life.

"Do you have some water?" Clara asked from behind him. It was the first words either of them had spoken since leaving the warrior camp.

"Yes, ma'am. I should've offered."

Henry stopped Harriet and climbed down by awkwardly swinging his leg over the mare's head. "Not used to riding this way," he muttered as he turned to help Clara dismount.

He paused with his arm half extended. There was dried blood on her face, and it was matting her hair. Her dress, once white but now a filthy no-color, was cut off just below the waist, revealing a pair of tattered drawers that were even dirtier than the dress.

"That blood from him?"

Clara nodded.

He extended his hand and Clara took it. A muffled cry of pain escaped her as she dismounted. Once down, she put her hands protectively over her exposed vagina. Henry saw that the drawers were completely open on the inseam—to make it easy to do the necessaries when you're in a dress, he figured. He also saw the reason it pained her getting on and off the horse: the inside of her thighs were chafed to the point of bleeding.

He realized he was staring, and averted his eyes. He walked past Clara and removed the canteen—the one given to him by a man named James "Red" Macklin one day on a dusty roadside in Missouri—from its place on his saddle. He handed it to Clara without looking at her, then began rummaging in his bulging saddlebags. "I have this salve, it's made from the roots of a gold colored flower. I put in on my hands sometimes in the winter and use it on the sores Harriet here gets on her hocks. I couldn't help noticing you could use some on your legs. It'll help heal them. If you don't squeeze so much with your legs when you're riding that won't happen—the chafing, I mean. Horses don't usually like it much anyway."

He handed her a tin which had originally held percussion caps but now carried the salve Standing Elk had taught him how to make. He reached back in the saddlebags and removed a pair of buckskin trousers similar to the ones he was wearing, a length of leather strap, and a small square of muslin cloth. "You can wear these, they'll be a sight too big for you but you can roll up the bottoms and cinch 'em up with this piece of bridle. I use this cloth for washing. I'll walk up here a ways and take a look at things if you want to clean up a little and put on the trousers."

"Why did you help me?"

"Seemed the right thing to do. We need to hurry up and get a move on."

"Will they find us?"

"I reckon not, if we're careful."

Clara began to weep. "Thank you…I don't know your name."

"Henry."

2

Clara washed her hair and face in the slowly running creek. Seeing the bloody tinted water running over the rocks made her stomach lurch. She thought of the gurgling sound Short Bull had made as he lay dying. Then she thought of the grunting sounds he made when he'd forced himself into her. Her body began to shake uncontrollably, and she sat down hard on the stony bed of the wash, her teeth clacking together painfully. Weeping again, she leaned to one side and vomited once. She waited that way to see if there would be more, but there wasn't. Soon both the shaking and the tears subsided. She told herself she wouldn't cry anymore. Her mother had once told her that she'd inherited her father's mettle—his *hardness.* She straightened herself up and searched for that hardness. She looked after Henry, who was further down the wash but still within earshot. He had his back turned. She wiped her mouth, then stood and walked several feet upstream where she finished washing the blood from her hair. She removed her ruined drawers and cleaned herself, then gingerly applied some of the pasty salve to the abraded skin of her thighs. It turned her skin a yellow-orange, but reduced some of the sting almost immediately. She put on Henry's trousers thinking she could easily have fit herself into one leg. *I must be a sight,* she thought, as she cinched the trousers up with the leather strap Henry had given her.

Seeming to sense she was finished, Henry started back up the wash. Clara watched him for a moment. She didn't know many colored people. Her father never hired them; he claimed they weren't trustworthy. The stableman who took care of their horses in Cornwall was colored. Lilith Davenport's head maid was also colored, and Clara thought she was wonderful. Thoughts of Lilith and the farmhouse in Cornwall brought on a wave of homesickness. She walked up and waited by the big mare.

"I've always loved horses," she said softly as Henry approached.

"Her name's Harriet. Are you hungry?" Clara shook her head. Henry nodded, and reached into his saddlebags and pulled out his only other shirt. Clara turned away and he quickly changed out of the bloody one; this he rolled up and stuffed back in the saddlebags. He untied Harriet and led her out of the wash. Then he climbed up and lowered a hand to Clara. This time she took it without hesitation.

"Where are you taking me?" Clara asked over Henry's shoulder.

"To Fort Laramie. We can arrange to get you back where you belong from there."

"That's where we were going when...when the Indians came."

"You want to tell me what happened?"

"I'd rather not talk right now."

"Fair enough."

3

They rode in silence for most of the day, each lost in their own thoughts. Henry stopped to let Harriet rest for awhile in the early afternoon. Clara reluctantly accepted some dried elk when he offered it. She ate the salty meat because she knew she should. She had no appetite.

There was about an hour of daylight left when Henry stopped at a place he called Horse Creek. The stretch of perennial stream was thickly treed on one side, with a low bluff on the other. He chose a spot against the bluff under a huge cottonwood that would provide decent concealment. Helplessly, his mind kept going back to another time when he'd searched for safe places to hole up.

"We should be at the fort, day after tomorrow. Could be mid-morning, but more likely late afternoon or evening; I'm not rightly sure which. I've never come this way before," Henry said, removing Harriet's saddle and setting it against the base of the bluff. "It'll be safer if we don't light a fire; the smoke can be seen a long way off. I hope you don't mind more dried elk—here, you can sit on this." He laid out his bedroll for Clara.

"Thank you...for everything."

Henry nodded and began rubbing down Harriet.

Clara sat on the bedroll and watched Henry as he carefully groomed the mare. Her shock was beginning to wear off, and she was curious about her rescuer.

"How did you get that scar on your face?" She regretted the question immediately. "I'm sorry, I didn't mean to pry."

Henry was silent for a moment. Then: "From a whipping, when I was a boy."

"Oh, that's horrible. You were a slave?"

"Yes'm."

"How was it that you came to rescue me? You weren't sent after me, were you? You couldn't have been hired by my father."

"No ma'am. I came to talk with my friend, Standing Elk. He's a Cheyenne, umm, Medicine Man."

"He told you, and you decided to help me?"

"Yes'm."

"Is he going to be angry with you?"

"If they figure it was me? I expect he will be. Only not for the reasons you might be thinking."

"For what you did to his chief?"

"Short Bull wasn't his chief. It's hard to understand the Indians' ways, even for me, and I lived with them. Standing Elk won't be angry because Short Bull is dead, or that you...were freed. He didn't like that Short Bull took you and he told me as much. He didn't do anything about it because it wasn't his place. He'll be angry with me because to him, it wasn't *my* place either. If the Dog Men find out what I did, they'll blame Standing Elk. He was the one who first brought me to them."

Clara gave Henry a truculent look. "Don't they know right from wrong?"

"Most do, some don't. Just like other folks, I reckon. But just like other folks, knowing right from wrong don't always mean they do right. Most Indians are fine people; kind like you wouldn't believe. I lived with the Cheyenne for a fair amount of time and never saw one of them do harm to another, and that's a lot more than I can say for other folks I've spent time with."

"You mean white people?"

"White *and* colored. My own father was killed in a squabble over a pair of shoes—least that's what I was told—and I once saw a slave strangle another slave just cause he thought the man was cozying up to the straw-boss too much and getting extra rations of corn flour. What I'm trying to say is, most Indians aren't like Short Bull any more than most white folks are like that fella who killed President Lincoln. No matter where you're looking from it was a terrible thing, him taking you like you were his to take…were there others with you? Your husband?"

"No. No husband." Clara wanted to avert her eyes again but didn't. "There were others. There was someone I loved very much. Like a father." Clara studied Henry's face. Then, much like Randall had fourteen days earlier and over three hundred miles away, she told her story. Not wanting to recount the details of her two weeks as Short Bull's captive, she ended with the Dog Men attack. Her composure, which she tried so stoically to keep, once again dissolved and she wept telling of Randall's death at the hands of the young Indian.

Henry listened without interrupting, even when he recognized John Elliot's name.

"I met your man," he said when she was finished. "In St. Joseph. I sometimes hire on with army supply caravans and tend horses. Anyway, they mostly just give me work they could have soldiers doing so I'll be around if they need a scout or interpreter."

"You've seen him? Is he well? Is he at Fort Laramie?"

"He was fine last I saw him. I was along on the supply caravan he came in to Fort Laramie with. He struck me as a thoughtful man. He spent a goodish amount of time writing letters… mayhap to you. I left not long after we arrived. I suppose it's been a fortnight or thereabouts."

"Do you think he's still there?"

"I couldn't say. There's a lot of comings and goings. If he isn't, probably someone will know where he is."

"Will you take me to him, if he isn't?"

"Well now, the army might be better—"

"I had some money, but it was in the wagon…"

"It's not about money, ma'am. I don't have a lot of use for it, truth be told."

"*Please.* I have to see John, and my father must have already sent word to whoever is in command at Fort Laramie. They may not help me. They might even try to send me back to

New York. My father has influential friends." Clara paused, looking deflated. "I'm sorry. I must seem ungrateful."

"No, ma'am, you don't. I'll see you to him, if I can."

4

Clara was running through the moonlit prairie. She looked over her shoulder, Short Bull's shadowed face loomed behind her. He reached for her, the tips of his fingers brushing her shoulder lightly before falling away. She ran faster, her breath coming in ragged gasps. His hand clamped on her shoulder and pulled her back. He pushed her down on her stomach. She tried to crawl away but he held her down with one hand on the back of her neck and forced himself into her. The pain was immediate and intense. He leaned over her, grunting, his heavy breath in her ear. His grunts turned to gurgles; hot blood splashed over her. She screamed.

Henry awoke from his thin sleep with a start. He looked around, momentarily disorientated, then grabbed the Spencer leaning against his saddle. "What is it?" he whispered into the darkness.

"Nothing," Clara responded, sounding shaken. "I had a dream. It's nothing, I'm fine now."

Neither one of them could go back to sleep. Henry wondered what he was going to do when they got to Fort Laramie. Hopefully Clara's lieutenant was still there. If he was, Henry could leave Clara with him then move on and locate William Bent for Standing Elk. If he wasn't, Henry was faced with the fact that he'd given Clara his word to help her reunite with John Elliot when he was supposed to be on his way to locate William Bent.

Clara lay under Henry's wool blanket wondering what she would tell John. Or would he know everything just by looking at her? Would he see something in her eyes and turn away in disgust?

She felt an irreconcilable mix of shame and anger. Everything she'd ever been taught pointed to Short Bull's physical violations being her fault. She could hear her father's condescending voice: *"You acquired exactly what you went looking for, Clara. Did you even fight? Or did you give in easily like you did with that detestable Elliot pup?"* There was another part of her that absolutely refused to accept the ignominy that accompanied Short Bull's actions. She was a victim, after all, and neither deserved nor would accept any blame. This time it was her mother who spoke: *"You're like your father in so many ways, my darling. You've his mettle; the very thing that elevated him from a poor, farmer's son to one of the wealthiest men in New York. It's a hardness which many men of great worth possess but is uncommon in women. Keep it hidden, it will serve you at times. If you display it openly it will cause you nothing but grief."*

Henry let an hour go by then stood. It was cold for June, and he'd given his bedroll to Clara. *Better off to be moving, he thought.* "Ma'am? We should be going."

Clara wanted to tell him to call her by her first name—he couldn't be but a few years older than she was, and she liked him—but years of propriety couldn't easily be shaken off. How would others react if she allowed a negro to address her by her given name? "Please call me Miss Hanfield, if you don't mind. Ma'am is how you would address my mother."

"Yes'm...Miss Hanfield. We should be going."

5

They ate a breakfast of dried elk—Clara ate her portion longing for an apple—and were moving before the sun was more than a promise on the eastern horizon.

Shortly after noon they saw the riders.

There were twenty-four by Henry's count, and they were coming from the opposite direction at a leisurely pace. They were Indians, but they were too far away for him to tell what tribe they belonged to.

"Shouldn't we flee?" Clara asked fearfully.

"We wouldn't get far if they wanted to chase us. Pull that rifle out and hand it to me. I don't think I'll have to use it—I never have before—but better to be safe."

What Henry didn't say was there was a chance that some of the Cheyenne Dog Men had gone out looking for Short

Bull's killer, making a circuit of the area, and were now heading back toward the lake.

Clara handed him the Spencer. He laid it casually across his lap where it could be easily seen without it looking like he was spoiling for a fight. The Indians had obviously seen them; they corrected their course slightly to ensure their path would meet Henry and Clara's.

He reached back and removed the field glasses from his saddlebags. "They're Sioux," he said a moment later.

Henry kept Harriet at a slow walk. He felt Clara's grip on his waist tighten as the small group approached. They stopped when they were about twenty feet away. Henry continued on until he was directly in front of them.

The group appeared solemn. The men were not yet in their decline, but the eight or so women appeared ancient. Henry said *"Hau,"* and let his eyes rest on a man with two eagle feathers in his hair. The man held an intricately decorated calumet in his lap much in the same way as Henry's rifle was resting in his. He raised his hand and said "Hau," in return, then regarded Henry and Clara silently while one of the few young men with the group urged his horse forward until it was side by side with Harriet. The young brave nodded curtly at Henry, then looked curiously at Clara, who kept her eyes fixed on Henry's back.

The man with the eagle feathers simultaneously spoke and made the hand signs for *I know you* at Henry. Henry searched his memory but couldn't remember ever meeting him. He was about to ask the man's name in Sioux—of which he could speak and understand only a handful of words and phrases—when the man spoke in English: "You have tobacco?"

Henry smiled and nodded. He twisted around and reached past Clara to get into his saddlebags, and handed the young brave a small hide bag with a drawstring. The brave dutifully took the bag to the man with the eagle feathers. The man looked inside and nodded. *"Philámayaye,"* he said, and slipped the drawstring over his wrist. He clicked his tongue twice and moved past Henry and Clara without another look. The others followed.

"What was he saying?" Clara asked as they rode away.

"He said he knew me."

"Do you know him?"

"Never met him, far as I recall."

"What would they have done if you hadn't given them tobacco?"

"Moved on, I reckon." Henry still had the pipe that Black Kettle had given him, but he rarely smoked it. He usually kept some tobacco with him to use as small tokens, though.

There was a very large tree in the distance. It drew their eyes with its unlikely presence on the featureless plain. As they got closer to its twisted and gray bulk, Clara thought she could see some color standing out against the weathered branches. "It looks like there's something in that tree," she said.

"It's the reason those people were here. It's a burial tree."

"A burial tree?...That's a *body* up there?"

"Yes. We'll stay away from it."

"Why would they put someone who died, in a tree?"

"Indians keep to themselves about death...I think it's so their soul can escape to the spirit world."

"Do you believe that?"

"It's not for me to say. It keeps the animals from getting to it."

"That's a dreadful thought."

6

"We should be there in another two hours, or thereabouts, " Henry said, as he looked off into the distance. Harriet was drinking from a rapidly drying-up seasonal creek, and Clara was trying to walk off some of the nervousness she felt along with the soreness in her legs and backside.

Clara had quickly grown comfortable with Henry and his calm and unexacting manner. She felt an icy stab in her stomach when she thought of facing other people, however. She looked at herself in her torn and filthy dress, and over-sized, hide trousers, and knew how everyone would look at her: with pity; with disgust.

"I don't think I can go into Fort Laramie like this."

Henry, who was leading Harriet back up to where Clara was standing, paused. After a moment, understanding dawned on his face.

"What do you want to do?"

"I don't know...look at me...I can't...you couldn't understand."

"I reckon you're right about that. But I'll help however I can. There's the sutler's—run by some nice folks—where we could get you a new dress. I know a Cheyenne woman who lives by the fort, she'd allow you could stay there while I went on in. I'll bring back the dress and some new shoes, and a horse with a proper saddle for you, then we could ride in together and look for your man. Begging your pardon, ma'am—*Miss Hanfield*, either way I have to get moving because I have other business that needs tending to as well."

"Yes. Yes, of course you do. But an Indian woman..." Clara trailed off, looking at her feet. After a moment she looked up at Henry. "Forgive me. If you trust this woman, then so shall I. And I will accept your offer, gratefully. I don't know when I will be able to repay you or the shopkeeper for the cost of the clothing and anything else that needs to be purchased. I can only offer my word that it will be repaid."

Henry smiled. "It's not much of a shop. Leastways not like they have down in St. Joseph or Independence—and, I reckon, New York. But they've got a fair amount of stock. It's necessities mostly, but they have other things. And you don't need to worry about the money, I get along just fine."

They arrived at the small camp of four lodges an hour later. Clara's heart was beating fast.

Henry pointed southwest and said, "The fort's just over that rise."

There were two old women hunched over a large piece of hide. One woman was poking holes in the edge and the other was weaving a hide thong through them. They looked impossibly thin to Clara. Henry spoke to the women in

Cheyenne. They looked at Clara curiously, then pointed out into the prairie.

"Go ahead and get down," he said to Clara, reaching his hand back to help her. After she had, he climbed down and retrieved his dwindling supply of dried elk from his saddlebags. He gave all of what was left to the two women. The women ejaculated in Cheyenne, and pawed at Henry. He said something softly, nodding his head reassuringly.

"We'll wait over here," he said to Clara, taking Harriet's reins and starting toward one of the lodges.

"Why, they're half starved," Clara said, looking over her shoulder at the women.

"Them and a lot of others."

"Why?"

"They can't hunt—not that there's much game around here anymore—and the army hasn't been delivering on most of what they promised. They have to walk all the way to Fort Laramie just to get turned away empty handed, or if they're lucky, a small sack of flour. These women don't have families, and what's left of their band went north sometime back." He stopped in front of one of the lodges, untied his bedroll, and released Harriet. "We'll have to sit here and wait for Owl Woman," he said, spreading out his bedroll.

Twenty minutes later an old woman wearing a deerskin dress came up from behind the lodge. She carried a small basket with a handful of what looked like miniature turnips inside. Clara observed that she walked with a pronounced limp. Henry stood and the woman greeted him warmly. Clara followed Henry's lead and also stood. Henry said: "Clara, this is *Mestaa'ėhehe;* you would say *Owl Woman*." Then Henry said something in Cheyenne to Owl Woman, ending with Clara's name. Owl Woman smiled and nodded.

After speaking to Henry in length, the woman walked off to where the other two women were still working with the animal hide.

"She'll offer to feed you while I'm gone. Please eat it. They don't have it to share but they'll share it anyway. I'll bring them back some food."

"I wish I had a book," Clara said, sitting down on Henry's blanket. Henry appeared not to have heard, and walked after Harriet who was munching grass some yards away.

He came back with Harriet in tow, and he was holding something wrapped in a small piece of wool cloth. He handed it to Clara, who looked up at him questioningly before unwrapping the item.

It was a book.

Clara stared up at Henry with frank surprise. "*A Christmas Carol!* My mother read this to me when I was just a child, and I've read it several times since. Isn't Dickens wonderful?...You're educated, then?"

"I can read and write well enough."

"Tell me, what was your favorite part."

"The part where his dead friend, Marley, comes to visit."

Clara laughed and mocked a man's baritone: *"Business! cried the Ghost, wringing its hands again. Mankind was my business. The common welfare was my business; charity, mercy, forbearance, and benevolence were all my business. The dealings of my trade were but a drop of water in the comprehensive ocean of my business!"*

Henry laughed. It was a rare occurrence.

7

Clara watched Henry ride away. He said she would be safe with the Indian woman, and she believed him, but she was still afraid. Although she'd only known him three days, she felt safe with Henry. And why not? Here was a man who had killed to rescue her, without knowing her or expecting any reward. He was kind, generous, *and* he appreciated literature. He was contrary to everything her father had ever said about negroes. How was a man like this regarded less than any other by the color of his skin? Yet, hadn't she still been unable to invite him to address her as Clara?

She looked over at the three women. They'd put the animal skin aside. Now they were stoking a small fire and preparing an iron cook-pot. Owl Woman limped here and there purposefully. Clara looked at the Dickens' novel. It was well-read but in fine condition. She thought of John and hoped they'd soon be reunited. She wondered how she should tell him he was to be a father. Soon there was the smell of cooking.

8

Henry was tired. More tired than he'd been since waking up in Standing Elk's lodge four years earlier. He'd slept fitfully ever since killing Short Bull. Clara wasn't the only one haunted by the Cheyenne Chief.

He let Harriet gallop for awhile—he'd always felt she was happiest when she was running—and it took him less than an hour to reach the sutler's store at Fort Laramie. The store was a sprawling building consisting of several add-ons to the original adobe structure. The current proprietors were an English couple by the name of Alden. They had arrived several years before, intent on Oregon, but had been forced to stay behind with their daughter who was ill with cholera. The girl eventually died. Seeing opportunity in the business, the Aldens had purchased it from the previous owner.

He tied Harriet to the hitching rail, removed his saddlebags, and entered the store. The interior smelled of old wood-smoke and dust. Ruby Alden looked up from her work: "Good afternoon, Henry. What can I do for you?" she asked in her thick, English accent.

"Afternoon, Missus Alden. I'll be needing a few things." He approached the long counter and set down his saddlebags. She wiped her hands on her apron and looked over the counter expectantly.

"I need ten pounds of flour, ten pounds of salt pork, five quarts of beans, a pound of dried beef...do you have any of those peach preserves left?"

"We do. And I have four dozen biscuits made this morning with fresh eggs."

"That sounds good. Two jars of the peaches, and a dozen of the biscuits...going to need some more tobacco...and a dress, fit for riding. The woman's a slight bit smaller than you are, begging your pardon. I'll need shoes to go with it; around this size..." he pulled a length of hide thong from his shirt pocket and stretched it out on the scarred, wooden counter, "...if you have them." She raised an eyebrow at this but said nothing.

"Also, does Mister Alden still want to sell that roan gelding he traded for awhile back?"

"No, I'm sorry. He sold it to a young sergeant from Massachusetts.

"I reckon I'll go see Seth Pritchard then. I'll need a ladies' saddle as well.

"As for the dress, there isn't much call for ladies fashion here, Henry; I have plenty of fabric but that's all…"

"Sell him yours." Came a man's voice through a partially opened door on the far wall, behind Henry. "It doesn't fit you anymore."

Frederick Alden, Ruby's husband, opened the door the rest of the way and stepped through.

"Good day, Henry," he said, walking up to the counter and lifting a hinged portion of it so he could walk through and join his wife.

"You haven't worn that dress in seven years, and you're not getting any smaller. Sell him the dress, and Grace's saddle. Although I must admit I'm curious as to what Henry requires them for."

"Oh, Frederick, we can't part with Grace's saddle," Ruby said.

"Grace has been gone eight years, dearest. We've got her other things. We don't need that old saddle, and I'd just as soon have someone get some use from it. Care to satisfy a dull storekeeper's curiosity, Henry?

"Thank you, Mister Alden, but it's not my place to say."

Frederick Alden looked disappointed. "Very well. Shall we say three dollars for the dress and eight for the saddle? I'll throw in a new horse blanket, free of charge."

"Sounds fair enough."

"Come with me, Henry, I'll show you the shoes," Ruby Alden said, sparing an irritated look at her husband. "Bring along that strip of hide, I'm sure we'll have something close."

After finding a pair of plain shoes that were nearly identical in length to the hide thong, Henry borrowed a pen and ink and purchased a sheet of paper and an envelope. He jotted a quick letter to William Bent stating simply that he was needed up on the Powder River. He signed it *Henry,* then addressed it to William. Afterward, he paid for everything and left the store to see about a horse while Ruby gathered the rest of his purchases.

Seth Pritchard was a recently mustered-out volunteer who'd spent his free time at Fort Laramie buying and selling horses and mules. He hadn't left Fort Laramie yet because he didn't have any place in particular to go (recently he'd been thinking of heading down to Texas, or maybe California). He was known to be a cheat if he could get away with it and would frequently take advantage of settlers passing through. He was also known to float loans to other soldiers at exorbitant interest rates. Henry didn't care for him, and due to Henry's skin color, the feeling was mutual.

Pritchard always considered himself a Union man, but he didn't like niggers any more than he liked injuns. He especially hated *smart* niggers.

Pritchard was camped a few hundred yards downriver from the fort. The short, big bellied man was sitting in front of his tent on a wooden stool when Henry rode up.

"Well, look who it is," Pritchard said without standing.

"Afternoon. I need a horse, if you have one for sale." Henry said, bringing Harriet to a stop.

"That so? Well, all I got's one for sale. I'm closing up shop here before long, now the war's over and they don't need me anymore. He's up under the shade of that tree; not the black, that one's mine. You'd just about disappear if you rode him."

Henry ignored the witticism. He urged Harriet forward a few steps and looked at the two horses tethered to a tree by the river. "That's the roan Frederick Alden was selling awhile back. Missus Alden told me he sold it to an army captain."

"That's right, only it was a sergeant. The sergeant wasn't much of a card player and needed my help more than he needed that horse. It's a fine saddle-horse. I don't reckon you could afford him, unless they're payin' negro scouts officer's wages now."

Henry said nothing and rode over to inspect the animal. After a few minutes he came back, knowing the horse would probably take all of the rest of the money he'd been indifferently stowing in his saddlebags for the past three years.

"I'll pay a hundred and fifty dollars," Henry said.

"That's a hundred and seventy-five dollar horse if ever there was one."

"Thank you anyway, then." Henry said and started away.

"Wait just a second. I didn't say I wouldn't sell it to you for a hundred and fifty. I just said it was worth a hundred and seventy-five."

Henry dismounted and removed the leather pouch he kept his money in from his saddlebags and counted out the money. "That bridle don't go with the horse unless you want to pay another three dollars."

Henry gave him the three dollars.

"You've done right well for yourself, learning to speak injun, haven't you?"

"Does he have a name?"

"What? The horse?" Pritchard bellowed laughter so hard he nearly fell off of his stool. "Let me get your bill of sale. Don't want you to be getting hanged for a horse thief."

9

Henry led the horse back to the store. The sidesaddle was sitting on the splintered porch. It was dusty, but appeared more than serviceable. He opened the door and entered. There was a tall, stoutly built man at the counter speaking to Frederick Alden, and three more sitting at one of the four tables on the far wall. The Aldens served coffee, tea, and Ruby's homemade biscuits as well as keeping a pot of beans simmering for hungry customers. Henry glanced at the men at the table and his blood froze.

Emmet Dawson was one of them.

He must have felt Henry's eyes on him, because he looked up from his coffee and stared at Henry, *hard*. Henry didn't see any recognition in the stare, but there was something else he could easily place: scorn.

"Can I help you, boy?" Emmet asked, rubbing his gray-flecked beard. Henry shook his head and turned away, but not before he saw Emmet's son (Henry couldn't recall his name) look up at him. Unlike his father, his mouth was agape with stark recognition.

Henry moved to the counter where his saddlebags lie next to his other purchases, his back to the tables. "Ruby! Henry's back," Frederick called out, not looking away from what he was doing.

Ruby came through a door-sized opening in the tall shelves behind the counter—where they kept a small stove for the coffee and beans—and walked over to where Henry was packing some of his purchases into his saddlebags.

"I'm sorry, Missus Alden, but I'm going to need two blankets," Henry said.

"Of course. I'll be right back."

"Could you bring them to me outside? I want to go ahead and get the horse saddled."

"You found a horse. Good. I hope the saddle will suit…I'll go and get the blankets."

"Thank you."

Henry threw his saddlebags over his shoulder and managed to stack everything else up in his arms. He carried the tower awkwardly to the door, and was just trying to get his hand out enough to reach the handle when a voice from behind him said: "Let me get that for you."

Henry turned his head and saw the tall man who'd been standing at the counter. He was smiling warmly.

"Thank you," Henry said, stepping aside so the man could reach the door handle.

Once outside, Henry set everything on the porch except the horse blanket, grabbed up the sidesaddle and hurried over to the roan. He looked over the roan's back at Harriet, who was tethered next to him, and stared at the Spencer rifle's stock poking out of its leather scabbard. He imagined walking back into the store with it and shooting Emmet Dawson and his son.

He forced the thought away and set to work.

"That was Frederick's horse," Ruby said, coming up behind him a few moments later. "How did you come upon him?"

"Seth Pritchard ended up with him somehow," Henry said, cinching the saddle straps. "Does he have a name?"

"No, I'm sorry. Frederick never names his animals." She patted the horse's neck then ran her fingers lightly over the saddle, almost lovingly, before turning back to the store.

"Take good care, Henry," she said.

"Thank you, Ma'am."

10

After wrapping the food he'd purchased in one of the blankets and tying it to the new horse's saddle, Henry mounted Harriet and headed toward the barracks. He stopped in front of a quartet of soldiers who were standing beside a wagon with a broken wheel.

"Afternoon. I'm looking for Lieutenant Elliot."

"Elliot? I don't recognize the name, but I've only been here three weeks," a man with corporal's stripes on his uniform answered.

"Sergeant Campbell, then?"

"What do you need the sergeant for, nigger?" a whip-thin soldier with a grease bucket in his hand asked.

"Eyes to your work, McCandles," the corporal said, without looking away from Henry. "Sergeant Campbell's over there." He waved his hand toward a small building some two hundred feet away. "Counting boots, I think," he added with a chuckle.

Henry rode over to where Sergeant Campbell and another soldier were dumping burlap bags full of boots out onto the ground and sorting through them. The same boots they'd loaded onto a wagon in St. Joseph back in April, Henry thought. It was now June.

"I figured you'd have already handed those out," Henry said.

"I did," Sergeant Campbell said, standing and brushing off his trousers. "These are new ones. Damn things fall apart after a couple good marches." He nodded his head at the packed horse. "You getting married or something?"

Henry was puzzled for a moment, then he smiled. "The saddle? No, not planning to any time soon. Do you remember that lieutenant who came in with us from St. Joseph? Elliot?"

"I remember."

"Is he here?"

"No, he isn't. He rode out a few days after he got here with a colonel by the name of Picton.

"You know where I can find them?"

"They headed down the Platte. Might have been seventy-five, a hundred of them."

"Shouldn't be too hard to find."

"If you don't mind me asking, why are you looking for him?"

Henry thought it over for a moment and didn't see any reason not to tell Sergeant Campbell about Clara.

"I found a woman. She'd been taken by some Cheyenne Dog Men; Short Bull. She and Lieutenant Elliot are supposed to be getting married."

"Was she coming here with a wagon and some escorts?...Hanfield?"

"That's right."

"Christ Almighty, She's got everyone and their brother looking for her. Where is she?"

"She's safe. I'd be obliged if you'd keep this to yourself for the time being."

"Why is that?"

"Well, it's not for me to say. I just want to see her to Lieutenant Elliot and let them sort it out."

"Henry, she's got men here looking for her. She comes from an important family back in New York. You don't want to be putting yourself in the middle of something like this. Especially being...being a negro. You want to get hanged like those Sioux? If you've found her, I'm obliged to report it to my superiors."

"Did something happen here?"

"What do you mean?"

"The Indians are gone—most of them anyway. And what Sioux?"

"Don't change the subject, Henry. That's army business. Tell me where the Hanfield woman is."

"Tell me what happened here."

Sergeant Campbell sighed. "There was another woman, she had a child with her. She was taken by some Cheyenne last summer—"

"Dog Men?"

"I don't know, probably. I don't know all of the details. Some Sioux ended up with her somehow—William Bent's son, George, says the Sioux ransomed her and the child from the Cheyenne so they could return them here as a gesture of peace. General Moonlight didn't see it that way, and had the two Sioux chiefs involved hanged. After that he started worrying about retaliation, so he sent most of the Indians that were here to Fort Kearny with a detachment of men. A bunch of them ran off before they got there; Captain Fouts ordered a pursuit, and he and four soldiers were killed. The rest of the army detachment gave up and sent word back here. General Moonlight rode out the day before yesterday with two hundred and twenty men to run them down."

Henry sighed. "He wanted to send more than a thousand Cheyenne, Arapaho, and Sioux to live on Pawnee lands? What did he expect would happen? There isn't even enough food there. They'd starve come winter...They're not going to let you treat them like prisoners."

Sergeant Campbell looked down at the soldier who was still on his knees sorting shoes. "Private Jackson, go take a rest. Get yourself some coffee or something." The soldier got up without a word and walked away. Sergeant Campbell watched him go, then turned his attention back to Henry. "You think I like watching what's happening to these people? Well I *don't*. But they're not helping themselves by raiding and killing and abducting white women and children. If they kill a soldier or a settler you can rest assured we're going to kill a hundred of theirs. You speak their language. Don't they know they can't win?"

"They're starting to understand that whites aren't going to be satisfied until they take everything worth having. Most of them would rather fight knowing they can't win than spend their lives confined to some piece of dirt where nothing grows and no game can live, waiting on the few crumbs thrown to them by their white masters. I expect there's going to be a lot more fighting before too long."

"Where's that put you?"

"Somewhere in the middle, I reckon."

"Since General Moonlight's gone, Captain Lange's in command. I can't say I like him much, so I try to speak with him as little as possible. I don't see why that needs to change today. I thought Lieutenant Elliot seemed like a decent enough man. Hopefully he'll move her as far from here as he can."

"I'm obliged, Sergeant."

"I can't help you if this turns into trouble for you."

"I wouldn't ask it. There is something else. Can you see this gets down to Fort Lyon? It's for William Bent. It's important he gets it." Henry pulled the envelope he'd addressed to Bent and handed it to Sergeant Campbell.

"I'll see it gets there, but there's no telling when he'll get it."

"I'm obliged."

"I'll be seeing you, Henry."

11

It was late afternoon when Henry returned to Owl Woman's camp. Clara was no longer reading Dickens, but was sitting next to Owl Woman and the two others, helping the women stitch small pieces of hide together. Owl Woman was leaned over, closely inspecting Clara's work. After a moment she raised her head and nodded her approval to Clara.

Henry dismounted and led the horses to where the women were sitting in a semi-circle.

"He's not at the fort. He left with some other men a few weeks back. We'll have to go find him." He began unpacking Clara's new horse.

"I hope these fit you," he said, handing her the cloth wrapped dress and the shoes. "There wasn't much to choose from."

"Thank you, Henry. Will you be able to locate John?"

"I reckon it'll be easy enough. You have some folks looking for you back at the fort, though. Might be best if I take you there while I go find him."

"No. I want to go with you. The only people waiting for me at Fort Laramie would be men sent by my father…Theo Brandt, I've no doubt. I have to see John."

"I thought as much. I just want you to know that it'll be more sleeping on the ground and eating dried meat, boiled beans, and whatever else I can hunt or trap—mayhap for weeks. I guess I don't need to tell you that some of the Indians might not be so friendly as those Sioux we came across. Also, they saw you with me. If the Cheyenne Dog Men are looking for whoever killed their chief and they pass through wherever those Sioux were camped…they'd be out to kill me."

"I want to go with you," Clara said firmly.

"No sense leaving until the morning." He handed Owl Woman a jar of the peaches, and she keened with excitement. "There's a jar for you too," he said to Clara.

12

Clara stood naked in Owl Woman's lodge looking down at her belly. It was protruding appreciatively. She rubbed it gently and wondered whether it was a girl or a boy. She picked up the dark green riding habit. It was of high quality but years out of fashion. It reminded Clara of something from the back of her mother's wardrobe. She put it on and discovered it fit reasonably well. She only wished for her undergarments. There was a matching pair of stockings wrapped inside the dress, and she slipped them on. The shoes fit even better than the dress, although she thought them to be of much lower quality—

housemaid's shoes. She smiled to herself imagining the stares she would have drawn in New York wearing such an ensemble.

Henry started some beans cooking with a little bit of the salt pork. Owl Woman added a handful of plains herbs, then admonished him to stir the pot. He gave the women all of the flour and the better part of the salt pork and dried beans. In return, they gave him a pair of unadorned hide moccasins.

"You're very kind," Clara said, coming up behind him. "Is there anything more to be done for them?"

"No. I bring some things when I'm this way. Someone else does too. They didn't kill the deer those skins came from. They could move closer to the fort, but they won't. They'd be reduced to begging, or they'd be sent somewhere else; could be someplace worse. I reckon they'll stay here as long as they can. I'll set some snares for them after supper."

Clara hunkered and leaned over the pot. "It smells wonderful. They gave me some sort of soup earlier. It was a little like onion, but it was watery and bitter. I ate it, as you suggested."

"It's a far cry from what you're accustomed to, I guess."

"Yes, it is. Randall used to cook onion soup for us on holidays. It was special to him; the recipe was his mother's. My father absolutely adored Randall's onion soup. I miss him—Randall, I mean. I always wished in secret that he was my father…now he's gone because of me."

13

Owl Woman brushed Clara's hair with a porcupine quill hair brush, then re-braided it in the dwindling twilight. Henry was out setting up snares. The old woman's touch was as gentle as her own mother's, and Clara felt another pang of homesickness. It passed as quickly as it arrived when she thought of her father. She would be perfectly happy if she never saw him again.

It was well after dark when Henry returned, and Clara had already retired to Owl Woman's lodge. The other women had gone to their lodges as well. He tended to the horses and then sat by the glowing embers of the night's fire, deep in thought. He wished for a smoke and conversation with Standing Elk.

14

Henry was up before the sun, and checking the snares by the first glow of dawn. He returned to the camp with three decent-sized jackrabbits and a gopher, which he gave to the woman tending the morning fire. Clara was up and making herself familiar with her new horse. Henry saddled the even-tempered animal and removed its hobbles. After speaking some words to Owl Woman in Cheyenne, Henry and Clara were on their way.

Twelve

1

"Good morning, Mister Eastman," Major Brighton said, entering the room after a polite knock on the door. Randall was sitting up in bed eating overly salty bacon and fried potatoes.

Randall looked up toward the voice—and the movement. His vision had returned enough for him to see shapes and vague, faded colors, but that was all.

"Good morning, Major."

Major Brighton walked over and sat in the chair next to Randall's bed.

"I've received word that I have fifteen hundred Indians on their way here from Fort Laramie. It seems General Moonlight fears an uprising due to his ill-considered hanging of two Sioux chiefs. His problem is now my problem. In light of this development, I will have to ask you to depart Fort Kearny. The doctor tells me you are out of danger, and I can no longer be responsible for your welfare." He took the nearly empty plate from Randall and replaced it with a large envelope. "My father was fond of saying 'The only true test of one's worth comes when no one is watching.' I never gave it very much thought until two weeks ago. There's more money in that envelope than I will earn as an army officer in the next several years. It was hidden inside the letters Clara Hanfield wrote to Lieutenant Elliot—who, I've been informed, is no longer an officer in the United States Army. The letters were given to me along with several other items, the day you were brought here. Nothing that appeared to have any value, of course. The Indians left only what they had no use for, and the officer in charge of the soldiers who found you ordered them to pick up everything scattered about and put it in the wagon with you. When they arrived, it was all brought to me. I wonder, if they'd removed the ribbon binding the stack of letters and looked through them—they weren't sealed, you see—would they have brought the money? Or would they have divided it amongst themselves? It's a question I'll never have the answer to. I can only answer that question for myself. And you have it there in your lap. I won't apologize for reading the letters. I only desired to better understand the events leading up to Miss Hanfield's abduction. Your wagon has been repaired, and I have eight men waiting to escort you back to St. Joseph."

"The wagon does not belong to me. Nor does this money."

"You were the only survivor of your party, Mister Eastman. If there are claims to any of this property, the responsibility lies with you to see them fulfilled."

"Miss Hanfield survived."

"You don't know that, and we've already been over this. My men lost the Indians' trail after three days. If she's alive— which I doubt— she could be anywhere. I'm truly sorry, Mister Eastman, but you must realize now that it was a fool's errand."

"Major Brighton?"

"Yes?"

"How old are you?"

"I'm thirty-four."

"Have you ever been in love?"

After a long pause, Randall watched the shape of Major Brighton rise. There were footsteps, and the sound of the door snicking shut.

2

"Mister Eastman? I'm Corporal McElroy. I'm to see you to St. Joseph," an unfamiliar voice said, entering the room. It had been less than an hour since Major Brighton's visit.

"I'm pleased to meet you, Mister McElroy," Randall said to the shadowy figure. "However, I have no intention of going to St. Joseph. Would you please tell Major Brighton that I wish you to take me to Fort Laramie?"

"Begging your pardon, sir, but Major Brigh—"

"Please just give him the message, young man."

"I'll tell him."

Randall watched the shadow leave. He was sitting in the chair by the bed looking across the room at a bright spot on the wall; *a window,* he thought. Twenty minutes later there was a single knock and the door opened.

"Hello again, Major Brighton." Randall said, knowing it was him by the lone rap on the door.

Major Brighton strode briskly across the room to where Randall was seated.

"Mister Eastman, it's time I was more clear on your situation, as you seem to have missed something. Some very serious allegations have been levied against you by some very powerful men. The only reason you aren't in shackles awaiting a noose or—if you were singularly lucky—in St. Joseph awaiting a train to take you back to New York to stand trial, is because your accusers believe you are dying of your wounds. In light of the overwhelming evidence that Miss Hanfield left home by her own volition and that your decision to accompany her was made strictly out your desire to protect her, both myself and Doctor Evans exaggerated the severity of your condition. Counterfeit justice can easily be purchased by men like Jonathon Hanfield, and if you are tried for any of his accusations, I assure you, you will be found guilty. I will not aid him. Fort Kearny's new commander will be arriving tomorrow or the following day, and he may not feel as inclined to risk his commission on your behalf as I have. Clara Hanfield is almost certainly dead. And if she isn't, she's no longer the same young woman you travelled this far to protect."

Major Brighton sighed.

"Go to St. Joseph, Mister Eastman. Corporal McElroy will help you find a nurse who you can hire to escort you to St. Louis, or Kansas City, or some other city where you can find the care you require. There is nothing for you here, and there is nothing for you at Fort Laramie. Good day."

He turned and walked toward the door.

Randall's nearly sightless eyes, now slick with tears, followed him. "Major?"

There was an audible sigh. "Yes?"

"You're a good man. Thank you for all you've done for me. Please give Doctor Evans my thanks and warmest regards."

"I'm afraid he left this morning. Goodbye, Mister Eastman."

Thirteen

1

It was an hour after dawn. Standing Elk let the gutted carcass of the doe slide off his horse. He spoke some words to Owl Woman, who nodded solemnly and pointed southward. He followed her gaze feeling troubled. He wondered what could have made Henry kill Short Bull for the white woman. Standing Elk may have convinced Short Bull to trade for her if Henry desired her, although he couldn't understand why Henry would. The woman would only bring trouble from the whites. Henry did not often speak in length. His words were few but his thoughts ran as deep as the rivers during the moon when the geese lay eggs. When he did speak in length, his words were worthy of ears. Henry was as Standing Elk in this way. He would find Henry. They would smoke a pipe and speak worthy words with each other.

Fourteen

1

Sergeant Campbell's expression was one of resignation as he watched Theo Brandt stride toward him across the parade yard. He wondered where Brandt's crony was; the southerner with the arrogant air of self-importance. Sergeant Campbell found Brandt distasteful in a way he couldn't describe. The man's eyes seemed to always be smiling, even when his mouth wasn't. He looked like a dandy, but the sergeant thought it would be a mistake to think he really was one. Brandt had been loitering about ever since the Hanfield woman was taken during the Indian raid.

"Go ahead and dismiss the men, Corporal," he said to the soldier standing next to him. He'd just finished issuing new Springfield rifles to a company that had arrived the previous day from Kansas. He took a few steps forward to meet Brandt. He knew what it was regarding, and didn't want the men to hear the conversation.

"Sergeant Campbell, it's my understanding that Clara Hanfield has been found alive, and that she is in the company of a negro scout who goes by the name Henry. May I ask why she wasn't brought here immediately after her discovery and rescue?"

"I couldn't say, Mister Brandt. You'll have to ask Miss Hanfield or Henry that question."

"I would love to do that but unfortunately they're not here, are they? And since you seem to be the only one the negro—"

"Henry. His name is Henry."

"You are the only one *Henry* saw fit to inform that Miss Hanfield was found alive. Did he explain to you how he managed to free her from her captors and why he didn't bring her here with him? And my employer—Miss Hanfield's father—will be interested in knowing why, when this...*Henry* came to you with the news, you did not dispatch men to see her safely back here?"

"Mister Brandt, I can appreciate that Mister Hanfield is worried about his daughter, and that you have to answer to him about the situation, but *you* might consider that you and Mister Hanfield owe Henry a debt of gratitude. He didn't bring the Hanfield woman here because she didn't want to come here. He's escorting her to where *she* wants to go."

Theo eyed him coolly. "Yes, to find John Elliot. I know. Captain Lange told me everything—here he comes now."

Captain Lange, a short, barrel-chested man with a wild and unkempt beard, walked purposely toward them. Sergeant Campbell steeled himself for what was to come. Whatever it was, he knew it wasn't good. When he reached them, Sergeant Campbell saluted. Captain Lange returned the salute, glanced uneasily at Theo Brandt, then returned his gaze to Sergeant Campbell.

"Sergeant Campbell, pick twenty men and go find that nigger and bring him and the Hanfield woman back here—Elliot too, if he's with them. Mind you bring them directly to me, even if General Moonlight has returned. You understand that, Mister Brandt? I want to see Clara Hanfield with my own eyes before you take her back to New York."

Theo Brandt nodded his assent. Captain Lange eyed Sergeant Campbell.

"You have something to say, Sergeant?"

"Yes, sir, I do. According to Henry, Miss Hanfield chose not to come here of her own account." He stole a look at Theo. "I'd say that makes it none of our affair. Besides, with so many men gone with General Moonlight, I don't see that we can spare the troops."

"Is that so, Sergeant? Mister Brandt, will you excuse us?"

"Certainly. I'll prepare my men to depart."

"Fine." The captain waited until he was out of earshot. "Sergeant Campbell, I don't care much for you, and I know you feel the same about me, so in most cases I would tell you I don't give a damn what you think about anything. But in this case you're right, so I'm going to give you an explanation: Jonathon Hanfield owns one of the largest shipping companies on the eastern seaboard. He entertains senators, congressmen and *generals*. His only daughter somehow managed to chase her childish infatuation all of the way out here only to get captured by Indians. I don't even want to think about what they may have done to her. Now she's roaming around the countryside with a nigger. Does that sound like a woman capable of making any decisions for herself? Now you go and find her and bring her back. I've given Brandt and his men permission to accompany you. Two of them are trackers, according to Brandt. I'd rather have someone I trust, like Jim Bridger, but he's off elsewhere. I want to be able to send word to Jonathon Hanfield that his daughter is on her way back to New York inside of two weeks. Now move your ass, Sergeant."

"Sir?"

"What?"

"Sir, they have almost a two day head start, and I'm not certain where exactly they went. I don't see how we can have her back here inside two weeks, if we can find them at all."

"I have faith in you. It's your ass otherwise."

2

Theo Brandt ducked his head inside the tent Emmet Dawson and his son James shared. The two were sitting on the canvas floor playing a card game.

"Prepare to leave. We'll be riding with a detachment of soldiers to follow the negro. Inform the Beadermans and meet me at the store in an hour."

Emmet handed his cards to James and stood. "Are you certain the young woman is even with him? Niggers are a dishonest lot, and you said yourself this sergeant never actually saw her. Perhaps he is after the generous reward you've been so proudly announcing."

"He was leading a horse with a ladies' saddle on it, and he's a known friendly to the Indians. She's with him."

"He's also an escaped slave who most certainly murdered his owner."

"Haven't you read the papers? The war's over and so is slavery, Emmet. If you have a grudge with the negro—if he's even the one you think he is—you can settle it once Clara Hanfield is safely under my protection."

"It's him," James said.

"That's wholly your business once you finish assisting me in mine. Which will happen sooner rather than later, I hope. I would like to quit this God-forsaken place at the earliest possible moment." Theo turned from the tent and called out over his shoulder. "One hour, gentlemen."

"In a hurry to get back to his tailor, huh, Pa?" James said.

"The Yankee is our employer. We should not speak ill of him, even in jest."

"Pa, are we ever going to go home?"

"We've spoken of this enough, James. There is nothing for us to go home to but the blackened remains of the house my father's father built, and a grave. You may choose to go back there someday; it's yours by birthright. I'll not step foot there again in life. For now, we have other matters. Go and tell Wayne and George it's time for them to earn their keep."

Two hours later the twenty-five men were heading southeast in search of Clara Hanfield.

Fifteen

1

John looked down at the remains of the four men who'd refused to follow Picton. He had no way of identifying them: they were stripped naked, their genitals and ears had been cut off, and there were no belongings. Their faces were bloated and streaked with dried blood. Huge, black flies crawled lazily over them. Nonetheless, John was sure he was looking at the four men who'd struck off for home shortly after the massacre in the very spot he now stood.

The massacre in which he himself had been a willing participant.

In the days following his departure from Picton and his band of raiders, John had travelled slowly and incautiously, both fearing and welcoming a similar fate to the men he now stood over. Henry would have understood.

Staring at the four men and the blackened and greasy looking pile of burned Cheyenne women and children, he became aware that there could be no atonement for the atrocity before him. He also realized that bathing in guilt and self-loathing would serve no purpose at all. He had to somehow stop Picton, and he should be making all haste to do so.

He turned from the scene and saw two riders heading toward him. Fear gripped him, and he was momentarily unable to move; the solitary perpetrator discovered standing over the evidence of an unforgivable atrocity.

The riders were too far away for him to tell whether or not they were Indians. He mounted his horse and waited.

2

"There's someone up ahead," Henry said.

Clara squinted her eyes. "I see. Do you think it's an Indian?"

"It isn't an Indian."

Henry reached back and slid out the Spencer rifle. He laid it across his lap and continued on. "We'll see who it is. Could be they need help."

It had been five days since they'd left Owl Woman's camp, and Henry was impressed with how well Clara adjusted to trail life after being accustomed to such wealth and privilege. She rarely complained—except for good-humouredly about the food—and could ride both well and for a long time. There were other things, however: The last three mornings when she'd walked off to do her necessary, Henry heard her retching. Finally, he asked her if she was well. She told him not to be concerned and that she was fine. He'd nodded but felt uncertain. Clara reassured him it was something that occasionally happened to a woman. He'd nodded again but felt no better about it. She also still awoke crying out every night.

Several minutes later they could see the man more clearly. He wore tan trousers and a blue shirt, and sat atop a bay horse—a big one from the looks. The shirt appeared to Henry to be the type a soldier would wear. The trousers and matching hat, did not.

When they were about three hundred feet away the man took off his hat and ran a hand repeatedly through his hair. Clara let out a strangled sounding cry off to Henry's left. He turned, alarmed, just in time to see her kick her horse into a run.

"Wait!" Henry called after her as he urged Harriet to follow.

3

John put his hat back on and returned his attention to the riders. Suddenly they were coming at him at a gallop; the lead rider well ahead of the other. He drew his pistol but was hesitant to aim it. *Something...* "That's a woman," he said aloud with wonder. Then: *"Clara?"*

No sooner had he said it than she was on him, heaving back on the reins and bringing the horse to a stop. John leaped off of his, the pistol falling forgotten from his hand. He ran to her.

Clara was laughing and weeping. She slid off of her horse and into his arms. "We found you. Oh, we found you."

They kissed—fiercely. She pushed his hat off of his head and ran her fingers through his yellow hair like she'd watched him do himself times beyond count. He reached up and took her hands in his and kissed each palm. Then he gently pushed her hands down and took a step back.

"Clara...I..."

"I came looking for you...do you still wish to marry me?"

"I...yes, of course. Clara, how did you..." he trailed off and looked over at Henry, who had stopped about twenty feet away and turned Harriet in the opposite direction.

"That's Henry. He saved my life, then he helped me find you... Henry!" she called to him. "Come on."

"Henry?" John said as he watched Henry turn toward them. "I know him. He's the negro scout I travelled to Fort Laramie with."

"He told me he'd met you."

Henry stopped Harriet a few feet from Clara and John, but he was looking past them, his expression turning to one of disbelief and horror. After a moment he dismounted and walked into the remains of the Indian camp without a word.

Clara looked after him.

"You don't want to look over there," John said, putting a hand on her shoulder and gently trying to turn her away. She took his hand in hers and followed Henry anyway. She was less than ten feet away when she stopped and put her hand over her mouth. "Oh, it smells awful," she said, turning away. She fought the urge to vomit and won—barely. She looked back over her shoulder.

Henry was standing in front of a blackened pile of—she knew what it must be, but didn't want to accept what her eyes were seeing.

She turned away again. "What is this?" she asked breathlessly.

"Let's walk a little farther away." John stopped, picked up his pistol, and holstered it. He took the reins of both his and Clara's horses and started away from the camp. Clara followed but felt powerless to stop looking over her shoulder.

"Where is your mother?...and your father? You couldn't have travelled here alone?"

"Randall accompanied me. Most of the way...he was killed by Indians. I was...I was taken captive."

John stopped and searched Clara's face. "My God, Clara. Tell me everything."

"I don't know if I can." She looked over her shoulder again. Henry was walking toward them, his head down. "At least not now, and not here."

John looked toward the camp, then back to Clara. He nodded. They waited for Henry.

Henry looked at John solemnly.

"Do you know what happened here, Lieutenant?"

John averted his eyes. "Yes."

"I'd be grateful if you'd tell me."

John stared at his boots for nearly a minute. Clara was about to say something when he pursed his lips tightly, nodded once to himself, and lifted his head. He looked at Clara, then at Henry.

"The militia I was with attacked this Indian camp. We killed everyone in it. Women and children mostly, and a few old men. I was misled, but I'll make no attempt to excuse my actions."

"Oh, John," Clara said, looking horrified. She reached out and put a hand on his arm.

Henry's expression was one of naked anger and disgust. His voice, however, remained even. "War's over. Regular army's in charge now. What's militia doing out here?"

"We were supposed to be looking for hostiles. We were hunting some Indians who killed some settlers up by the Platte River. We came across this camp, and Frank Picton—he's a colonel, or was...I just realized I'm not certain which it is— ordered us to attack."

"Like Big Sandy Creek..." Henry said mostly to himself. He looked at Clara. "I'll lead you two back to Fort Laramie." He turned and started away to where Harriet waited."

"Wait. Please. He was about to attack another Indian camp, west of here. Seven days ago or thereabouts; I seem to have lost count. I refused to take part. That's when I left. He's going to resupply at Fort Laramie, then he plans to go north...he said to the Powder River. They're going to raid more camps. He's attempting to incite a war with the Indians. I have to try and stop him.

"Well, I wish you luck," Henry said without turning. "There's nothing I can do about it, and to be plain, I can't say I'd help you if I could."

"I can't take back what I did, but I can't let it continue without doing something. Aren't you friends with the Indians?"

Henry stood with his back to John and Clara and stared silently out over the prairie. Finally: "Things aren't so simple as that."

"John, perhaps you should let the army sort this out," Clara said. "You could wire your father. He could speak to someone."

"Clara..." John's voice wavered, and a single tear spilled from his eye. "I shot a woman who was running for her life. She was carrying a child...I killed her. I killed them both. I don't know how I'll live with this, but I know there *will* be no living with it if I don't do something."

Clara began to weep. She glanced at Henry. "John, I'm going to have our child."

He stared at her, mouth agape, crying openly now. He stepped forward, took her in his arms, and buried his face in her neck. That's wonderful news, Clara. We'll find somewhere to begin our life together. But first I have to stop Picton."

"Does the army know what he's doing?" Henry asked, turning to face them.

"I honestly don't know."

"How many men does he have?"

"About sixty-five. He might get more when he reaches Fort Laramie."

"There weren't many men there—at least when we left— and the ones that were, were all regulars. Does he have more on the way?"

"I don't know. It's possible...Clara was right. I'll wire my father. He might be able to help."

"That's good, I suppose, but if what you're saying is true, it could be too long of a wait for some." Henry was silent for a moment. "You left them seven days ago?"

"It could have been six, and I wasn't travelling very fast."

Henry wanted to ask why but decided to leave it alone. "Can you find Fort Laramie from here?"

"Yes."

Henry's eyes darted to Clara for the briefest moment before moving back to John. "Are you sure?"

John caught the look. "I am a trained cavalryman, and I keep my eyes open." He pointed north and slightly west. "A day's ride to the river, then we follow it. Satisfied?"

"Pardon me Lieutenant, mayhap you should listen—"

"I'm not a soldier anymore."

"Right. You give Miss Hanfield your pistol and keep your rifle out in plain sight. If you see any Indians, don't run, just keep moving same as if you didn't see them. If they come up on you, nod, smile, and offer them some tobacco." Henry put up his hand as he saw John was going to speak. "I'll give you the tobacco, but before you give it to them, hold it up and then run your finger down your face like this," Henry ran his finger over his scar. "When you do it, say *Nótaxemâhta'sóoma* then *Henry*. Hold up the sack, run your finger down your face, then say *Nótaxemâhta'sóoma*, then *Henry*."

John tried to repeat Nótaxemâhta'sóoma several times, but couldn't seem to pronounce the difficult vowels. "What does it mean?" John asked.

"Something the Indians call me. It's not important."

"Nótaxemâhta'sóoma," Clara said, almost perfectly.

"That'll do. It may or may not help. You'll have to hope they take the tobacco and go. If they try to take anything else from you, start shooting because they were going to kill you anyway. You'll be less likely to see anyone if you stay off the river until you get close to the fort. You can follow it from a distance" He shot a look back at the camp. "Were those four men part of this?"

"Yes...and no. They signed on with Picton but left shortly after the...after the attack here. They wouldn't kill women and children."

"It seems like good folks die in unfair numbers and men like this Picton—*and Emmet Dawson,* he thought—keep on taking breath. Where did you leave him and his men? I want to see this other Indian camp with my own eyes. I'll meet you back at Fort Laramie. You'll have questions to answer, I expect. There were some men looking for Miss Hanfield—from her family—but I reckon everything will be fine seeing she's with you now. How much food do you have?"

"Not much."

"I'll leave you with some."

4

Henry rode hard and reached the remains of the Arapaho camp in four days. He was loath to push Harriet, but she was a strong animal and if everything John Elliot had told him was true, his errand was an urgent one.

He smelled the buffalo long before he saw them. Once he reached the top of the low hills he could hear the flies buzzing as if he were locked in a room full of them. Looking down on the carcasses he wondered why so many animals were killed and left to rot.

When John first told of his part in the killings at the Cheyenne camp, there was a moment when Henry wanted to kill him. The urge had vanished as quickly as it arrived, but it left Henry feeling conflicted about the man. He'd admitted to the murder of innocents, and who was Henry to inflict justice on him? John's remorse and desire to stop more killing seemed veritable, and in the end Henry decided that stopping more killing was what mattered.

The scene at the Arapaho camp affected Henry in a deeper way than the charred and unrecognizable remains of the Cheyenne had. He wept openly as he walked Harriet past the bodies. Instead of being piled up and burned, the Arapahos were laid out in three neat rows on the horse-trampled ground. All of them—including two children not long out of infancy—

were scalped. Their belongings were slashed, tattered, and strewn about the prairie.

From the camp the men's trail was easy to follow, and it was clear they were on their way back to Fort Laramie. Henry wondered why John hadn't come this way as it was closer to the fort by days. He decided it must have been as simple as John choosing to go back the way he'd come because he'd feared getting lost. It showed good sense, in Henry's opinion.

Several miles north of the Arapaho camp he came upon two fresh, unmarked graves. *It cost them something, at least,* he thought, looking down at the mounds of naked earth. *Good.* He looked north. He figured Clara and John should only be a day away from Fort Laramie if they didn't run into any trouble. He guessed he'd arrive two days later if he took it easy on Harriet. He would. She'd earned it.

5

Clara and John only travelled five miles that first day before stopping. Considering how much they'd longed to be reunited, there was little conversation during the ride. What talk there was, was strained and regarded matters of little or no consequence. Clara was unsettled by John's revelations, though she told herself his intentions had to have been noble. As he said, he'd been misled. John would never deliberately harm anyone without just cause. She also desperately wanted to tell him of the violations she was forced to endure at the hands of Short Bull, but was afraid of how he would react. Would he turn away from her in disgust?

For John's part, he was ashamed. He wondered if Clara could ever feel the same about him after what he had done. He wanted to know about her captivity. His mind ran wild thinking about all of the horrible things she might have been forced to endure, but he was unsure of how to broach the subject. He should be comforting her.

And there was the child.

Neither could bring themselves to discuss the child when their future together seemed so uncertain.

They stopped for the night near a clump of scraggly, medicinal smelling bushes. The bushes didn't provide much cover, but the weather was warm nearing hot and there wasn't a cloud in the sky. The scrub did provide a place to tie the horses and slight break from the wind.

John laid out their bedrolls side by side, and Clara sat down while he got some of the dried beef.

"I had a jar of peaches, but I'm afraid I ate all of them," Clara said with a faint, apologetic smile.

"Peaches," John mused. "If I had a jar, I'd eat them all too. It seems like years since I've had a proper meal." He sat down next to her. "Clara, what's the matter?" She had begun weeping softly.

"I have something I have to tell you…but it's difficult."

"There isn't anything you can't tell me."

"I want to believe that."

"Then do." He reached out and put his hand to the side of her face. "Because it's true."

She told him everything, including details she hadn't felt comfortable sharing with Henry. John lay on his back next to her and watched the sky change from a brilliant blue, to a sooty gray, to a liquid black glowing with the brilliance of an uncountable number of stars. When she was finished he said: "I love you with all of my heart, Clara. Nothing can ever change that, but I have to stop Picton and bring into the light what's happening out here. I don't presume to understand the Indians, but it stands as self-evident that the Indians are not all devils like some would have us believe. I owe this debt at the very least. Afterward, we can go wherever you wish. We can be married as we have always planned, and raise our child away from our fathers' petty disputes and heavy-handed lordship over us…that is, if you'll still have me. I've done a terrible thing. Something that will haunt me for the rest of my life. I wonder if I deserve your love."

"You're a good man. You will always have my love."

6

They awoke with the sun, cradled in each other's arms. John shared out some of the dried beef and they both ate, albeit unenthusiastically. Desire for Clara had crept up on John shortly before he dropped off to sleep, but he didn't attempt to act upon it. He knew that now wasn't the time, and he was prepared to wait as long as Clara needed. He thought she would let him know.

Clara was jolted awake in the early hours of the morning with the same nightmare about Short Bull. John was fast asleep with his arm over her. His nearness comforted her, and she soon dropped off and slept dreamlessly until dawn.

After their breakfast John showed a reluctant Clara how to use his pistol. He had her practice dry-firing because he didn't want to risk gunshots drawing unwanted attention to them. He did his best to explain recoil to her so she would be prepared for it in the event that she actually had to fire it with live ammunition.

The lesson turned out to be unnecessary.

They spotted the soldiers around two that afternoon; twenty-five to thirty riders by John's estimation as he squatted in the grass, peering through his field glasses. The soldiers were moving along the river, travelling in the opposite direction of Clara and John. The two were travelling parallel to the river but about a mile away, as per Henry's advice. Assuming the troops had come from Fort Laramie, John thought they should ride to meet them.

The soldiers halted when they saw the two riders heading in their direction. As Clara and John neared, four riders broke away to meet them. Clara was disappointed but not surprised when she saw that Theo Brandt was one of them.

"Miss Hanfield, I'm happy to see you are alive and unharmed." Theo said. He cast a dark look at John. "Your father will be very pleased. He's been worried and is anxious for your return to New York."

"You can tell my father I'm not returning to New York and that he should no longer concern himself with my affairs,

Mister Brandt. I'm afraid you've travelled a long distance unnecessarily."

Sergeant Campbell saluted John. "Lieutenant Elliot," he said.

"You don't need to salute me, Sergeant. I'm not a soldier anymore."

Sergeant Campbell looked nonplussed. He turned his attention to Clara. "Miss Hanfield, I have orders to escort you back to Fort Laramie. Captain Lange wishes to speak with you." He turned back to John, "He'll want to see you too, Lieutenant…ahh, Mister Elliot."

"We were already on our way to speak with General Moonlight." He regarded Theo Brandt coolly. "I'll make it clear to you right now, Mister Brandt, Clara isn't going anywhere with you."

Theo smiled smugly but remained silent.

7

John told an increasingly disconcerted looking Sergeant Campbell about Colonel Picton and the raid on the Cheyenne camp. He omitted nothing. At John's request, the sergeant had agreed to ride a short distance ahead with John and Clara so that John could tell the story out of earshot of the other men. Theo Brandt eyed them with suspicion as they rode ahead.

"I knew there was something not quite right. No uniforms, Confederate prisoners, no drills. I asked Captain Lange what Colonel Picton and his men were doing, and he said 'keeping the trails safe.' "

"Is that what he said?" John mused. "That's the army's work, isn't it? Picton claims he's been tasked to do what the army can't."

"And what's that?"

"Start a war."

Sergeant Campbell was silent for some time. "You said he had you sign your discharge papers because the army couldn't be involved in what he was doing. Did he have some of his own? Is he still a colonel?"

John sighed. "I don't know."

8

They arrived at Fort Laramie the day after Henry had stood staring in silent disbelief at the slaughtered and mutilated Arapahos. Clara was provided a room in the officer's quarters along with a basin of hot water to wash with. Afterward her and John were given a hot meal. Around four in the afternoon they were summoned to a small office overlooking the parade grounds. Captain Lange sat behind a cluttered desk looking irritated and out-of-sorts.

"There's been quite a commotion over you, Miss Hanfield. Please sit down." He motioned to a lone chair in front of the desk. John remained standing.

"You appear to be in good health. Your family will be happy to know it. I was told that you were rescued from your Indian captors by the colored scout, Henry?"

"Yes I was. I am in his debt."

"Truly—"

"Captain Lange, we were hoping to see General Moonlight," John interrupted.

Captain Lange glanced at John impatiently. "General Moonlight is chasing renegades. I will have to suffice. As I was saying, Theo Brandt, your father's…representative, has left a five hundred dollar reward for Henry to show your father's gratitude. How was it he was able to free you?"

"He…he killed their chief."

"Did he? I wouldn't have expected that, knowing how friendly he is with them."

"Captain, I'd like to discuss Colonel Picton with you," John said. "It's a matter of some urgency."

"What does Colonel Picton have to do with Miss Hanfield?"

"Nothing, but if you're finished questioning Clara—you can see she is well—I'd like to bring some disturbing events to your attention."

"I'm sure your *urgent matter* can wait a few more minutes. Now, Miss Hanfield, I'm ordering a detachment of men to escort you and Mister Brandt to St. Joseph where you can secure transport back to New York—"

"She's not going back to New York," John said angrily just as Clara was saying the same thing.

"Corporal Harnett?" Captain Lange called out.

The door opened almost immediately, and a young soldier with a smattering of orange freckles across his nose and cheeks hurried in. He looked at the captain, then at Clara and John. His expression went from one of mild alarm to confusion.

"Corporal, arrest this man and get him out of here."

"Sir?"

"You heard me, Corporal."

The corporal drew his pistol. "Your sidearm," he said, holding his free hand out for John's pistol.

"You're arresting me on what charges?" John asked.

"Who said I'm charging you with anything? Get him out of here, Corporal. Now."

John glanced at Clara who was staring at him wide-eyed.

He smiled at her reassuringly and carefully removed his pistol from its holster and handed it butt first to the corporal. The corporal shoved it in the waistband of his trousers, then used his own pistol to motion John to the door.

Clara leaped from her chair, sending it clattering to the floor. *"No!"* she cried and grabbed onto John's shirt. "He hasn't done anything wrong and neither have I (the money she took from her father's study flashed briefly in her mind). We are leaving."

Captain Lange got up, came around his desk and took Clara firmly by her arm. "Holster your pistol, Corporal. Miss Hanfield, Mister Elliot will be freed as soon as you are well on your way back to New York. You can believe me when I say that I'd rather run barefoot through a briar patch than have anything to do with your personal affairs. The way things are, I've been ordered to see you off with Mister Brandt and that's what I'm going to do. Corporal, take him to an empty room in the officer's quarters and post a guard outside. Mister Elliot, if you make trouble I'll have you put in shackles."

"Clara, we were wrong to come here," John said. "I'm sorry."

"Move, Corporal. And find Lieutenant Blake and send him over."

Corporal Harnett took John by the arm to lead him away, but John shrugged loose. He gently pried Clara's fingers from his shirt and squeezed her hand while he leaned over and kissed her on her cheek. "I'll come for you," he said as he released her. He nodded to the corporal and started toward the door. The corporal followed and closed the door behind them. Captain Lange released Clara, then righted the fallen chair. He stood holding it for her, but she only stared at him with blazing eyes, her lips pursed so tightly they nearly disappeared. After a moment he walked around the desk and sat down.

Clara moved over to the window and gazed out at the empty parade grounds, wishing not for the first time that she'd been born a man.

Twenty minutes later there was a knock at the door.

"Come ahead," Captain Lange said.

A soldier in his mid-twenties with a thick, sandy colored moustache and ice-blue eyes stepped in and saluted. "You wanted to see me, sir?"

The captain returned the salute. "At ease, Lieutenant. Pick twenty men—not the ones who just came in with you, take some who haven't been out in awhile—and ready them to escort Miss Hanfield and her guardian to St. Joseph tomorrow morning."

The lieutenant glanced at Clara. "Sir, I just got back this morning—"

"Did I ask you to speak?"

"No, sir."

"Then close your mouth. You're going because I trust you. It's very important that Miss Hanfield makes it safely to St. Joseph. Ready your men, outfit a wagon, and meet me back here for supper. Dismissed, Lieutenant."

9

Captain Lange surrendered his own quarters to Clara and left a guard outside the door. She paced the room angrily, at one point overturning a trunk full of the captain's belongings—

mostly letters—and then kicking them across the floor. Afterward she felt childish and tired. She sat on the narrow pallet and wept. The next thing she knew she was being awakened by a knock at the door. She sat up. The knock came again, followed by a tentative voice. "Miss Hanfield?"

Clara stood and walked to the door. She opened it a crack. It was Sergeant Campbell.

"It's time to go, Miss Hanfield. There's a wagon waiting for you."

"Sergeant, you must know this is wrong. Can't you help us?"

"What I know doesn't matter much, Miss Hanfield. I've got orders and I have to follow them. I'll be back in fifteen minutes."

"John said he thought you might be someone he could trust."

Sergeant Campbell looked down at his shoes, turned, and walked down the short hall to the stairs. Clara shut the door and stood with her back to it. She looked at the mess on the floor for a moment, then got down on her knees and began picking up the scattered letters and other trappings of Captain Lange's life at Fort Laramie.

10

Sergeant Campbell returned as promised, and silently led Clara out to the waiting escort. It was just after sunrise. Theo Brandt sat atop the wagon next to a soldier. He flashed his winning smile; the smile she'd always distrusted when he came to discuss business matters with her father. Often he would stay for dinner, and he would sit and smile that smile at her and her mother. "Your father and mother will be happy to have you home," he said. Clara ignored him and climbed into the wagon. Once inside, she looked out at Sergeant Campbell.

"The horse I travelled here on, it belonged to Henry. Will you see it's returned to him?"

"I'd be happy to."

"Will you look after John and make sure he's not mistreated?"

"I'll do what I can for him."
"Goodbye, then."
"Goodbye, Miss Hanfield."

11

Henry rode into Fort Laramie forty-eight hours after Clara had departed with Theo Brandt and twenty-one soldiers. He corralled Harriet, and walked toward the Alden's store anticipating a cup of coffee and hopefully some biscuits before looking for John Elliot and Clara Hanfield. He was about halfway to the sutler's when he was approached by a red-haired corporal—Harnett, he thought his name was.

"Captain Lange wants to see you."

Henry looked at the store, then back at the corporal. "Now?"

"He said the minute you got in. He's had the whole fort watching for you."

Henry raised his eyebrows. "Where is he?"

"He's in General Moonlight's office. Follow me."

They cut across the parade grounds and into a small building adjacent to the officer's quarters. Corporal Harnett led Henry into the same small office that Clara and John had been brought to two days before.

"Hello, Henry," Captain Lange said from his seat behind General Moonlight's desk.

"Morning, Captain," Henry replied warily.

"Dismissed Corporal. Sit down please, Henry."

Henry sat.

Captain Lange leaned across the desk and held out a small leather sack. Henry looked at it, then at the captain. "Go ahead, it's yours," Captain Lange said, giving the sack a shake. It produced a musical jingling sound. "There's a hundred dollars gold in there. The Hanfield woman's father put it up in appreciation for what you did."

Henry took the offered money figuring he would give it to Clara. "I reckon they made it back here, then?"

"Safe and sound. Miss Hanfield is on her way back to New York—where she belongs if you ask me. A woman of her upbringing has no business on the frontier."

Henry stood. "Well, thank you." He turned to go.

"General Moonlight will want a report on the Indians who captured Miss Hanfield and murdered her escorts. He'll also want to know how you freed her and where they're located."

"It was Cheyenne Dog Men, twenty-five or thirty braves. They were camped on the White River. Only chance I came on them. I traded a knife for her."

"A knife?"

"That's right. I reckon they only took her because they didn't want to kill a woman."

"Is that a fact?"

"That's right."

"That's not exactly how Miss Hanfield told it. You be careful what line you're walking. Everyone mostly leaves you alone and you're afforded courtesies most coloreds would be envious of…just remember whose side you're on."

"I'll be mindful."

12

Henry wondered where John Elliot was. Captain Lange made no mention of him, and Henry didn't want to appear interested. After all she told him, he couldn't see Clara Hanfield deciding to go back to New York, and certainly not without John. Something wasn't right. He began looking for Sergeant Campbell.

As it turned out, Sergeant Campbell found him. Henry decided to go ahead and get the cup of coffee he'd wanted, and was sitting at one of the small tables in the Alden's store when Sergeant Campbell walked through the doorway.

"Thought you might be here," Sergeant Campbell said, as he removed his hat and walked over.

"Biscuit?" Henry asked as Sergeant Campbell sat down.

"Don't mind if I do."

"Would you like some coffee, Benjamin?" Ruby Alden called from somewhere out of sight.

"Yes, thank you."

Henry had a faint smile on his face.

"That's my name. She calls me by it because it's her brother's name." He dropped his voice to a near whisper. "I need to talk to you."

"I was intending to find you once I finished here. I wanted to think about a few things first."

"Does it have anything to do with Clara Hanfield?"

"A good portion of it."

Ruby Alden arrived with a steaming pot of coffee and a tin cup. "Here you are, Benjamin. Would you like some more, Henry?"

"No, thank you, Missus Alden."

"You two should really try tea. It's quite delicious. Give me a shout if you need anything else." She walked away and disappeared behind the counter and into the store's small kitchen area.

"What did you want to talk to me about?" Henry asked.

"Is it true what John and Miss Hanfield told me about Colonel Picton—who may or may not even be a colonel. At least not anymore. Did he really attack a Cheyenne camp full of women and children?"

"Yes. Then he and his men attacked an Arapaho camp down near the South Platte. Killed and scalped every single one of them. Seventy-three, by my count. Twenty-four of them children."

"My God. And you saw this for yourself?"

"That's right."

"I thought he was telling the truth," Sergeant Campbell mused.

"Who?"

"John Elliot."

"Where is he?"

"I'll get to that. Captain Lange sent me and some men out to chase you and Miss Hanfield down after I told him you'd found her. Her father has quite a reach. Well, we ran right into her and John by the Platte; that was our second day out. John told me about the Cheyenne camp and everything Frank Picton said to him. But yesterday when I told Captain Lange what John told me, he laughed at me. He said Colonel Picton and his men arrived here to resupply the same day I went after you and Miss Hanfield, and that Picton had said a Cheyenne war party attacked him and his men unprovoked. Then he said that John refused to fight, and fled the field. Captain Lange says Colonel Picton and his volunteers are doing important work—like keeping dogs around your chicken yard; a deterrent. He said Picton's protecting settlers, and that John Elliot is a liar and a coward."

"You think Captain Lange knows what Picton's really doing?"

Sergeant Campbell paused, seeming to think the question over. "No. No, I don't. I don't believe he knows much about anything. This post is a calamity—a disgrace, truth be told. What with the war, and the war ending, officers in and officers out, soldiers in and soldiers out: volunteers, regulars, galvanized Yankees, Indians. I don't like Captain Lange much—I don't believe anybody does—but he follows orders, plain and simple, and there are a lot of orders coming from a lot of different places right now."

"Would he send out some men to have a look at the Arapahos?"

"I already asked if he'd let me take some men to either verify or refute John's claims. He said I'd have to take it up with General Moonlight when he gets back if I'm that determined to ignore the chain of command and make an ass of myself."

"Will the general send someone?"

"Not on your life. He hates Indians. If anyone's privy to what Picton's up to, it's him."

"Isn't there someone else we could tell?"

"I'm only a sergeant, and you're a scout. There's no one."

"Where is Picton now, and where is John Elliot?"

"Picton moved out four days ago, north. John's in the officer's quarters. Captain Lange put him under arrest until Miss Hanfield and that smiling-eyed dandy, Brandt, are far enough away that he can't catch up and cause any trouble. The captain sent a twenty-one man escort with them to make sure they reached St. Joseph safely."

"Who's Brandt?"

"Theo Brandt. He's the one I told you about. Him and three other men have been here for weeks, camped just down the river. He's employed by her father, and travelled all the way here to bring her back to New York. I don't know where the other three went. They weren't around the morning Miss Hanfield left, and their camp's gone. My guess is once Brandt found out he was getting an army escort, he didn't see the point in paying them any longer."

Sergeant Campbell took a bite of his biscuit and a sip of coffee. He looked over his shoulder toward the counter to make sure they were still alone, then turned back to Henry. "I'm going to let him escape, tonight. I need you to take his horse and gear downriver and wait for him."

"I was intending to let Harriet rest until this evening, then I was going to ride north. I have to track down Colonel Picton and warn The Cheyenne before there's more killing—if there hasn't been already. I'll wait a couple more hours, I suppose— no more than that— if you reckon he wants to come along, but it's my guess he'll go after Miss Hanfield before he does anything else. Though, if it's like you say, I don't see what he's going to be able to do for her. Probably just get himself arrested again, or worse, shot. Why are you helping him? You could put yourself in some hot water."

"During the war I always felt I was doing what was right. Since I've been here…I don't know. I have half a mind to go with you myself, only I'd be in a lot more than just hot water if I did. John got a letter, it had been waiting here for him for a week or more. He told me it says his father shot himself dead back in New York. It's a shame... anyway, John seems like a good man. It's not much for me to forget to post a guard on his room tonight. I can't give him his weapons or other gear without giving myself away, so he'll have to make do. Whether he goes with you, or goes after Miss Hanfield is up to him. He wouldn't be doing wrong either way, would he?"

"I reckon not."

13

Lieutenant Blake called a halt. Clara climbed out of the back of the wagon, her legs stiff from the long ride. It wasn't even mid-morning but it was already hot. Her stomach was paining her more than usual, and she was feeling particularly tired and out-of-sorts. Her mood since departing Fort Laramie the previous morning had alternated between anger and despondency. The anger re-emerged every time she looked at Theo Brandt's face. Her father's henchman (that was how she thought of him) attempted to spark a conversation with her on several occasions. Clara ignored him. He appeared unperturbed, even when she afforded him a blistering look before turning away. She walked up the column to stretch her legs. Soon she would have to do her necessary, and possibly vomit. For now she fought back the latter and ignored the former. To Lieutenant Blake's credit, he'd been stopping the column in places with trees or tall brush nearby. She was supplied with a chamber pot, but the thought of using it in the wagon with men on horseback only a few feet away horrified her. She would rather endure the stares at her back as she walked off behind the trees—these from the soldiers who otherwise went out of their way to avert their eyes from her.

The wagon was midway between the column of mounted soldiers. Clara reached the front of the line and turned back. Lieutenant Blake, who was at the head of the column, tipped his hat to her and said, "Good morning, Miss Hanfield," as she moved past. She nodded an acknowledgement; she didn't blame him for following his orders, but she didn't want to speak to him, either.

A searing pain suddenly shot through Clara's abdomen, doubling her over. The pain was followed by a wave of faintness. The world's color grayed-out. She stumbled and fell to her knees. Warmth rushed from her vagina; blood soaked into the thick fabric of the riding habit and ran down her legs into her boots. The thirsty prairie soil between her feet turned the color of old bricks.

"Here, now!" a soldier exclaimed as he watched Clara first drop to her knees, then fall face first in the dust. He and several other soldiers—including Lieutenant Blake—dismounted and hurried to her side. Theo Brandt's attention had been elsewhere but he turned at the soldier's shout. Irritation crossed his features as he climbed from the wagon and strode briskly to the cluster of soldiers standing over Clara.

"Move back, please," he said. "Miss Hanfield, what's the matter?" He stopped short and stared open-mouthed at Clara.

"Reese, help me turn her over," Lieutenant Blake said to the soldier next to him. "The rest of you, back away."

They gently turned Clara over. "Oh, lord," the soldier said, seeing where her blood had soaked through the dark green skirt.

"Let's get her into the wagon," said Brandt, kneeling.

"You men! Move those horses, now. And get that wagon up here," Lieutenant Blake called out.

The lieutenant looked at Brandt. "What happened? Has she been wounded? Is she ill?"

"Neither that I'm aware of."

Clara moaned, her eyes fluttered open. Her look was one of confusion. She tried to push herself up.

Lieutenant Blake put his hands on her shoulders. "You lie still. We're going to help you into the wagon. Have you been wounded recently?"

Clara began to weep.

"Miss Hanfield—" Brandt began.

"Get away from me!" Clara screamed at him.

The wagon was driven up alongside Clara. "Let's get her inside," Brandt said softly, when what he really wanted to do at that moment was put his hands around Clara's throat and strangle the very life from her. He would have no choice but to take her back to that filthy military outpost with its stinking privies, uneducated plebes, and foul-mouthed unfortunates. He could only imagine what kind of man the doctor was. Regardless, it wouldn't be the doctor Jonathon Hanfield blamed if Clara died.

The three men lifted Clara and carried her to the wagon. She was still weeping. The soldier who had been driving crawled inside and helped guide her in. Once done, Lieutenant Blake began giving orders.

"Reese, I want you and Dunbar to ride back to the fort and collect Doctor Clark. We'll start back that way as quickly as is prudent."

"What do you think's wrong with her, Lieutenant?"

"I don't know. Get moving and don't spare the horses. Private Rains, bandages, now."

The lieutenant turned to Brandt. "Move away from the wagon, Mister Brandt."

"What are you talking about?"

"I want to speak with Miss Hanfield, and it's plain that you trouble her."

"She is my charge, Lieutenant."

"I beg to differ, Mister Brandt. She is *my* charge until which time we return to Fort Laramie. Now, please move away."

Brandt started to move. "You'd do well to mind your tone, Lieutenant Blake."

"I'll take that under advisement."

A young private handed Lieutenant Blake a bundle of cotton fabric. He took it without a word and walked the few steps to the back of the wagon. Clara was lying on her side with her arms covering her face.

"Miss Hanfield, I need you to tell me if you are wounded.... Miss Hanfield—"

"Leave me alone." Clara knew about the morning sickness from Lillian, the kitchen helper who allegedly informed Clara's father about Clara and John. Lillian's mother had suffered from it while pregnant with Lillian's younger brother. The morning sickness was *all* she knew about being pregnant. Nonetheless, there was no doubt in her mind; she'd lost the child.

Lieutenant Blake was uncommonly discomfited. He was married and knew of his wife's monthlies, but only in the vaguest sense. His wife was always secretive about the whole business. He thought the Hanfield woman had bled too much for it to be that, but he had no way of knowing for certain. He examined the floor of the wagon, it didn't appear there was any additional blood. There was quite a lot on her skirts and shoes, however.

"Miss Hanfield, if you're bleeding, we need to stop it or you will die. I'm going to toss in these bandages. Please hold them tightly over...over the wound. We're taking you back to Fort Laramie." He tossed the bandages. They landed near her head. She reached out and took them but didn't move to do anything with them.

"Thank you. Now please go away."

Lieutenant Blake closed the canvas and did as he was asked. "Let's move out," he said.

14

Henry watched from the porch of the Alden's store as the tired and ragged looking procession of soldiers filed onto the Fort's grounds. He assumed this was General Moonlight and the two hundred something men he'd departed with intending to run down the Indians who'd refused to live at Fort Kearny. Henry couldn't help but smile. The men were on foot. He imagined dozens of braves sneaking into the soldiers camp in the early hours of the morning and running off with their horses. He wondered how far the general and his men had to walk. His smile faded with this last thought. From what he'd learned about General Moonlight, Henry didn't think he'd let the incident go unpunished. He sighed. Things were getting worse.

He was dozing when Sergeant Campbell woke him twenty minutes later. We've had some luck. I guess you've noticed the fort's numbers have grown in the last hour. It was General Moonlight. Indians took their horses. They had to walk back some seventy miles. The commotion will make it easier for me to cut out John's horse. Why don't you get yours ready and tie it up by the corral. I'll bring out John's and tie it up next to yours. Then you can be on your way. I'll have him meet you a mile up the river after dark."

"Fair enough."

"Good luck, Henry."

15

"You hear they sent the doctor out for that woman everyone was making such a fuss about, Sergeant? They sayin' she might be dead."

Sergeant Campbell lost his count of the horses in the corral. He lowered his tally sheet. "Who told you that, Private Macklin?"

The private, a man from Tennessee who only six months before had been a Confederate soldier, spit tobacco juice. A goodish amount dribbled down his stubbly chin. "I went over to look in on the doctor—my corns have been paining me something fierce—and he was gone. Corporal over there—I cain't remember his name— told me the doctor lit out with a pair of Yank—sorry, a pair of *cavalrymen* right before noon. They told the corporal she was bleeding like a slaughtered hog, and there wasn't no hope she'd make it back here alive. Funny ain't it? After all the trouble on her account."

Sergeant Campbell handed the private a pencil and a scrap of paper. "Count them again, and write the number so you don't forget. I'll be right back."

"I cain't write."

Sergeant Campbell was already walking away. "You best not forget, then."

16

It was early evening by the time the wagon carrying Clara and Doctor Clark arrived back at Fort Laramie. When they reached the fort, the wagon was driven to the small adobe hospital while the hot and tired escorts saw to their mounts.

Doctor Clark and the wagon's driver escorted Clara up to the hospital with Theo Brandt right behind. They entered into a small vestibule. To Clara's right there was a short hall that opened into a large room lined with beds. From what little she could see, it looked as if all but one of them were empty.

Doctor Clark thanked the soldier and dismissed him. Then he told Brandt there was no need for him to wait; that he would send for him if he was needed. Brandt thanked him and walked out. He saw no need to stay as the doctor had already explained to him what happened: Jonathon Hanfield's daughter was a slut. Theo Brandt, however, had no intention of being the one to tell him. He went looking for Captain Lange.

"You can rest in here," the doctor said to Clara, as he opened a small door off the vestibule. "It's just a storeroom, but I sleep in here on occasion. The laundress just washed the sheets, and they're good ones. I brought them with me all the way from Vermont. I'll have you stay awhile, but as long as there's no more bleeding you should be able to resume your journey east the day after tomorrow...I already mentioned it to Mister Brandt, but I'll speak to Ruby Alden about finding you something else to wear. For now I have a nightgown you can put on. Give me a moment, I'll just go get it."

The tiny, dimly lit storeroom was cluttered with crates and cabinets. There was a small window, high on one wall. Dust motes danced in the minimal sunlight it provided. Clara moved to the corner and sat down on the edge of the narrow bed. A crate marked *Morphine* served as a bedside table. There was a single candle set in melted wax on top of it.

After a few minutes the doctor returned with a plain white gown over his shoulder, and an enamel basin full of water in his hands. He set the basin on the morphine crate, and laid the gown at the foot of the bed.

"I thought you might want to wash up a little better than we were able to do in the wagon." He removed a small square of fabric from his pocket and dropped it into the basin. "I'll go and see Ruby Alden about a proper dress, and I'll have some food brought a bit later. I was obligated to tell Mister Brandt what happened to you. It's up to him if he feels compelled to tell anyone else. I won't be speaking of it again."

Clara couldn't bring herself to look him in the eye.

He walked toward the door.

Finally she forced herself to speak. "Thank you, Doctor."

"I do what I can," he said without turning.

17

Doctor Clark returned some time later with a plate of beef, potatoes, and onions, and a pitcher of water. Clara was lying in the bed. She'd changed into the over-sized nightgown and had the bed sheet pulled up to her neck.

"I'm still trying to find a dress for you. Ruby Alden at the store is trying to locate one. I'm confident we'll find something before you leave here."

He set the plate and the pitcher on top of the morphine crate, then picked up the wash basin from the floor. The water in it was dark red. He walked out and returned a few moments later with a cup, a chamber pot and several matches. He put the chamber pot on the floor at the foot of the bed, and set the matches and the cup on the morphine crate.

"How are you feeling? Will you eat something?"

"Better, thank you. Doctor...do you know if John Elliot is still here? He...I arrived here with him. He was put under arrest—"

"I'm sorry. I wouldn't know anything about that. Would you like me to get a message to Captain Lange or General Moonlight?"

"No. No, thank you. Thank you for the food."

"You're welcome. I'll look in on you later."

18

Clara awoke with a start. It was completely dark and she was momentarily disoriented. There was a thump from somewhere on the other side of the door, then she heard a voice call out in a muffled shout/whisper: *"Clara!"*

At first she couldn't credit her own ears, but then it came again, *"Clara!"* It was followed by a second voice: "Shhhh…"

"John?" Clara said to the darkness.

"Here…she's in here."

The door opened. Clara's eyes had adjusted enough to see two shadowy figures enter. She threw off the sheet and sat up. "John? I'm here."

John rushed over and kneeled in front of her. "Dear God, Clara. What happened? Are you hurt?"

"Our child…" Clara burst into tears. "Our child is gone."

"Oh, oh, Clara, darling, I'm so sorry. This has all been my fault."

"I'm sorry. I truly am, but we have to go—now. Miss Hanfield, can you walk? Can you ride?"

"Sergeant Campbell?"

"Yes. We have to leave, right now."

"I can walk."

"Then come on and follow me."

John took Clara's hand and led her out of the storeroom. There was a little more light and John saw she was dressed in only a nightgown, and barefoot as well. "Clara, your clothes—"

"They're covered in blood."

"Get them anyway, John. We can wash them later, in the river," Sergeant Campbell said.

"Clara, where are they?"

She led him back into the storeroom.

"That you, Doc?" came a voice from deeper in the hospital. "Doc, my leg's on fire. Doc?"

"Hurry," Sergeant Campbell hissed.

Clara and John came back out of the storeroom and Sergeant Campbell turned for the door. He opened the door slightly and looked across the parade grounds at the cavalry barracks, several men stood outside talking. He looked right, then left. "Come on," he said, opening the door and walking down the porch steps. At the bottom he turned left and walked briskly to the end of the building where he turned left again. He could hear Clara and John right behind him.

Once behind the building they were completely obscured. The horses were tied by the river, about two hundred yards away. They would be exposed for a short period before they reached them, but the moon was waning and the night was very dark.

"You can still go back. Maybe you won't be blamed," John said without much conviction.

"I've made my decision, for my own reasons. We need to hurry, Henry won't wait. You two go; straight that way and up the river. I'll be right behind."

John started off. It took a great effort for him not to run. Clara pulled back against his grip and whispered, "Let go, you're hurting me." He released her hand but kept looking back to make sure she was following.

They reached the river, and the horses. There were only two, one was the roan Henry had purchased for Clara. Sergeant Campbell mounted the other one. "That isn't an army horse, is it?" John asked, while helping Clara up on the roan.

"I may be a deserter, but I'm not a horse thief. This one is mine. Come on."

John climbed up behind Sergeant Campbell because it would be too difficult to double on the sidesaddle.

John turned to Clara. The white nightgown gave her a ghostly look in the faint moonlight. "Are you certain you can ride?"

"Yes. Please, can we get away from here?"

"Follow me," Sergeant Campbell said.

19

Henry looked up when he heard the voices. Not one, but two horses. He stood and walked over to Harriet. Keeping an eye on the approaching silhouettes, he eased the Spencer rifle from its scabbard.

"...should be getting close."

"He *did* give you his word he'd wait?"

Henry relaxed. He gave a short whistle.

"Henry?"

"That's right." He returned the Spencer to its scabbard. "I reckon some things changed," he said when they got close enough for him to identify them. "Hello, Miss Hanfield," he said.

"Hello, Henry."

He turned to the pair riding double. "Lieutenant...Sergeant."

"John. Please, just John from now on."

"Good to see you, Henry. Though I didn't think it'd be so soon. I guess since we're all just citizens now, you might as well start calling me Ben."

Henry smiled faintly in the darkness. "That may take some getting used to, and I reckon citizen isn't what the army will be calling you. Your horse is over here, John. I really have to get a move on."

"We're going with you," Clara said.

Henry looked up at her, then at John.

"We've already decided. I have to see this through, and we'll not be parted again," John said.

Henry was silent for a long time. At last he said: "I guess I'll be going on alone. You do what you believe is right." He turned to Benjamin Campbell. "Sergeant...*Ben,* I don't know your reasons for being here but you're welcome to come along with me. I won't be responsible for what might happen to Miss Hanfield, and, respectfully, Miss Hanfield, you'd slow me down and I just can't have that. I've lost too much time already." He turned toward Harriet.

"They'll be looking for us. Where are we supposed to go?" Clara asked.

Henry stopped and turned back. He sighed and regarded Clara. "You're wearing nightclothes."

"I have her dress and shoes right here. They need to be laundered," John said.

Henry turned back to John. It was too dark for John to see the open anger on Henry's normally impassive face. "There might be fighting."

John climbed off of Ben's horse. "We've spoken of it."

Henry was silent for a time. Finally he walked to Harriet and untied her. "I scouted up ten miles before it got dark. They followed the river. We'll go that far, then wait for sunup."

20

Clara, John, and Ben explained everything to Henry as they rode northwest up the Platte River, one picking up the narrative where another left off. Henry listened in silence, he was deeply saddened to hear of Clara's loss. It only reinforced his feeling that she shouldn't be along, and intensified his anger at John for insisting that they go.

John told of the letter he received while confined in the officer's quarters. It was from his father's closest friend and business associate. The letter told of his father receiving notification that his federal shipping contracts would not be renewed as usual come their expiration in July. Three days later he received a letter from his bank calling in all of his loans due to his imminent insolvency. He shot himself at his office on the docks that same day.

They stopped several hours before dawn at a sizeable copse of trees. Henry suggested everyone try to get some sleep. No one did. When it was light enough to see, John took Clara's dress and shoes down to the river and began washing them. When Henry saw what he was doing he removed something from his saddlebags and followed.

"Blood's probably not going to come out. This might fade it some, though."

John was hunkered by the quickly moving water. He turned and took the offered cake of soap.

"Thank you."

Henry nodded, then turned to go.

"You think I'm wrong for bringing Clara?" It was almost a rhetorical question.

"Yes."

"What would you have done? Would you have left her there?"

"It doesn't make any difference, what I would have done. You can keep the soap."

Henry walked the short distance back to the trees and stopped dead.

"You just keep coming, nigger," Emmet Dawson said, pointing a rifle at Henry. "James, go get the one by the river and bring him up here with the rest." Emmet glanced quickly at the Beaderman brothers. "Gentlemen, you are experiencing divine providence first hand—come on now, boy, kneel down here next to these other two. After all these years, God has put you in my path once again. This time His justice will be served."

"Like the justice you served on Eliza?"

"Your whore only reaped the harvest she had sown."

Henry let out a wail of rage and rushed at Emmet. Emmet turned the rifle and hit him in the forehead with its heavy stock. There was a hollow sounding thud, and Henry fell to the ground.

"George, tie him," Emmet said. "Then tie the rest of them."

"What's this all about?" Ben Campbell asked.

"Clara!" John called, breaking into a run.

"You hold on or I'll shoot you," James called from behind him.

John ignored him and knelt by Clara. "What is this? I know you. All of you," he said angrily.

"This nigger," Emmet kicked Henry in the side, "is an escaped slave."

"Slavery's been abolished. Or haven't you heard?" Ben said.

"I will not explain myself to a Yankee."

George Beaderman approached Ben. "Give me your hands and shut your mouth, Yank, before I shut it for you."

"War's over too, you ignorant pie eater. Your side lost," Ben said vehemently.

George pulled his pistol and aimed it at Ben's face. "Mister Dawson, I'm going to shoot this blue belly scum."

"Please do, George."

The report was deafening. Clara, who was only inches away, could barely hear her own scream as she watched the back of Ben Campbell's head explode outward in a spray of blood and brains.

Ben's body pitched sideways into the dust, and Clara watched in horror as a tendril of smoke rose lazily from the hole in his forehead. George Beaderman turned the pistol on John. "Now, you want to give me your hands, or you want a ball in your head too?"

After George Beaderman tied John and Clara's hands, he tossed John's pistol aside and holstered his own. He then helped his brother and James Dawson lift Henry onto a horse they'd culled from their captive's string. Ben's horse.

"No!" Clara shouted frantically. "Theo Brandt must have informed you that my father is very wealthy. Please, take us back to Fort Laramie. I'll send a wire to him—"

"Tie his hands. Quickly, he's waking…" Emmet Dawson turned to Clara. "I have every confidence Mister Brandt will pay us whatever reward we desire for your safe return, Miss Hanfield. It was fortuitous that we recognized your horse and saddle in the nigger's possession. Otherwise we would have hanged him yesterday afternoon and been done with it. I suspected he was waiting for you. Perhaps you have a taste for the darkies."

"I'll kill you," John said.

"George, finish hanging this nigger then gut-shoot the other Yankee. His nigger-loving jezebel can watch him die."

"Mister, whatever you think I did, you're mistaken," Henry said, swaying slightly on the horse. "I was a free man then, and I'm a free man now. Only difference is, now I'm not afraid of you, or what you're about to do."

James threw the noose over a thick branch and slipped it over Henry's head. Henry didn't struggle.

"You can reunite with your black whore in hell," Emmet Dawson said, and slapped the horse in the thigh.

Clara shrieked as the horse bolted out from under Henry. John struggled to his feet, only to be knocked back down again by Wayne Beaderman's boot. Henry's legs flailed and kicked out wildly. Clara managed to stand. Emmet Dawson stumbled toward her. He was clutching at something protruding from his throat. Blood was gushing from his mouth and he was making choked, retching noises. On his face was an expression of bewilderment. He dropped to his knees.

"Pa!" James shouted and started toward his father. He only made two steps before letting loose a scream and falling to the ground. He twisted and writhed and moaned in pain. His hands reached fruitlessly for the arrow in his back.

Wayne and George Beaderman spotted the lone rider and started shooting; all other concerns were forgotten. The rider was coming fast, and straight at them.

"Lie down on the ground, Clara," John shouted as he struggled to his feet again. "It's Indians." He ran to Henry and tried to get underneath him. Stars exploded in his vision as Henry kicked him in the face with one thrashing boot-clad foot. He tried to get under him again, "Henry…Henry stand on my shoulders!" he yelled up to him. Henry didn't seem to hear.

Standing Elk's horse charged forward. He nocked another arrow, aimed, and let it go. This time the arrow missed, and he calmly slung the bow over his shoulder. He lifted the revolver Henry had given him more than four years before from where it hung from his neck by a rawhide thong. Sliding his body down the left side of his horse to where he was nearly lying on it, he clung to the animal with one hand and held the pistol with the other.

"Shoot the goddamn horse, Wayne! Shoot the goddamn *horse!*" George shouted at his brother seconds before Standing Elk's charging mare trampled over him, cutting off his voice forever. Standing Elk pulled himself upright and heaved back on the reins. He wheeled and fired the pistol. The bullet took off Wayne Beaderman's right ear. Beaderman dropped his rifle and started running toward the river. Standing Elk shot him in the back.

Henry's struggles were weakening. Standing Elk rode up and cut the rope where they'd tied it off to a low branch. Henry dropped to the ground in a heap. Clara got up and ran to him. John stood several feet away, massaging his jaw. He stared at Standing Elk warily.

Standing Elk dismounted, unslung his bow and quiver of arrows from his shoulder, and leaned them against a tree. James Dawson cried out weakly. He was crawling toward his father. Standing Elk strode over to him, batted away his hat, and grabbed a handful of his hair. He yanked back—hard—while simultaneously removing the elk-horn handled knife from the sheath on his leggings. James Dawson let out a womanish scream of fear and pain. Standing Elk dropped to one knee and quickly swiped the knife across his throat before releasing him and letting him collapse to the ground. His legs kicked weakly for several seconds before becoming still. Standing Elk stood. John was staring at him, wide-eyed. He spared John a brief glance, then dismissed him. He walked to where Henry lay unmoving in the dirt and squatted next to Clara, giving her a curious look before nudging her aside. She recoiled from his touch but stayed by Henry. Standing Elk leaned over and put his ear by Henry's mouth. He began singing something under his breath. It was simple and melodious, and consisted of mostly vowel sounds. After a moment he turned to Clara and said, "Water."

Clara stood, but John was already awkwardly taking the canteen off of his saddle with his tied hands. Ben Campbell had loaded the horses with food and water before sneaking John out of the officer's quarters. *He risked a lot,* John thought sadly. He stared down at Ben's body.

"Give it to me," Clara said, taking the canteen from his hand. He looked up, startled from his thoughts, but said nothing.

Clara stood over Standing Elk. Holding out the canteen with her bound hands. He was probing around the back of Henry's neck with one hand.

"Is he going to live?" Clara asked, her voice wavering.

Standing Elk stood, grunted something Clara couldn't understand, and walked to his horse. He untied his medicine bag from around the horse's neck and returned to Henry, wordlessly taking the canteen from Clara before squatting back down beside his friend and beginning to sing again. He removed a small, folded piece of hide from his medicine bag and dumped the brown, powdery contents into his hand. Setting the bag down, he removed the stopper from the canteen with his teeth and poured a few drops of water onto the powder. He set the canteen aside and used a finger to mix the powder into a paste. This he spread over the thick, angry looking weal on Henry's neck. With a satisfied nod, he stood and walked over to the broken and battered body of George Beaderman.

"Excuse me." John said, walking over and standing next to Clara. "Do you speak English?"

Standing Elk acted as if he didn't hear. He picked up George Beaderman's pistol and examined it briefly before setting it aside and removing Beaderman's belt and holster.

"You're Standing Elk," Clara said. It wasn't a question. "Please. Will he live?"

Standing Elk stood. He put George Beaderman's belt around his waist and holstered the dead man's pistol. He pulled his knife from its sheath and approached Clara and John. John stepped protectively in front of Clara. Standing Elk reached out and took him firmly by one forearm and flicked the knife through his bonds. He handed John the knife, hilt first, then pushed him aside, though not roughly. Standing Elk studied Clara's face. "He will live," he said, then started off toward the body of Emmet Dawson. He stopped short to pick up a pistol.

"That's my pistol," John called after him while cutting Clara's bonds with Standing Elk's knife. Standing Elk examined the Remington, then looked at John. He turned his attention back to the Remington after affording John the same dismissive look he'd given him just minutes before.

"It's his," Henry croaked. He pushed himself up to a sitting position. Clara ran to him. Standing Elk glanced his way, then took one last look at the pistol. He dropped it to the ground and walked over.

"Haaahe, Nótaxemâhta'sóoma," Standing Elk said, sitting down cross-legged in front of Henry.

"Haaahe," Henry returned hoarsely. Then switching to English: "You're going to call me that now?"

Standing Elk smiled almost wryly. "I gave you this name."

Henry looked past Standing Elk, his expression changing from one of reserved gladness to one of sorrow. He stood, wavering slightly before finding his balance. He walked over and stared down at the body of Ben Campbell.

Standing Elk came up beside him.

"You killed all of them?" Henry asked.

"Héehe'e."

Henry nodded. "We have to get moving, but first I want to bury him."

"This is what the whites do. Then you hunt whites who kill Indians." Both were stated with Standing Elk's familiar matter-of-fact way.

"You know about the Cheyenne and Arapaho camps?"

"Héehe'e."

"How long have you been following me?"

"Since Hotoa'ohtšéhe'kėstaestse was killed for a white woman. His son, Ho'neoxhaaestse, says he will kill the one who killed his father. He says the one who killed his father is…óvahe…a coward."

"Do you say the same?"

"Short Bull took what was not his. You should not speak so much. Your voice needs to heal. I will prepare a pipe while you put the white soldier in the earth."

Standing Elk walked over to Emmet Dawson. "This was their Chief?"

Henry nodded. Standing Elk removed Emmet Dawson's pistol belt and pulled the pistol from the holster. It was a Colt Navy, identical to the one Henry had given him. He re-holstered it, walked back over to Henry, and handed it to him without a word.

21

Henry and John went about the task of burying Ben Campbell. They worked slowly and in silence. Henry was suffering from the worst headache of his life, and John was preoccupied with his guilt: his guilt for murdering the Cheyenne woman and her child, his guilt for his father's suicide, and his guilt for not immediately taking Clara as far away from the God-forsaken prairie as their horses would take them. Both men were digging with knives and their hands. When they were finally finished, it was shallower than Henry would have liked. Clara offered to help gather rocks for a cairn, but she was flushed and tired looking. John told her they could manage without her and suggested she sit in the shade of a tree and rest. Standing Elk filled his pipe, set it aside, and began stripping Emmet Dawson and his men of everything he deemed useful. Clara looked away when he started removing their clothes.

"Shouldn't we bury those men as well?" John asked.

Henry glanced at the bodies. "No."

"Why is he taking their clothing?"

"Couldn't say."

"I'm going to take Clara away from here—now, today. South, to Colorado for a start. Then to Texas or California…I'm sorry, Henry, I should have done it before."

Henry stopped and looked at John. "Sometimes doing right isn't so simple as you'd think. You want to believe everything is a choice between right and wrong, but it isn't. Sometimes you have to choose between right and right. Seems like it'd be easy. For some reason it never is."

"What if your choices both seem wrong?"

"I reckon you should feel lucky that's not what you're faced with. Come on, let's bring him over here."

After they dragged Ben's body into the grave, Henry covered him with his bedroll. They backfilled until there was a short mound, then gathered rocks from the river for the cairn.

"Either of you want to say anything?" Henry asked John and Clara.

"Perhaps you should." John said.

"I reckon not."

Henry walked over to where Standing Elk was sitting on the ground and cutting the dead men's clothing into long, thin strips. Clara and John followed. Standing Elk looked up from his work as they approached.

He spoke in English: "I will ride and gather many warriors. You find these Indian killers. If they did not follow the river, leave these for sign."

"They'll be easy enough to find without those," Henry said.

"I will not be searching for them. I will be searching for you."

Henry looked puzzled.

"He doesn't want Picton to know he's coming with an army of Indians," John said. "You locate Picton, then just track him from a long distance. When Standing Elk arrives with his warriors, they'll still have the element of surprise."

Henry nodded. "How long?"

Standing Elk waved a hand. "Many days."

John looked at Clara. "I want to get you to a city. Denver, for now."

"They need you," Clara replied.

"You heard him. He's going to gather an army of Indians to go after Picton and his men. As for whoever set him and this awful scheme in motion, I'll write a letter to the Secretary of the Interior demanding an investigation. We can post it when we reach Denver. Clara, you don't look well. I'm a fool. This is no place for you. This is no place for either of us."

Clara was silent for a moment. Finally, she looked at Henry and smiled. "Henry, thank you for everything you have done for us. I won't forget you."

"My pleasure, Miss Hanfield."

Clara turned to Standing Elk. "Thank you for coming to our aid, and for saving this good man's life—twice now, from what I'm told."

Standing Elk stared up at Clara but said nothing. He stood up and walked over to the pile of belongings he'd taken from Emmet Dawson and his men. He selected a Burnside rifle along with about twenty cartridges wrapped in a piece of oilcloth, and presented it to John. John took the rifle and ammunition, and after a short deliberation walked over to his horse and removed his cavalry sword. The elaborately decorated sword had been a gift from his father. He hadn't worn it a single time since leaving the military academy, not even when he rode into the Indian camp expecting a battle. He caught Henry's eye on the way back; Henry gave him an almost imperceptible nod.

He held the sword out to Standing Elk who took the offered gift, removed it from its scabbard, and examined it closely. He held it up in the air; the dappled sunlight filtering through the trees flashed brightly on the immaculate blade. He uttered a satisfied grunt and returned the sword to its scabbard.

He put a hand on John's shoulder and nodded once. "Épéheva'e….It is good."

22

Three hours later they were prepared to go their separate ways. After discussing it with Standing Elk in Cheyenne, Henry convinced John and Clara to take the two best horses out of the four the Dawson's and Beaderman's had been riding.

"If one of yours comes up lame, you'll have another—and one to carry your supplies. I don't need much, and neither does Standing Elk, so we loaded up most of what food and water is here for you two. If you stick to the way I told you, you won't likely run into anyone before you reach Colorado. Just make sure the horses drink their fill at the water stops, because it's a long way between them."

John extended a hand. "Good luck."

"Thank you," Henry said, shaking it.

Clara threw her arms around Henry and hugged him fiercely. "My dear, Henry. Thank you."

Henry was momentarily taken aback but returned the embrace with a faint smile. The smile faded when he felt the side of Clara's face.

He gently broke away. "You feel feverish."

"Well, it's hot. You should try wearing one of these." She waved her hand over the thick riding habit. John had finished rinsing it out in the river before he helped Henry bury Ben Campbell. Afterward he laid it in the sun to dry. It was still damp in places, the blood stains had faded, but were still clearly visible.

"You should have a hat, anyway," Henry said.

John turned to Clara, "You can wear mine. I'll cut a piece of the nightgown you were wearing and line the inside so it will fit better."

"There's no cause to worry over me. I'm a bit tired but feeling quite well otherwise."

"I guess you should be on your way, then," Henry said.

Clara and John mounted their horses. Henry tethered the spare to Clara's, and the pack horse to John's.

"Wait, almost forgot," Henry said, and strode over to Harriet. He removed a small sack from his saddlebags, then returned and handed it to Clara.

"There's a hundred dollars in there. My reward for rescuing you."

"I can't accept this. You deserve ten times as much…" She smiled ruefully. "Theo Brandt told me he'd been offering five hundred. It appears you've been cheated."

"I'd still like you to have it. You'll need it in Denver."

"Thank you, Henry."

"My pleasure, Miss Hanfield."

"Please, call me Clara."

Henry smiled. "My pleasure, Clara.

Sixteen

1

Following Picton and his men wasn't difficult. The signs from the nearly seventy riders and the handful of pack-horses were plentiful. The remnants of their camps stank of urine and feces. There were discarded whiskey bottles, bean sacks, scraps of cloth, and the greasy looking remains of burned out campfires.

Picton's trail exited the river and headed roughly northwest less than two days out of Fort Laramie. Henry thought Picton might sweep around and pick up the Bozeman Trail, but he didn't. He began tying strips of cloth to scrubby bushes and tree limbs to mark his passage for Standing Elk.

He found the dead Sioux three days after parting company with the others.

The corpses were lined up just like the Arapahos had been. Fourteen of them, all braves, mutilated by Picton's men, then picked over by scavengers. Henry figured the Sioux had been on a hunt. He dismounted and walked Harriet down the line of bodies. He wondered not for the first time what was in men—or missing from them—that made them capable of such acts. He wondered if he had the right to claim he was any different. Hadn't he himself struck—and possibly killed—another man to take what that man possessed because he believed he needed it more? The questions were troubling. He thought of what Standing Elk had said as they sat and smoked while watching Clara and John fade into the shimmering distance.

He coughed smoke. His throat burned like he'd swallowed an ember.

"Do not breathe in the smoke. It must rest in your mouth, then you may set it free," Standing Elk said in Cheyenne.

Henry did as he was told. He drew in the smoke and held it in his mouth for a few moments before opening it and letting the smoke drift slowly out. Standing Elk nodded his approval. Henry passed the pipe, but Standing Elk just held it in his lap.

"The white man only knows desire, Nótaxemâhta'sóoma. He knows nothing of contentment. His heart is dry and withered, and he seeks to revive it with that of which has no

medicine. He is careless and wasteful, and places himself above and apart from all other things. The white soldiers murder without regard, but themselves are spiritless and go screaming into their own deaths as they were born into life. The white father would take all of our hunting grounds and leave our children with stomachs full of air and hearts full of hate. There can be no peace with such men. We will kill this murderer of The People, but it will not stop the whites. There will be more. Many more."

Henry thought about Short Bull. He thought about his father, whom he didn't even remember. He thought about Picton and the men who followed him. He thought about the man by the river. Henry understood then, that there was something in Standing Elk's words that belonged to all men.

2

The next day he found their campfires still smoldering. He was close.

Seventeen

1

Clara was bleeding again. She'd taken a piece of the cotton nightgown and put it between her legs when they stopped to water the horses. Now, less than two hours later, she could feel blood dripping down her leg. The wad of fabric had completely soaked through.

"I'm afraid I have to stop," she said.

John was travelling just ahead of her. He twisted around in the saddle. "Can you make it to those bluffs up ahead? We'll find some shade there."

"Yes."

They reached the line of bluffs about twenty minutes later. Towering red sentinels overlooking a dry and empty landscape. They came to a place where two bluffs met and there was a deep U-shaped divide between them. The sun was low in the west, and John thought it as good a place as any to stop for the night. He urged his horse toward the cleft and stopped just inside. It was shaded from the afternoon sun, and easily ten degrees cooler than out in the open.

John dismounted and hurried around to assist Clara. He helped her down. Her face was a sickly white except for the angry looking red blotches high on her cheeks.

"Please walk away," she said. "Go and look around. You can return in a little while."

"Clara, what's wrong?"

"I'm bleeding," she whispered, as if someone might overhear.

"Oh, no. What can I do? Let me help you."

"No. Please, just go. I'll be fine."

John hesitated.

"Please," she repeated.

He nodded. "Just let me tie up the horses."

2

As soon as she felt he was far enough away, Clara removed the canteen from her horse and walked in the opposite direction with one hand pressed between her thighs to keep the blood-soaked cloth in place. She made for a pile of house-high rocks that had at some point separated themselves from the bluffs. As soon as she was behind them she let the bloody remnant of the nightgown drop. It made a sickening *sploosh* sound when it hit the ground. Clara removed the stopper from the canteen with a shaky hand. She bent and lifted the hem of the riding habit; a wave of dizziness washed over her, she dropped the canteen and uttered a breathless, "Oh, no," before fainting.

3

"Clara? Clara, darling?"

Clara's eyes fluttered open. John was kneeling over her. He was wetting a scrap of cloth with water from his canteen. He laid it on her forehead. It was blessedly cool.

"I'm so hot," she said.

He put his hand behind her head and gently lifted it. "Here, drink a little."

She pushed the canteen away. "Oh, John. I should have stayed in New York. I should have waited for you to return. So much has happened. I'm responsible for Randall's death. Kind, gentle, Randall. I'm so sorry. And the sergeant—Ben. He…he—"

"He was doing what he believed to be right. So was Randall. None of this is your fault. If there is blame to be placed, it should be placed on me. *I'm* the one who should never have left New York. I should have protested the ridiculous punishment levied on me without process. I should have pushed my father to provide me with proper legal counsel instead of worrying over the Elliot's good name being shamed in the newspapers. We're here, now, and we're together. I will never let you out of my sight again. I love you, Clara. Now please, drink some water, then I'm going to carry you out of the sun where you can rest."

She nodded her head and he brought the canteen to her lips. He could feel the heat emanating from her face on the back of his hand. He pushed back the tears that threatened to come and set the canteen aside.

"I'm going to lay out a blanket for you." He hurried over to the horses and removed a bedroll. He spread it out in the shade of the narrow divide then returned for Clara.

"All you need is some more rest, darling," he said as he gently lifted her. "We have plenty of food and water; we'll stay here until you're well again." He knew there was no water for the horses, but thought they could endure two or three days and still carry him and Clara to the next hole. He laid her down on the blankets. There was a smear of blood on his shirtsleeve where he'd had his arm underneath her. He'd seen the bloody remnant of the nightgown lying next to where he'd found her. He retrieved what was left of it from her saddlebags and tore it into several pieces.

"Clara, you're still bleeding," he said, squatting next to her. "Can you put this between your legs?"

She nodded and took the wad of cloth from him. He turned his head away.

4

Clara worsened during the night. She floated in and out of consciousness, sometimes muttering things John couldn't understand. He stayed awake and kept exchanging the fever-heated cloths on her head and neck for cool ones. Twice he changed the saturated wads of the nightgown, but by dawn the flow of blood had stopped almost completely. He drew some hope from this.

By noon she seemed a little better. She drank a fair amount of water, and even took a few small bites of dried beef. John thought her color was better and she felt a bit cooler.

Though she slept most of the day she was clearheaded and in better spirits during the times she was awake. John spoke softly to her of the hours they'd spent walking by the lake near her family's farm at Cornwall. She even laughed a little when he brought up the time when a large and ill-tempered gander had bitten him and then chased him into the water. They agreed it was only a matter of time before she would be strong enough to travel.

Later that night her fever intensified to the point that she was completely delirious. She shouted curses at her father and swiped feebly at the air. She had fits where she wept uncontrollably. John finally stripped off the heavy riding habit. Its stench of blood, urine, sour sweat, and something foul and unnamable nearly made him vomit. Tossing the soiled dress aside he could scarcely believe the amount of heat coming from Clara's body. He upended one of the canteens over her, and she began to shiver. Her teeth chattered so loudly he feared they would break. John laid himself beside her and put his arms around her. He held her close; despite the shivers, her heat was enough to break a sweat on him. Soon the shaking passed and she fell into a fitful sleep. John held vigil, wetting scraps of the cloth and wiping her body down. At some point in the early hours of the morning, he dozed.

When he awoke, Clara was dead.

5

John sat in front of the grave with the pistol's muzzle pushed firmly against the soft skin below his chin. Tears blurred his vision. He attempted to pull the heavy sidearm's hammer back, but it slipped from his blood-slicked hand and clattered to the ground. He squeezed the tears from his eyes and looked dumbly at his fingers. They were raw and still bleeding from pulling stones from the rocky soil. He lowered his hands and stared at the grave.

"I'll be with you soon," he said. Fresh tears spilled from his eyes.

He picked up the pistol and slid it into its holster, then walked to the horses and began removing all of the gear (excluding his own) from them and letting it drop to the ground. "Go on, you're free," he said, releasing the horses.

John Elliot mounted his big stallion and rode away.

Eighteen

1

Henry watched the men through his field glasses. It was less than an hour from sundown, and they were setting up camp near a stream at the base of some bluffs. Earlier he'd almost been spotted by an Indian—probably a Pawnee—who was watching Picton's back-trail, but the Indian had been distracted by something farther away and to Henry's left. Henry had dismounted and coaxed Harriet to the ground where he lay next to her with his arm over her neck. The Indian, who was only a few hundred feet away, caught the movement in his peripheral. His eyes passed over Henry several times before he turned his horse and moved on. The encounter told Henry that Picton wasn't as careless as he'd begun to believe he was. He wondered how many scouts Picton had watching his flanks.

2

The next morning, well before sunup, Henry rode east for five miles before turning north, skirting well around Picton's camp. He decided it would be best for him to stay in front of Picton and his men. That way he could warn any Indians in Picton's path. He rode parallel to the bluffs, figuring that Picton would follow them, at least for awhile. Henry thought the stream running along the bluffs ran to the Powder River. It was likely there were Indian camps along it. He guessed Picton's scouts would know that, even if Picton didn't.

He stopped frequently to leave sign for Standing Elk. Henry hoped he was able to gather enough braves to defeat Picton and his gang of murderers. The lake with the blue flowers was only a three day ride from where Emmet Dawson had just attempted to kill Henry for the second time. If the mixed band of warriors were still there, then Standing Elk should already be on his way. If not, there was no telling when he might arrive. If the Indians *were* still at the lake, and the Dog Men with them, Henry knew it might mean him coming face to face with Short Bull's son, Brave Wolf. He chose not to brood on the possibility.

Early the following afternoon he saw the dark lines of smoke rising lazily from a place where the bluffs took a pronounced bend to the northeast. Here the dust-colored, flat-topped hills with their brome and sagebrush covered lowlands began to give way to higher mountains mottled with pine and fir as they marched their way off into the distance.

Knowing he was easily a day and half ahead of Picton's scouts, Henry cut northwest, heading for the bluffs. It was likely a Sioux camp, he thought, the midday smoke from tanning hides.

He entered the camp two hours later: Cheyenne, not Sioux. They'd fled north after hearing about the murder of their kinsfolk at Big Sandy Creek. As was common in the spring and summer months, most of the men were on a hunt. According to an old man named Spotted Bird, the men had been gone for three days. He gestured animatedly with one scarred and misshapen hand as he told Henry in Cheyenne how there had been little game on the journey north, how they had survived on roots and what was left of the white man's treaty flour. Finally they had to eat some of their horses. Spotted Bird blamed the whites for the lack of game. He claimed they scared it all off to force The People to live where the whites wanted them to live; where they were told they could hunt but there was no game; where they could eat only flour, beans, and sick beef; where they could easily be killed when the whites no longer wanted to share any of the land with them. Henry told him of Picton. Spotted Bird asked Henry if he, Nótaxemâhta'sóoma, was going to help them battle the white-man warrior. Henry frowned at the old man's use of the now familiar name.

"I will help you," he said.

Forty-one women, nineteen children, five old men, and seven boys still two or three years from manhood remained in the camp. Escape was Henry's first instinct, but there weren't enough horses to make a run for it—less than a dozen—and Picton was too close for them to make a go of it on foot.

They would have to stay and fight.

3

Henry distributed what little dried meat he had left, then he asked the women to put out the fires (they were cooking big pots of some sort of pungent smelling porridge) and gather all of the rope and hide thongs they could find. The teenage boys and old men brought what weapons there were: five bows, two war-clubs (one with a broken head), and eleven bone-handled knives. Soon a pile of arrows began to grow—Henry thought around thirty—though a few were missing some fletching. Everyone went about their tasks and did as he asked without question. He was saddened a little by the eagerness of the seven not-yet-men to face the white warriors. They were already boasting about their victories and dreaming of the stories that would be told about them.

The plan was a simple one. Henry wasn't a soldier, nor a wily tactician. He wasn't anything. He was, he thought, as he surveyed the scrubby prairie, a man without a place, a purpose, or a people.

4

He spotted John with his field glasses about two hours shy of sunset. Clara wasn't with him. Henry mounted Harriet with a sense of foreboding, and rode out to meet him. He knew she was dead before John could open his mouth.

"Clara's gone."

Henry lowered his head.

"Ahhhh, God, Henry. Why her?"

"I can't say."

"Is God punishing me?"

"I reckon not…" He felt like there was more but let it go. "Picton's less than two day's ride from here. His scouts are going to find this camp tomorrow evening or the following morning unless he changes direction. It don't seem likely that'll happen. I'm going to try to help these people."

"Your friend…Standing Elk?"

Henry shook his head. "There aren't any fighters here. A few boys, and a few men too old to draw a bow."

"What do you intend to do? I'm with you, regardless."

"I'll show you. Might be you can tell me if I'm being foolish."

5

The camp was set close to the bluffs in the crook made by their sharp bend to the northeast. A narrow but fast running stream hugged the contour of the rocky face. Lodges were scattered about; a lot less than there should have been for how many people there were. Henry guessed families were sharing lodges. Something he would have found unlikely just four years prior.

When Henry and John neared the camp, Henry pointed to the women laboring over holes they were digging with knives and broken pieces of lodge pole.

John stopped and surveyed the women. "You're going to try to tumble their horses? You're going to have to dig a lot of holes."

"Yes. And I've got a few lengths of rope I thought I'd use to trip some of them up."

"You might get a few, if you conceal it well enough, but Picton has more than sixty men— *experienced men* who can ride and shoot. How far are the holes from the base of the bluffs?"

"A little farther than my rifle can shoot. I figured I'd aim at the ones who make it through, try to make every shot count."

John removed his hat and ran his fingers through his hair. "We should try and get these Indians away from here."

"There's nowhere to go, and no way to get them there if there was."

John dismounted and walked over to where a young woman was digging a hole in the stony soil with a paddle-shaped piece of driftwood. She looked up at him questioningly, and he gave her a reassuring smile. He stared down at the hole for a moment, then looked back at Henry. "Tell them to dig the holes smaller and closer together. And have them concentrate mostly on the south end and work their way to the north. Picton will almost certainly ride straight on from the south."

They rode the rest of the way into the camp. The old men and the seven young braves were repairing arrows and talking animatedly. They fell silent and stopped what they were doing, eyeing John suspiciously as he dismounted. Henry climbed down from Harriet and they turned their attention to him, looking at him with something close to awe. He put a hand on John's shoulder and said, "Néséne."

"What does that mean?" John asked quietly.

"I said you were my friend."

"Am I?...your friend?"

"I reckon."

The group looked dubious but returned to their work. After a moment a boy of about thirteen rose and walked up to Henry. He held the previously broken war-club. It had been repaired. A smooth, heavy rock from the stream had been seated and bound to the carved wood handle. He held the hammer out to Henry and spoke in Cheyenne: "I am Little Mouth. This belonged to my father. He was a great warrior and hunter. He is there," the boy cocked his head once toward the sky then stood silently with the hammer held out in both hands. "You will defeat the white warriors with this."

Henry stared at the hammer but made no move to take it. The boy lowered his eyes. He was clearly disappointed, but he stayed where he was, arms outstretched.

After a long moment Henry took the club. The boy smiled brightly, then turned and ran back to the group. There was laughter and exclamations.

"This location would be easily defensible if you had adequate weapons and a dozen good men with rifles. Nestled where it is, in the bend of these bluffs, Picton can only come at it from one direction."

Henry regarded John seriously. "Do you reckon they'll lose their taste for it if we kill ten or fifteen of them on their way in?"

"No. No, I do not. Your weakness will be apparent. They are going to kill you and everyone else here. Where are they camped?"

"South, along these bluffs. Forty miles back, give or take...unless they've been riding hard. But he's been keeping near regular days, so I don't have reason to believe they have been."

John turned and climbed back on his horse. He looked down at Henry, who wore a slightly bewildered expression.

"How did you get that scar?"

Henry ran his hand over his stubbly left cheek, letting his fingers glide over the smooth, irregular line where no hair would grow. "Tip of the overseer's whip. I was a still a boy."

John looked out at the horizon. "My family never kept slaves. Not even my grandfather's grandfather. I truly believe the practice to be unconscionable. Still, up until now I have never regarded a negro in the same way that I would a white man. It isn't a subject I ever put any thought into, it's only…circumstances. I've spent my entire life surrounded by men of wealth and purpose, and have never met a finer or more noble man than you, Henry." He twisted around and retrieved an envelope from his saddlebags. "Would you do something for me?"

"If I can."

"If you survive this, would you post this letter for me?" He held the letter out toward Henry.

"What are you going to do?"

"I have to cut off the head. I'm going to tell Frank Picton that I have reconsidered my position, then I am going to shoot him. With him dead, this will end. For the present, at least."

"I reckon they'll kill you."

"It's nothing more than I deserve. And if my death means these people are spared, then perhaps it would be a small measure of atonement. I'd like to think so."

Henry wondered if there was such a thing.

"Will you post the letter?"

He took the offered envelope. "I will. If I can."

John removed the Burnside and the bundle of cartridges from underneath his bedroll. "Here, I won't be needing this, but you might." He turned the horse. "Good luck to you, Henry. And thank you, for what you did for Clara."

Nineteen

1

"Scouts are coming back. Got another rider with them, Colonel," Bill Taylor said, while handing the field glasses to Frank Picton.

Picton raised one bushy eyebrow. "Is that so?" he said, taking the glasses and raising them northward.

After a long moment he muttered, "Curious indeed. It appears our discontented young officer has returned, Mister Taylor. It is a world of wonders."

"The men won't want to follow him, Colonel."

"The men will do as I tell them. If the…ahh, lieutenant, has had a change of heart, he will be permitted to demonstrate it."

"Yes, sir."

"We'll stop here for the night. Bring me my southern whiskey. And have a pull, yourself."

2

Fifteen minutes later John rode into camp under the curious and mostly contemptuous eyes of Picton's men. Conversations ceased, and tasks were momentarily forgotten as he passed. Frank Picton was several yards away from the bustle and dust of the newly struck camp, seated in a folding chair under the only tree in the immediate vicinity. He had a wool blanket on his lap with a book lying on it. In his left hand he held a small tin cup, he lifted it in John's direction. "The prodigal son returns."

John stopped about fifteen feet away and dismounted. He smiled, took two steps toward Picton, and drew his sidearm.

"Beware the ides of March," Picton said, while dropping the cup from his left hand and bringing up the ten gauge coach gun with his right. The reports were nearly simultaneous; the crack of John's pistol shot was swallowed by the roar of the big double-barrel. John was pushed backward, his mid-section ripped open, his bowels spilling from the wound and onto the dusty ground as he landed in a sitting position with his legs splayed. He vomited up blood through his nose and mouth, then lifted his hand and looked at the pistol with dazed and cloudy eyes. Picton stood, blood staining his red shirt a darker maroon. He dropped the shotgun and took a few staggering steps toward John. John caught the movement; his eyes cleared, and his confused expression transformed to one of rage. With great effort he leveled the pistol at Picton. Picton's eyes flicked quickly over John's shoulder just as another shot thundered. The front of John's head exploded outward, bits of bloody skull and brain flecked Picton's trousers. John Elliot's lifeless body crumpled ungracefully to the rocky Dakota soil.

Picton couldn't remember the man's name. He was a southerner. Was it Emerson?...Henderson? Or perhaps it was Denison? "Thank you, young man. Now please find Doctor Paulson and...never mind, here he comes now."

John's bullet carved a notch in the left side of Picton's neck. Richard Paulson, the veterinarian turned field-surgeon, told him that if the bullet had been an inch to the right it likely would have severed his jugular vein, then minced his spine before it blew out the back of his neck.

After Paulson finished bandaging the wound and took his leave, Bill Taylor asked Picton how he knew John was set on assassinating him.

"I knew no such thing," Picton said. "It's merely prudent to be prepared for more than one eventuality. My bottle of whiskey and a second cup were every bit as ready as the shotgun."

Twenty

1

The sun was sinking low in the west as Henry sat perched on the rocky outcrop thirty feet above the camp. Using a stunted pine that was stoically clinging to the thin soil of the outcrop as cover, he watched Picton's scouts through his field glasses. Two of the scouts were Pawnee, the other two, white men. They were less than a half-mile to the south, at the base of the bluffs. One of the whites had field glasses of his own and was looking through them in the direction of the camp. After a moment he passed the glasses to one of the Pawnee. A short but animated conversation followed, and soon they turned their horses and headed back to the south.

If John killed Picton, these men shouldn't be here, Henry thought. *John is dead and Picton is coming.*

He was saddened by the likelihood of John's death, but it was Clara he mourned. She hadn't left his thoughts since John had arrived with the news. In the short time Henry knew her, he grew to love her; not in the way a man loves a woman, but in the way he imagined a father must love his daughter, though he was far too young to be hers.

He scrabbled down the side of the bluff to where Harriet was tethered by the creek, untied her, and walked her over to where Spotted Bird sat sharpening a knife on a flat stone. The old man's gnarled fingers worked the blade across the stone with practiced precision. Outside of the seven young braves, who were working with their bows in seclusion behind a thicket of cottonwood trees across the stream, the rest of the camp had resumed their normal routine— at least under casual inspection. The truth was, that morning four women packed up a lodge and took one of the horses—presumably it belonged to one of them—and their children, and fled. The remaining women and old men stole fearful glances at each other and paid close attention to Henry's every move. He often saw them scanning the horizon, most likely with hope their men would return from the hunt. Only the young children seemed unaffected.

"They're coming," Henry said in Cheyenne. "Tomorrow. I will return soon."

Spotted Bird nodded his head without looking up from his work.

Henry mounted Harriet and rode out to follow the scout's back-trail. He didn't expect the attack to come before the morning—more likely in the afternoon—because the scouts were almost surely several hours ahead of Picton and the rest of his men. It could be as late as midnight before they even reached him to share their discovery.

But he had to know for certain. What if Picton and his men were only two or three miles south of the camp? As unlikely as he thought it was, it was still possible. If they were that close, they may not wait for tomorrow. They could attack before the sun completely dropped over the horizon.

He guided Harriet down the middle of the stream to avoid the holes the women had dug and then concealed with sagebrush, grass and twigs. It was good work—three day's worth. If you didn't know they were there, they were almost invisible. He decided he'd follow the back-trail for two hours. If he didn't come upon Picton's camp by then, he would assume Picton stuck to his usual pattern and was well behind his scouts.

2

When Henry returned it was still two hours before midnight. The seven young braves and some of the old men were dancing and singing by the light of a fire. *War dance,* Henry thought desolately. He noticed Spotted Bird wasn't among them. Henry sat far away from the sacred event and ate some of the stew the women had saved for him. It was a bitter tasting brew made from boiling certain roots and seed-pods for hours until they were soft enough to eat. It's what they were cooking when he first saw their smoke from afar. Not tanning hides, but cooking the only food they had available to them.

He was at odds with himself. He wanted to send the women and children a few miles to the northeast to wait out the attack. But if he did, the camp would look abandoned—or nearly so. If Picton believed there was only a handful of Indians in the camp, he might not send in his full strength, or worse, think something was amiss. Henry couldn't have him sending men out into the surrounding area. He needed Picton to come at the camp with all of his men and at a full charge. Henry cursed to himself, something he rarely did. He wasn't a soldier, not a dark warrior as his Cheyenne name would imply. He wished John would have stayed. John was a soldier. Henry knew he'd left because there was little hope that two men with rifles and a few boys and old men with bows could turn Picton's attack. It was bitter medicine. He would talk with Spotted Bird. Perhaps Spotted Bird could pick twenty women to take all of the children away from the camp. It wouldn't make any difference if Henry and the others failed; the children would die just the same as if they would have remained in camp. But it was a chance. And it would still leave over thirty people to make a show of numbers for Picton's field glasses—thirty people who were almost certain to die.

Tossing out almost half of his stew, Henry rose and walked to the lodge Spotted Bird shared with his granddaughter's family. He was curious but wouldn't dishonor Spotted Bird by asking why he wasn't attending the ceremony. Instead, he explained what he wanted. Spotted Bird listened carefully, then rose and began walking through the camp from lodge to lodge. By midnight, eighteen women and all of the children save the seven young braves were walking northeast along the stream.

Henry removed the Spencer from its scabbard, and a box of ammunition from his saddlebags, then walked back to Spotted Bird's lodge. He spent the next thirty minutes having Spotted Bird load, unload, then reload the rifle. The elderly Indian's malformed hand was surprisingly dexterous, and he mastered the task swiftly. Henry planned to fire the seven-shot Spencer empty, then fire John's single-shot Burnside while Spotted Bird reloaded the Spencer. He rarely missed, even when shooting at a moving target, and his plan was simple enough. He hoped that if he shot enough of the men who made it past the holes, the rest might turn back before they ever got the chance to kill an Indian.

3

Dawn.

Henry, Spotted Bird, and an old man named Fast Horse watched Little Mouth and the other young braves practice with the bows. All of their faces were painted for war. The old men, also painted, watched intently. There were seven boys and only five bows. Spotted Bird and Fast Horse would choose who used the bows, and who would stay at the thicket with the old men to protect the women with knives and clubs.

Once it was decided—Henry thought only two of the older boys actually shot well—and the arrows divided among them, Henry had the chosen five follow him. There were several small outcroppings at different heights above the camp, four of them provided fair cover. Two were low enough—about fifteen feet—for the inexperienced bowmen to be within their range. He pointed at these and instructed the two most accurate bowmen to climb up to them and wait for the attack. The remaining three—including Little Mouth—he staged among the lodges. There was little cover otherwise.

Once the bowmen were in place, Henry helped Spotted Bird climb up about thirty feet to an outcropping almost directly above the cottonwood thicket. Once Spotted Bird was situated, Henry climbed back down and collected the two rifles and all of the cartridges for them: twenty-seven for the Burnside and thirty-three for the Spencer. He looked down at Emmet Dawson's pistol on his hip, and without any deliberation he set down the rifles and ammunition, removed the belt, and walked over to where Little Mouth was sitting against a lodge. Henry took the Colt from its holster and removed the percussion caps, then he showed a wide-eyed Little Mouth how to cock and fire the pistol. He explained the best he could in Cheyenne that the pistol should be used at close range. He picked up several rocks and threw them about twenty feet to emphasis this point. Satisfied that Little Mouth understood, Henry replaced the percussion caps, slid the pistol into the holster, and showed Little Mouth how to fasten the belt. Little Mouth frowned when the belt simply slid down his thighs and landed as a ring around his feet. Henry chuckled and gestured for Little Mouth to give it to him. Little Mouth stepped out of the belt, bent, and picked it up. He looked at it but made no move to give it back to Henry. Henry held out his hand, and after a moment the boy reluctantly handed it over. Henry drew his knife and Little Mouth took a step back. Henry smiled and quickly drilled two more holes in the belt with the tip of the blade. Still smiling, he handed the belt back to Little Mouth. This time it fit.

Henry gathered up the rifles, ammunition and his canteen, and climbed back up to the outcropping. The space was tight for both him and Spotted Bird, but they were well-concealed behind a wagon-sized boulder that had broken away and fallen from somewhere farther up the bluff.

Outside of venturing out to forage, which Henry warned them against, the women began going about their work as they would on any other day. Morning cook-fires were kindled though there was little to cook, and water was drawn from the stream. They were aware that they were in danger from the white men, and Spotted Bird had instructed them to hurry across the stream and hide behind the cottonwood thicket if the warning signal was given. They weren't aware, however, that their appearance of normalcy was important. It was a concept that Henry simply couldn't translate into Cheyenne. The women went about their business normally, because it was all they knew.

The sun was high and hot when Henry finally saw the riders.

They were coming from the south along the stream at the base of the bluffs and moving slowly. Henry knew from his outings with the army that this was to keep down the dust to conceal their advance. They stopped at the same spot the scouts had on the previous day. The distance was too great to discern features through the glasses, but Henry thought he knew who Picton was nonetheless. There was a man at the front on a bay horse. He was wearing a red shirt, and most of the activity seemed to be centered around him. It appeared he was lifting a pair of field glasses. Henry lowered his own and slid back behind the boulder.

"Soon," he said to Spotted Bird in Cheyenne, who nodded solemnly and picked up the Spencer. Henry leaned back around the boulder and raised the glasses. Picton's men were fanning out to cover the entire opening in the L shaped bend of the bluffs, cutting off any chance of escape. *There's nowhere to go, anyway,* Henry thought.

Picton wasted no time, he and his men charged forward. Henry turned and shouted behind him, "Now!...*Hétsęstseha! Hétsęstseha!*

Spotted Bird let loose with a call that sounded similar to the yip-howl of a coyote. It was immediately echoed by the two young braves who were perched on outcroppings, and the three down below among the lodges. The women dropped what they were doing and hurried across the stream to the spurious safety of the cottonwood thicket where four old men and two young ones barely out of boyhood, armed only with knives, were prepared to die protecting them.

Henry took the Spencer from Spotted Bird and went down on one knee as close to the boulder as he could push his body. The dust cloud following the charging riders was immense. The ground shook, and the sound of hundreds of hooves beating the earth was like thunder. Faster horses began to pull ahead of the rest, and he had time to think, *I'm a damned fool,* just as several of the lead horses went crashing and tumbling to the ground.

Henry opened fire.

He hit five of the first seven he shot at, and did it in less than thirty seconds. Spotted Bird was already grabbing the Spencer and shoving the Burnside into his hands before he could even get turned around. It wasn't fast enough; riders were entering the camp. He fumbled open the bundle of ammunition for the Burnside and set it on the ground in front of him as he watched a rider run his horse into a lodge at the edge of camp. The lodge collapsed and the horse and rider with it. The horse clambered up and ran off, the rider stood and drew his sidearm, searching for a target. Henry shot him, levered the rifle, removed the spent cartridge, and loaded another. Shots started ringing, the dust was beginning to make it hard to see. Some of the riders were dismounting and entering lodges, others were charging for the stream and the thicket of cottonwoods.

Henry shot the first rider to make it to the stream, but there were a dozen more right behind. He levered the Burnside again just as Spotted Bird tapped his shoulder, snatched the empty rifle away and handed him the Spencer. The riders were already across the stream and coming around the flanks of the thicket. Henry stood and switched places with Spotted Bird, he couldn't defend the women from the side of the boulder he'd been shooting from. He had a clear line of sight over the rest of the camp, but the boulder itself blocked his view of the cottonwood thicket. He lay down on the edge of the outcrop and looked for a target. The women were scattering in all directions as the riders descended upon them, swinging their sabers and firing pistols. Shouts, curses and screams of agony melded into an unintelligible cacophony of human depravity and suffering. Henry shut out the screams and fired the Spencer. The riders, almost directly below him, were easy targets. He shot three before anyone realized where he was. Finally, one began shooting back. Others joined in. The angle was poor, though, and they were on horseback. Not a single bullet came close. Henry shot two more and the rest began to flee back across the stream. He stood and switched places with Spotted Bird again, exchanging rifles as he did. All of the riders were fleeing the camp. Henry saw two more horses go tumbling as they attempted to gallop over the concealed holes. He fired at one of the fallen riders as he untangled himself from the injured horse and scrambled to his feet. The shot was pushing the Burnside's range, however, and the bullet puffed the dust several feet away from its intended target. Henry let him go.

For the moment, it was over.

Henry raised the field glasses. Picton—if he wasn't injured or dead—and his remaining men were riding northeast at a gallop, along the stream. *The children!* Henry thought in a panic. *Why would he ride north?* The women probably didn't walk the children more than a few miles. If Picton's men didn't stop, they'd run right into them. He turned to Spotted Bird and pointed northeast. "Nótaxevé'ho'e," he said. Spotted bird looked flummoxed for a moment, then understanding dawned on his creased and sun-weathered face. He put a hand to his chest and nodded. Henry nodded in return.

They climbed down the bluff and hastily strode past the bodies of the slain and injured. The air was thick with the smell of blood and gunpowder. Fast Horse, two of the young braves, and at least ten women lay dead near the thicket. An equal number of Picton's men lay strewn among them, either dead or mortally wounded. Unharmed women tended to the injured while the remaining few males snatched up firearms and tried to retrieve as many arrows as they could. One of Picton's men screamed in agony as a brave pushed, pulled, and twisted the arrow in the man's side in an attempt to free it. Another was being bludgeoned to death with a rock by a woman as several others stood over her and watched. A shot was fired and Henry spun around. One of Picton's men was lying on his back and aiming a wavering pistol at the group of women. Henry raised the Burnside just as Little Mouth walked up to the man and unceremoniously shot him with Henry's pistol. He squatted and began removing the man's possessions.

There were three of the men's horses milling around the stream. Henry asked Spotted Bird to catch them. Meanwhile he searched quickly among the bodies and dead horses for rifles. He passed over a Springfield and some other make he didn't recognize before finding a Spencer with just over half a box of ammunition on a groaning horse with a broken leg. There was a man pinned underneath, dead. Henry shot the horse.

He hurried back to where Spotted Bird waited with two horses. Apparently the third had ran off. He handed Spotted Bird the Spencer and the ammunition, then ran across the stream, mounted Harriet, and rode back. Little Mouth was standing next to Spotted Bird. He was holding Henry's pistol, belt, and holster in his hand, and had another around his waist. He handed it up to Henry, who took it and quickly checked the loads. Only four shots fired. It meant Little Mouth had understood when he'd explained the pistol's range; the boy didn't waste any shots.

Spotted Bird held up the reins to one of the horses, and cocked his head toward Little Mouth. Henry looked around; he was hoping for one of the older braves. Aware he was losing precious seconds he nodded his head. Little Mouth whooped loudly and leaped up onto the horse. Spotted Bird struggled, but finally got mounted. He muttered something derogatory in Cheyenne about the white men and their saddles, and kicked the horse forward.

4

About a mile and a half northeast of the Cheyenne camp, Frank Picton raised his hand and slowed his horse down to a walk.

"They were just waiting for us, Colonel. Goddamn red sons-of-bitches dug goddamn holes," Bill Taylor said unbelievingly.

"I'll ask you not to use the Lord's name in such a manner in my presence, Mister Taylor. Post two reliable men with fast horses by that tree at the creek's edge. Tell them to stay out of sight. If they see anyone leaving the savage's encampment, they're to rejoin us forthwith. Give them your field glasses."

"Why—"

"Do it *now,* Mister Taylor."

"Yes, Colonel."

Taylor turned his horse to do as he was bid. Picton stared forward. He was red-faced and angry beyond measure.

Several minutes later, Taylor rode up alongside Picton. "I sent McMurtrey and Highley. I would've sent Pendergrass, but he's dead...so's Hill. Red sons-of-bitches."

"An Indian—much like a nigger—can learn to shoot a rifle, but he does not possess the intelligence, dexterity, nor the patience to be its master. And the traps, although a rudimentary defense, required planning beyond their aptitude."

"Are you saying there were white men back there shooting at us?"

"I'm saying that the late Mister John Elliot seems to have found at least one pair of sympathetic ears. Ears I intend to have hanging from this very saddle by this time tomorrow. How many men did we lose?"

"Sixteen."

"Unfortunate. Hill, you say?"

"Yessir. Colonel. We're going back, aren't we? I mean, white men or not, there couldn't have been more than two or three rifles and a handful of bucks shooting arrows."

"One rifle. And a very well positioned sharpshooter in possession of it. We'll halt shortly and wait until nightfall. He'll lose most of his advantage with the sun...what in the...Taylor, look over there. There are red devils by the creek. Tell the men to arm themselves."

5

The women snatched up the youngest of the children and ran when they saw the riders, but there was nowhere to hide and they couldn't outrun horses. Picton had them herded back together on a grassy area next to the stream. The women held the infants protectively.

Picton dismounted and walked back and forth in front of the Indians, rubbing his beard thoughtfully.

"Rider coming, Colonel. Moving fast," a man called out.

"Looks like McMurtrey's roan," Taylor said.

"Perhaps we'll not be forced to wait after all," Picton muttered to himself.

A few minutes later, McMurtrey rode up fast, reining in the roan, hard. He stopped short in front of the huddled women and children.

"Three of 'em come outta there riding hell bent, Colonel," McMurtrey said breathlessly. "They're coming this way."

Picton stood facing his frightened captives and drew his pistol. "Of course they are," he said, and opened fire.

6

Henry heard the shots over the hoof beats of the galloping horses. He pulled hard and brought Harriet to an abrupt, sliding stop. The rapid staccato of the rifle and pistol shots echoed from the bluffs, slowly tapering to nothing. Finally, there was one last shot. Its lone echo faded, leaving a silence so complete as to be an abomination.

Spotted Bird and Little Mouth had also stopped, though several yards in front of Henry. They walked their horses back. Spotted Bird met Henry's eyes, his expression was grave. Little Mouth still looked eager, impatient even.

Henry looked at Little Mouth and spoke in Cheyenne. "You must go west for one day, then north. Find more Cheyenne, Arapaho, or Sioux. Tell them what happened here. Do not stop at the camp."

"I want to fight the white warriors. I am not afraid."

"If you wish to help your people you must do this."

Little Mouth looked at Spotted Bird, who was gazing steadily at Henry. After a moment, he turned to Little Mouth and nodded. Little Mouth whooped loudly, kicked his horse up and rode off.

"The white warriors killed the children," Henry said.

"Yes," Spotted Bird agreed.

Henry took his field glasses from his saddlebags and scanned the base of the bluffs. He found them, not far off, at the edge of the stream. The man in the red shirt was staring back at him through his own pair of glasses. Henry wondered what he was thinking.

7

Frank Picton lifted his field glasses. There were two riders, not three. A nigger and an Indian—an *old* Indian from the looks. He turned to Cal McMurtrey, "You said there were three riders, I only see two."

"There were sure enough three of them, Colonel. Garrett Highley saw 'em, same as I did."

Picton raised the glasses again. *There.* One was fleeing. The sharpshooter, had to be. *Elliot's Indian loving accomplice.* He handed the glasses to Taylor and began reloading his pistol.

Take ten men and go after those two. One's a nigger—undoubtedly the one who dug all of those holes—the other's an old Indian. The rest of you mount up, we're going after the recreant who murdered our companions from hiding."

"Pardon, Colonel, but there was an awful lot of squaws and pups here. There's bound to be men somewhere. You sure you want to split up?"

"Mind yourself, Mister Taylor. Do not question me again."

"Yessir."

8

Henry watched the roughly forty men separate into two groups. The larger one, led by Picton himself, rode southeast. The smaller group started toward him and Spotted Bird.

They're going after Little Mouth, he thought, though he couldn't understand why. After a moment's deliberation he turned Harriet and rode off eastward—*fast*—and on a course that would put him between Little Mouth and Picton.

He rode nearly a mile, then slowed Harriet enough that Spotted Bird could catch up. When Spotted Bird came up alongside, Henry pointed at him, then pointed southeast—away from the Cheyenne camp. Spotted Bird nodded and turned his horse southeast.

It had the desired effect. The men chasing them veered and followed Spotted Bird. Henry continued eastward. Minutes later he was directly in Picton's path. He slowed, leaned forward and rubbed Harriet on the neck. "I'm sorry," he said, then he straightened up, pulled the Spencer from its scabbard, turned north, and rode straight at them.

9

Frank Picton felt only perplexity as the rider turned toward him. He couldn't see whether it was the nigger or the Indian who was about to give up his life for John Elliot's fleeing collaborator. He guessed the Indian. This was an act of loyalty, and he knew that niggers rarely possessed the capacity for it. Indians, at least, would try to protect one another. He withdrew his pistol and charged ahead.

10

The distance was closing quickly, but Henry had enough time to hope that if he succeeded in killing Picton, the other men would cry off and leave Little Mouth and the survivors at the Cheyenne camp alone.

When he felt he was within the Spencer's range, he forced himself to wait a little longer, even after Picton's men began firing at him. Finally he raised the rifle. He recalled the first time he was allowed to hunt buffalo with the Cheyenne, and let his hips absorb the now familiar rhythm of Harriet's gait. He aimed, fired…and missed.

Henry levered the rifle and raised it again. White-hot pain exploded in the left side of his chest. He fumbled and almost lost the rifle. Nearly on top of them, he quickly aimed and fired again. The shot went home, taking off the bottom half of Picton's face. He saw this just as Harriet ran headlong into the oncoming riders. More fire lit up Henry's right shoulder, and the Spencer went tumbling to the ground as his right arm dropped uselessly to his side. Harriet grunted and stumbled to the left, Henry, nearly losing the saddle, grabbed a handful of her mane just as she regained her gait.

Then they were past.

11

Blood was running freely over Frank Picton's hand as he raised it to where his lower jaw should have been. He felt a flap of something lying against his neck that could have been his tongue. He held the hand up and stared at the blood in rage and disbelief. *It was the nigger. How could he…*

Frank Picton toppled from his horse.

12

Henry spared a look behind. A dozen men or slightly more had turned to give chase. Harriet was flagging. He thought she might be shot. He pushed her anyway; they would die if she stopped.

13

Harriet was walking. *Have I been asleep?* She was nearing the bluffs— which weren't really bluffs anymore but mountains. Henry turned, the pain from his chest was immediate and intense. *Broken rib,* he thought dazedly. There was no one following him. He looked down, there was a small hole just below and to the left of his breast. He tried to move his right hand to examine it, but his arm wouldn't move. The lower half of his tan shirt had turned a deep red. He felt hot and out of sorts. There were trees ahead, and he could see the stream glistening through them. He could hear the water, running fast. Eliza was there, next to a large pine. She was beckoning him.

Twenty-One

1

The tracks of the thirteen horses and riders joined with another group, several miles to the north of where the old Cheyenne with the twisted hands had been killed, scalped, and left lying in the dust.

The riders, near forty in all, had then rode south. Brave Wolf and the other Dog Men, along with Red Cloud and his his two hundred warriors would follow and kill them. Standing Elk would stay behind with the boy and see to the old man. Perhaps afterward, he would find Nótaxemâhta'sóoma.

Twenty-Two

1
New York, New York. May 23 1866.
Jonathon Hanfield set down his pen with a scowl and looked up from his work when he heard the familiar creak of his study door.

His eyes widened, then narrowed. "Where is Clara?"

The figure in the doorway reached back and pushed the door closed.

"Now you just wait—"

The pistol shot was deafening. Jonathon Hanfield's words were replaced with an inarticulate gulping sound. He started to rise, then sat back down heavily before slumping forward onto his desk blotter. Randall Eastman stood in silence, gazing at his former employer with his head slightly cocked to one side—a habit he'd developed due to the sight never returning fully to his left eye. Finally, he let the pistol drop to the floor, turned, opened the door, and walked out of the room. He didn't see Louisa Hanfield standing on the stair landing with her hands on the wrought iron railing.

The carriage driver looked impatient as Randall strode down the walk.

"Where to now, sir?"

3
Secretary of the Interior's office, Washington D.C. Jan. 10 1866.
"Carl, please have this letter forwarded to Mister Usher. That windbag vacated this office nearly a year ago, and he still receives more correspondence here than I do. It's a wonder these men out west can even name our current president."

4
Lawrence, Kansas. Feb 12 1866.
John Usher wadded up the two sheets of paper and tossed them into the fireplace. His expression was thoughtful as he watched the flames consume the letter. He lifted the envelope and stared at the name written on it for a long while. *John Elliot.* He would have some quiet inquiries made, though the letter was dated from the previous summer, and John Elliot was likely as dead as Frank Picton must be. What Picton did before he vanished seemed to have been effective, however. It was like he had said all along: *All the Indians need is a little nudge.*

The envelope soon joined the letter, and he returned to the huge cherry-wood table in the center of the room. He bent and ran his hand over his scale model of the future Union Pacific Railway, Eastern Division's central plains railroad—*his* railroad.

5
Near Carthage Mo. June 3 1866.
Clarence Masterson ran up to the main house and rapped once on the door before opening it.

"Mister Hoyt?" he called excitedly.

"Come in and shut the door, Clarence," answered a spectacled man who was seated at a tiny desk next to a stone fireplace. "And mind your feet." He put down the newspaper he was reading and turned toward the door.

Clarence, the Hoyt farm's foreman, hastily stamped his boots on the doormat. "Mister Hoyt! There's a nigger out here says he's got a horse and saddle and some other things belong to you."

Andrew Hoyt removed his glasses. "Is that so?" His hand went unconsciously to a thin scar just above his right ear. "What does this man look like?"

"Well, he's a sight, for certain. Rode in here like he was the Almighty himself. Got a scar on his face as thick as a bridge rope, and he's wearing two pistols. You want I should get the rifles?"

Hoyt was silent for a long moment. Clarence was about to repeat the question when he finally spoke. "I don't think we'll need the rifles. See to his animals and bring him in. He's probably thirsty."

Acknowledgement

Writing is not as solitary as one would think.

This novel would not have been possible (at least in any form that would be worth reading) without my mom and dad, for whom I owe absolutely everything; Chazz, Casady, Chelcy, and Cheyenne, for their unwavering support; Sarah for her honesty, even when she knows it will ruffle my fragile feathers; Sage Adderley-Knox for being an all-around awesome person, and for believing that I have something to offer.

Thank you.

RIP Bradley Knox. I would liked to have known you better.

Made in the USA
Middletown, DE
25 May 2020